An
Island
Far From
Home

BOOKS BY KATE HEWITT

FAR HORIZONS TRILOGY

The Heart Goes On

Her Rebel Heart

This Fragile Heart

AMHERST ISLAND SERIES

The Orphan's Island

Dreams of the Island

Return to the Island

The Island We Left Behind

THE GOSWELL QUARTET

The Wife's Promise

The Daughter's Garden

The Bride's Sister

The Widow's Secret

STANDALONE NOVELS

A Mother's Goodbye

The Secrets We Keep

Not My Daughter

No Time to Say Goodbye

A Hope for Emily

Into the Darkest Day

Kate Hewitt

An
Island
Far From
Home

bookouture

Published by Bookouture in 2023

An imprint of Storyfire Ltd.
Carmelite House
50 Victoria Embankment
London EC4Y 0DZ

www.bookouture.com

ISBN: 978-1-80019-922-4
eBook ISBN: 978-1-80019-921-7

To Isobel and Jess, thank you for working on this book with me, and providing a seamless transition! To many more books!

CHAPTER ONE

AUGUST 1941

Kingston, Ontario

"Oh, come now, Rosie, don't you want to? I mean, really want to? Deep down?"

Rosie Lyman laughed at the good humor—and more than a little mischief—glinting like gold in her cousin Violet's hazel eyes as she shook her head. "Do I? Really, deep down, honest-to-goodness want to?" she replied teasingly. "No, I do not."

"*Oh!*" Violet let out a theatrical groan as she flung herself backwards on her bed, arms and legs starfished for maximum melodrama as she stared up at her bedroom ceiling as if gazing into the very heavens themselves. "Of course you don't. You really are so very *sensible.*" Spoken like an insult, and yet with deep affection.

"I'm afraid I am," Rosie agreed cheerfully. She sat next to Violet on her bed and gave one outflung arm a conciliatory pat. "But why do you want to, as it happens? Join up, I mean?"

Just about two months ago, on the twenty-seventh of June, the Canadian government had finally—after several years of earnest petitioning from various women's auxiliary volunteer services across the country—announced it would be forming an official military body for women, the Canadian Women's Army Corps, or CWAC, in order to "free a man to fight," or as one recruiting poster had put it, "to serve so men might fly," something that was much more necessary nearly two years into the war, with more and more Canadian boys heading over to England by the day. Hundreds of pilots in the RCAF had fought in the Battle of Britain, and there was even talk of Newfoundland possibly being attacked by the Germans. The war felt closer than ever, a shadow over them all, although one, Rosie thought, Violet usually wanted to shake. Always up for fun, her cousin seemed one of the least likely people to join the Canadian Women's Army Corps and serve her country.

Officers in the newly formed CWAC were now touring the country to recruit volunteers, traveling all the way out to British Columbia, as well as to the farthest reaches of Nova Scotia and New Brunswick, holding meetings and socials in various cities and towns in an attempt to appeal to women who were "serious-minded and sensible" to enlist in the CWAC. Kingston's recruiting center was holding such a meeting that night—a social in one of the dance halls on Division Street, and Violet wanted Rosie to go with her.

"Why wouldn't I want to join up?" Violet returned, lifting her head from her bed briefly to stare at Rosie with a surprisingly fierce light in her eyes before she dropped it down again. "I want to go somewhere—*see* things—wear a smart uniform—"

"The only thing I think you'd likely be seeing is a latrine or a laundry basket," Rosie returned as she rose from the bed to tidy up some of Violet's tossed-about clothes. She'd come to her cousin's house on Centre Street at her urgent summons, and also because Violet had been her best friend since her family had moved to the small and gracious city of Kingston from Amherst Island when Rosie had been thirteen, and despite their many and obvious differences, they'd been nearly inseparable since.

Violet, having lived in Kingston for several years by that point, had seemed confident and worldly-wise to shy and timid Rosie, even though she'd had a certain amount of experience of her own, from her childhood days in New York City, as well as a winter spent in Los Angeles for her brother's health when she was only seven years old.

She and Violet had both had somewhat tumultuous childhoods, Rosie reflected as she hung up one of her cousin's discarded dresses, Violet still sprawled out on the bed before her. Their fathers Lucas and Jed Lyman were brothers and as different from each other as Rosie and Violet were; Jed, quiet and taciturn, and Lucas, Rosie's dear dad, more laughing and light. Lucas was an academic turned lawyer who had set up his own small law office in Kingston, offering legal aid to farmers as well as advice to the government. Once, he'd been a high-flying lawyer for one of the top firms in New York, but he'd lost his position and most of his money during the Crash of 1929.

Rosie still recalled, with a shudder of memory, their furniture piled in the street, the shabby one-room bedsit in Harlem where they'd had to live while her father got what work he could and her mother joined the breadlines, both of them trying their hardest simply to keep body and soul together. Most of all, she remembered the fear that had lined her stomach like acid, that constant swoop of anxiety through her whole body, her entire world turned to chaos as just about everything she'd known had been taken away, replaced by a void of uncertainty.

But then they'd moved to Amherst Island—the place where both her parents had grown up—in 1930. And, after nearly a year of that sort of life, it had been a wonderful relief and a much-needed sanctuary, even though at first the winters had been hard and luxuries scarce, her father leaving his law degree behind to farm a few acres of rented land while her mother,

Ellen, acted as the island's nurse. They'd lived there for five years before a job opportunity for her father had allowed them to move to the more conveniently located Kingston, where Rosie and her younger brother Jamie had gone to high school.

Jed, Violet's father, had had a surprisingly similar path, if not the same kind of ambition as his brother; he'd reluctantly left the Lyman farm behind when he'd married Violet's mother, Louisa, who'd come from a well-to-do family in the States. Then he had accepted a position in her father's bank in Vermont, even though he wasn't the sort of man to sit behind a desk, or tot up a column of numbers. Just like Lucas, he'd lost everything during the Crash, and he had ended up farming back in nearby Seaton before a position had arisen in a bank here in Kingston and Jed and Louisa had moved to be closer to family.

It had felt important back then, Rosie knew, to gather your loved ones close, when all else had failed or fallen. It felt even more important now, with the headlines full of war and men marching off to battle just about every day.

And yet, while she was very grateful for her cousin's friendship, she had no real desire to sign up to the Canadian Women's Army Corps and spend the rest of the war scrubbing latrines or washing woolen socks, "to free a man to fight," although she suspected her cousin, who loved to embrace every madcap scheme going and seemed to think it would be good fun, would do her best to convince her otherwise.

"That's simply not true, you know," Violet exclaimed as she scrambled up from the bed to reach for a leaflet she'd tossed onto her bedside table a few moments earlier. She waved it in front of Rosie's nose, full of certainty. "It won't just be scrubbing or sweeping. Look what it says here. They want educated women to be clerks, stenographers, typists, telephone operators, even drivers—"

Rosie twitched the leaflet from Violet's fingers. "And cooks, canteen helpers, cleaners and laundresses," she finished reading before she handed the paper back with a firm shake of her head. "Is that really what you want to be doing for the war effort?" Violet didn't even make her own bed; her family had a maid for all the housework.

"It won't all be sweeping and scrubbing," Violet replied with a shrug, and Rosie raised her eyebrows.

"You know how reluctant the army was to let women organize anything official," she pointed out. "We were the last country in the Commonwealth to have a women's corps at all. They aren't about to let women do anything truly important, and I can't see you wanting to scrub and slave away for the next few years in some faraway military base, out in a cornfield in Manitoba or something like that! Besides," she added with an attempt at a playful look, "what about your studies?"

Violet lifted her chin, eyes flashing. "What about them?"

"Oh, Violet." Rosie suppressed a small sigh. Both she and Violet were about to start their second year at Queen's, Rosie studying History and Violet English. But while Rosie adored her studies, and was content to have her nose buried in books, Violet could take or leave them, and often did so, with happy abandon, whether it was a jaunt out ice skating when the lake had frozen over, or some high jinks at the university, already notorious for its undergraduates' pranks.

On the first of April last year, Rosie recalled, Violet had been in the rowdy group that had driven all the way to Watertown, in upstate New York, to put up signs, written in florid Georgian script, declaring that the surrounding lands had been repossessed by the Crown, effective immediately. The prank had made some of the national newspapers, and incurred Violet's parents' considerable dismay, especially when she and the other pranksters had been called up in front of the dean of the university. Even after the sternest of dressing-downs, and having to make a public apology, Violet had been insouciantly unrepentant.

"It was just for fun," she'd told Rosie, who had shaken her head and laughed, even though she'd been more than a little shocked by the whole escapade. "I don't know why everyone has to get in such a palaver about it."

Foolhardy jaunts aside, Violet, smart as she was, did not take the same delight in her studies that Rosie did. She found books boring and considered her professors to be fusty and dull. Rosie had done her best to help her cousin along through their first year, so Violet had at least passed her final exams, but she realized now that she wasn't at all surprised that Violet would happily abandon her course to gallivant after some new adventure, even if it would be likely to be nothing more than sweeping and scrubbing. She just wasn't sure she wanted to be dragged along with her.

"What does the rest of it say, then?" Rosie asked as she took back the leaflet once more and scanned its typed lines. Yes, there was a good deal about women recruits wearing suitable uniform, although no details were given, except that if a uniform was not yet available, they would be provided with "some distinguishing mark." Likewise, there was very little about where they would live—only that they would be billeted "when suitable accommodation can be made ready." "But they make it clear you won't be paid as much as a man," Rosie pointed out, and then read aloud, "'Women will be paid at somewhat lower rates than those authorized for soldiers.'"

"Well, honestly, Rosie, you can't expect us to earn the same as a man risking his life," Violet protested as she twitched the leaflet from Rosie's fingers and tossed it aside impatiently.

"What about the same as a man who is washing the same socks?" Rosie returned with a touch of asperity. She knew women weren't paid the same as men in any field, but that didn't mean it was fair or right.

Violet sighed. "All right, yes, but so what? Of course women won't be paid the same. They never are. It could still be fun, especially if we did it together." Her eyes lit up as she leaned forward. "Some girls in the year above us have already enlisted, and they say it's going to be *such* a laugh. There are all sorts of socials—parties and dances, with all the dishy servicemen—"

Rosie let out a huff of skeptical laughter. "That's hardly the point of the thing, though, is it?"

"I'd rather shine a pair of shoes than write an essay," Violet flung back with more dramatic bravado, Rosie thought, than certainty. She knew which she would prefer.

"If you're so keen to do something for your country," she suggested, "why not do more with Queen's Voluntary Service Corps?" The group had been formed midway through their first year, and Violet had been one of about thirty members, with Rosie coming along occasionally, mainly for moral support.

"All they've done is knit and roll bandages," Violet replied, with a touch of scorn. "I thought it would be so much more than that, but it was completely dull. Anyway, you know it's not the same."

"No," Rosie agreed, "it's not, but now that an official organization has been formed, perhaps they'll do more interesting things. Women everywhere will." Even if it remained just washing and scrubbing, typing and filing. Perhaps as the war went on, things would change and women would be given more opportunities, more power?

"Women everywhere except you," Violet pointed out, and Rosie flushed a little at the implied rebuke.

Was she being selfish, in dismissing her cousin's idea so quickly, simply because it sounded like another of Violet's madcap schemes? No matter what went on in the world, dishes needed to be washed, socks knit, floors scrubbed, perhaps more than ever with a war on. Men were certainly doing their part, and several dozen boys at Queen's had already joined up voluntarily to fight overseas. A few months ago, the prime minister had introduced the National Resources

Mobilization Act, which had called for a national register for home defense, a decision approved by almost everyone, although some contemptuously called such conscripts "zombies," wanting more men actually fighting overseas, where it really mattered.

Since the Act's formation, there had been plenty of talk about conscription to fight, and although it hadn't happened yet, Rosie felt sure it would one day, a thought which made her tremble for all the boys she knew at Queen's who would have to leave their studies to take up arms. Right now, the war felt comfortably far away, but it wouldn't forever. It was getting closer every day, and burying her head in the sand and insisting she needed to stay at her studies was not, perhaps, the most patriotic response.

"I'm going to the dance tonight," Violet announced grandly, flinging her arms wide and doing a little twirl. "And I just might join up right there and then." She gave Rosie a decidedly beady look. "And you're coming with me, Rosie Lyman!"

"I'll come to the dance," Rosie conceded, although she didn't particularly like dancing all that much. She wasn't very good at it, never quite knowing what to do with her hands or feet, or where to look. Still, she was content to play cheerful wallflower to her cousin's gorgeous lily—a role she took on amiably often enough. "But no promises about joining up," she added, like a warning.

"Well then," Violet returned, her eyes glinting with humor, along with an alarming amount of determination, "it sounds like I've just about got you convinced!"

That night, the dance hall on Division Street was buzzing with a throng of would-be women recruits and the men eagerly attending them—a mix of Queen's students and training pilots from the recently built RCAF base at nearby Collins Bay, as well as cadets from the Royal Military College on Point Frederick, and one of Queen's rivals in sports.

Still, thanks to the war, there were quite a few more women present than men, most of them seeming more interested in joining up than kicking up their heels with their hopeful partners. There was a long line by the table in the back, where a beady-eyed officer was handing out forms.

Rosie smoothed down the front of her day dress in navy cotton with white piping as she looked around with some apprehension. Small talk had never been her particular forte, so she tended to avoid parties like this, and besides, next to Violet, she suspected she was practically invisible.

She glanced at her cousin, elegant in a dress of dark green silk, with puffed sleeves and a shirred waist, her golden-brown hair done in an elaborate style, one foot already tapping to the music as she looked around the room in expectant assessment. Rosie suspected that right now her cousin, at least, was more interested in dancing than filling out a form, never mind agreeing to several years of service who-knew-where.

"Shall we get a drink?" Violet suggested as she started to move through the crowd. "I'm sure there's only lemonade, but I'm parched."

Dutifully, Rosie followed her cousin through the noisy throng, wincing as someone's elbow accidentally connected with her ribcage, and a woman brayed a loud laugh practically in her ear. She really would have rather been at home, reading a book or talking to her father about his work; she'd been helping him in his office all summer, and while it had been nothing more than some typing and filing so far, she had unspoken hopes of one day doing more. Much more.

Or, she thought, she could have been playing bridge with her younger brother Jamie; her parents were always happy to make up a four, and Rosie loved the game, the endless, interesting strategy of it. At seventeen, Jamie was thankfully too young to think of joining up yet, and, in any case, a weak chest when he was small would most likely scupper his chances now. Rosie suspected her mother was secretly glad of the fact; she'd always coddled Jamie a bit, since he'd had so many close calls as a child, his breath rattling through his lungs as he gasped for air. Thankfully, he was in much better health now, although Rosie knew her mother still worried about him.

"Here we are," Violet said cheerfully, handing her a glass of the predicted lemonade. "Now, who looks interesting?" Her narrowed gaze scanned the room of undoubtedly eligible bachelors, half of them in uniform, and Rosie swallowed a laugh.

"I thought the stall over there with that dragon of an officer was what interested you," she remarked, nodding toward the hatchet-faced woman in stiff-looking navy at the back of the hall.

"All in good time," Violet replied airily, her gaze continuing to move over the crowd. "We can't come to a dance and not dance, after all."

"I can," Rosie replied, and Violet gave her a scolding sort of look.

"Really, Rosie, you're too much! When are you going to learn to enjoy yourself?"

"I do," Rosie protested, "but you know I've never been much of one for—" She stopped her explanation because the band had started up again and a cadet had already approached Violet and was now whisking her away to jitterbug. Her cousin tossed a somewhat apologetic look over her shoulder at Rosie, before she began twirling and twisting with happy abandon.

As Rosie glanced around at all the dancing couples, she doubted she'd be asked to dance even once that evening, and she told herself it was a good thing. She'd long ago made peace with her unremarkable looks—light brown hair, rather wispy, and hazel eyes that were more mud-colored than Violet's golden, glinting ones. Her figure was trim enough, but without any of the buxom curves that were feted in magazines and movies, and as for flirting... when Violet had once, in a fit of impatience that Rosie didn't try to chat up the fellows, tried to teach her to bat her eyelashes, she'd hooted with laughter as Rosie had blinked and squinted and pretty much looked as if she'd had just gotten a speck in her eye.

"He'll be handing you a handkerchief, not trying to steal a kiss," Violet had said, shaking her head, and Rosie had rubbed her eyes ruefully.

"I'm not interested in any of that, Violet. You know I'm not."

"Not interested," Violet had replied with her usual shrewdness, "or too scared to try?"

Rosie had merely scoffed, and thankfully her cousin had dropped it. They hadn't talked about it since, and Rosie was glad not to. She had her studies to think about, after all.

She took a sip of her lemonade as her foot instinctively tapped to the music, just as Violet's had.

"Are you thinking of joining up, too?"

Rosie turned to see Vera, a cheerful, friendly girl from one of her history lectures, smiling at her in expectation.

"No, no," she said quickly, and then felt guilty for being yet again so swift to reject such a notion. "But my cousin Violet is thinking about it," she added, with a smile. "I'm just here for moral support."

"Well, I think it sounds awfully exciting," Vera told her in a confiding manner as she took a step closer to Rosie. "Although a bit scary, for sure! Apparently, we're going to have to go through basic training just like the fellows... all the drills and exercises and getting muddy and the rest of it." She gave a shudder of apparent enjoyment.

"Sounds like a real laugh," Rosie replied, trying to muster her enthusiasm, and Vera grinned.

"Oh, I bet it is. Lots of parties and things, and of course all those soldiers around..." Her voice had dropped to a cheeky, conspiratorial whisper.

Rosie frowned. "I thought the soldiers would be billeted elsewhere?"

"Well, they are for basic training, but that doesn't stop us getting a little friendly, does it?" Vera returned with a wink. "Nothing *too* shocking, mind..."

Rosie thought Vera's knowing grin rather suggested otherwise and she tried her best not to blush. She had little experience of such things, as Violet liked to point out, but she didn't think she was a *complete* innocent. She heard things, at least—some gossip from Violet and the other girls at Queen's. How much of it was actually true was another matter, but judging from the gleam in Vera's eye, at least some of it was.

There had been, Rosie recalled, a deep reluctance on the parts of both the government and the general public to form the Canadian Women's Army Corps in the first place, because it was thought unseemly for women to serve in such a way, and people—men in particular—feared it would encourage "fast" behavior. While Rosie didn't hold much truck with that sort of talk, she suspected many would look at someone with Vera's attitude as evidence of their fears.

"So you're definitely going to join?" she asked, and Vera gave a firm nod.

"Beats studying, doesn't it?"

No, it does not, Rosie thought, but decided not to say. Again, she felt that prickle of unease, a flash of guilt. Should she be falling into step with her sisters-in-arms, willing to wield a toilet brush the way a man did a rifle? And yet surely, she thought a bit desperately, she could serve her country better by training to be a lawyer rather than working as a skivvy...

"I did it!"

Flushed with triumph, Violet appeared before Rosie, cadet

decidedly not in tow, a piece of paper brandished in one hand like a trophy.

"You did what?" Rosie asked, blinking.

"You joined up?" Vera chimed excitedly, nodding toward the paper in Violet's hand. "Oh, I'm going to right now, as well!"

"Come on then, girls!" Seeming determined to make it a jolly affair, Violet linked arms with both Vera and Rosie. "Off we go!"

Rosie tried to pull her arm from her cousin's, but Violet held fast. "Violet," she protested, "I told you, I'm not—"

"You can at least take a look," Violet replied, pulling Rosie more firmly in by her side. "Just a look!"

"But, Violet—"

"I'm not taking no for an answer!"

Despite her faltering protests, Rosie found herself cheerily marched between the two women toward the table at the back of the room where the beady-eyed officer waited with a clipboard full of forms. She listened in growing trepidation as the officer asked Vera all sorts of questions—was she eighteen?—the age had recently been lowered from twenty-one— over five feet, in good physical condition?—equivalent to Army Standard A— had completed her High School Entrance, and lastly, but perhaps most importantly, was she "of good character with no record of conviction of an indictable offense"?

Vera answered merrily to all of them, and Rosie had the strange feeling that her two friends considered the whole thing the most wonderful lark. Did they have no idea what they were signing up for—at the very least, a few years—"as long as the conflict shall last"—with no choice in the matter of where or how they served?

"Well, young miss," the officer asked Rosie, jutting out her chin, "what about you? Are you ready to enlist and free a man to fly? Do your duty to God and your country? I assure you, there is no better place for a Canadian woman to serve."

"I..." Rosie stared at her helplessly. In the face of the woman's unwavering and challenging stare, her explanations about pursuing her studies seemed feeble indeed. Feeble and, she realized, selfish.

"Come on, Rosie," Violet cajoled, grabbing her arm. "I've signed up already, so we can do it all together. I can't imagine going without you, and it really will be so much fun."

No, it won't, Rosie thought as a pen was thrust into her hand. *At least, I don't think it will be...*

"Do it," Vera cried as they both pushed her forward. "We both have now. Come on, Rosie. Do it!"

CHAPTER TWO

FEBRUARY 1942

Kitchener, Ontario

"We're almost there!"

Violet rubbed the smeary glass of the window, peering out at the dark night as the train rumbled toward the military base in Kitchener where the newest group of CWACs would be doing their six weeks of basic training. Next to her, Rosie shifted in her hard wooden seat, her back aching from being jolted across the province in the freezing cold for the last six hours, yet she couldn't help but feel a nervous little thrill of excitement at the prospect of finally arriving at their destination.

Most of the other recruits were cheerful and eager to arrive at the base and start their training, although Rosie remained a bit anxious about the uncertainty of it all. During the long train journey, she had listened to the other girls' banter and gossip, quietly sharing in the sense of fun and camaraderie, the gales of laughter and thermoses of tea passed around to keep them warm as the train journeyed west, to sixty miles past Toronto... but she'd wondered, at least a little, what on earth she was doing here.

Violet hadn't been able to strong-arm her into signing the form on the night of the dance, but her cousin, in her usual, determined style, had chipped away at Rosie's resistance until she'd felt it would be wrong not to go; in fact, she'd almost —*almost*—been looking forward to it.

In their last conversation before she'd finally signed the paper, Violet had told her point-blank Rosie was reluctant simply because she was scared.

"Scared!" Rosie had repeated, trying to sound dismissive. "What on earth would I be scared about?"

"All of it," Violet had flung at her. "Doing something new, something strange, and most importantly, something you might not even be good at." Her eyes had gleamed as she'd nodded. "I know you, Rosie Lyman. You don't want to try unless you're sure to succeed." Violet's hands were planted on her hips, her expression fierce as she had stared at Rosie across the rumpled mess of her room—she'd asked her over to go through her wardrobe, deciding what to take to basic training and what to leave behind. Rosie already suspected, thanks to her Aunt Louisa's fashion tastes, most of her cousin's wardrobe would be in the latter category, a froth of silk and satin tossed gaily onto her bed. "You've always been scared to do anything new or strange," Violet had stated, a grand pronouncement that rather stung.

"I'm not—"

"I don't blame you, what with everything you experienced when you were small," Violet had continued, her voice gentling, and Rosie had flushed, not particularly wanting to be reminded of those days. She knew she had been rather timid as a child; with her brother's weak chest, life had always seemed precious and fragile, and even more so after her family had lost everything in the Crash. She hadn't liked trying new things; she'd valued certainties and safety, and still did. And some might say she was shy... But that didn't mean she was *scared*. "Even if that's true what does that have to do with—" she had begun, only to be cut off by Violet's exclamation.

"Oh, Rosie, I wish I had half the brains you do, you know." She had reached for her arm, pulling her toward her for a quick, affectionate hug. Rosie had hugged her back, yet was unable to meet her cousin's eye. "But Rosie," Violet had continued earnestly, "the world is so much bigger than Kingston, or Queen's. And while I do think it's important to serve king and country—and I *do*—I think enlisting could be good for you. I think you need a little adventure in your life! A little challenge. It could wake you up, maybe."

"I'm perfectly awake, thank you," Rosie had replied, knowing she sounded defensive. But goodness, Violet made it sound as if she were sleepwalking through life!

"Don't you *want* to go," Violet had broken in earnestly, "if I do? We've always done everything together, Rosie. Queen's will be as dull as dishwater without me!" She'd given a cheeky grin, and Rosie had let out a little laugh.

"That will certainly be true—"

"We could have so much fun together, Rosie, like the two musketeers!"

"I think it's three," Rosie had replied dryly, but she was smiling. She was, she'd realized, more and more tempted by Violet's proposal. She would miss her cousin and best friend dearly if she left, and really, the way Violet talked, it seemed churlish, as well as unpatriotic, to refuse to join up—and so now here she was, with all of it finally about to begin.

Many of the girls on the train, Rosie knew, had enlisted out of fierce patriotism, while others, like Violet, really did just want an adventure, and they felt they were sure to have it while in the

CWAC. Others, Rosie discovered, just wanted an escape from home.

"My mum wants me to take care of the little ones every day, all day," one woman from Gananoque had told Violet and Rosie rather grimly as she'd huddled in her coat, her chin tucked low. "And there are *five* of them. And my father won't let me have any callers—not even from church. It was up at dawn every day and in bed after supper. I couldn't wait to get away. Anything is better than that."

"You poor thing," Violet had said, squeezing her hand. "You'll have loads of fun, I'm sure. It's all going to be an absolute *gas*, I know it is!"

Rosie had her doubts about that, but she had kept quiet and smiled in sympathy at the young woman. "I'm sure you'll have many more opportunities here," she'd offered, and the woman had smiled at her gratefully.

"I know I am hoping to."

No matter what she'd told Violet earlier about wanting to stay at her studies, over the last few months, Rosie had come to realize the situation wasn't as simple as that. Students at Queen's would be required to do six hours of mandatory service anyway, and classes were likely to be interrupted, thanks to the number of boys determined to enlist.

And then there had been the disappointment from her father...

It still hurt to remember how he'd nipped her fledgling dreams in the bud. After working in his office all summer, Rosie had finally got up the courage to tell him her true dream—of one day joining him as a lawyer, Lyman and Daughter proudly written on the sign outside. Her father, although as kindly as ever, had explained how that wasn't likely to happen anytime soon.

"Darling," he'd said, "you know that the work I do, dealing with farmers and men of the land. They're an old-fashioned bunch, pretty stuck in the mud, to tell you the truth, and they don't like change. As far as they're concerned, women belong in the kitchen or garden. I'm not saying it's right," he'd added quickly, as if he sensed her protest, "but they're traditional, and more than one set of eyebrows has risen, I can tell you, at simply seeing you out here, with your typewriter!"

"Is that meant to make me feel better?" Rosie had asked, an uncharacteristic spurt of bitterness entering her voice. She'd known farmers were old-fashioned, but if her father explained the situation, perhaps they would come around, in time. "Things will change, Dad," she'd said, "you know they will, and especially with this war. Women will start to do all sorts of things—drive ambulances, repair engines, maybe even fly planes —" She'd sounded, Rosie had realized, like Violet going on about the CWAC. According to her cousin, women would be able to train for all sorts of trades, avenues that weren't open to them in civilian life. Avenues better than this one—filing and typing with no hope of advancement.

"And practice law, I'm sure," her father had agreed, his eyes crinkling at the corners as he smiled at her, warmly now. "I've no doubt, Rosie, and I think you'll make a wonderful lawyer, one day. And I would never say never, to have you joining my practice... after all, Lyman and Daughter does have a nice ring to it." He'd tilted his head, so clearly trying to appease her, and yet failing, because Rosie had wanted his enthusiasm, his unbridled excitement, not this cautionary approach, as good as a warning or even a straight-out no.

"But don't get my hopes up, because of the fusty old farmers you deal with?" she'd finished, trying not to sound as hurt as she felt. She'd been reasonable enough to acknowledge that her father had a point, even if she hadn't liked it. Farmers *wouldn't* want to deal with a young woman, fresh out of law school, the ink barely dry on her degree. But that didn't mean they couldn't try, if her father got behind her one hundred percent... something she now understood he wasn't willing to do.

"Something like that, I suppose." He'd reached over to pat her shoulder. "I'm sorry, darling. I don't mean to pour cold water all over your hopes, I really don't. Maybe one day it will be possible. The world never changes as quickly as we want it to."

"It will only change if we make it," Rosie had returned. "If we step out and *do* something, and force it to happen." She'd lifted her chin. "'If it's right for men to fight for their freedom,'" she quoted, "'it's right for women to fight for theirs.'"

"Emmeline Pankhurst?" he'd guessed, and Rosie had nodded defiantly. Her father had simply sighed and shaken his head, seemingly defeated, the conversation clearly over.

Rosie had, with Violet's urging, enlisted the very next day.

Now, however, not for the first time, she wondered if she'd acted at least a little bit in haste. She'd had plenty of time to consider the matter, as they'd continued with their studies while they'd waited to be called up for training. In the end, Rosie had told herself she'd done what she'd done and she'd make the best of it, do her duty and maybe even see a bit more of the world—starting with a freezing train to Kitchener, Ontario.

Her cousin had made at least a dozen friends since they'd climbed aboard this train, chatting and laughing and squeezing into the seat, while Rosie had been happier, as always, to listen and watch. The recruits were a motley bunch—a mix of raw-boned farmers' daughters and gum-snapping city girls, the talk wilder than anything she'd ever heard before, although all in good humor. Violet certainly seemed happy enough to join in, and Rosie managed to smile and nod along, doing her best not to blush. Violet had been right, she certainly was outside of her comfort, but she would not give her cousin, or anyone else, the satisfaction of seeing that.

Violet, of course, wasn't fooled.

"You don't need to look so disapproving," she'd whispered to Rosie halfway through their journey, and Rosie had stiffened in surprised affront.

"I don't," she'd protested. "I'm just listening, Violet." But her cousin was already leaning forward, chiming in with one of her own stories, while Rosie did her best to look interested and friendly. Violet had never been bothered by her quietness before, she thought, even as she resolved to make even more of an effort.

"My dad was ever so mad I was enlisting," one woman confided. "He wanted me to stay on the farm, for sure! Who's going to milk the cows now? Not me!" She glanced around at them all a bit defiantly, as if daring them to argue.

Rosie's own family had taken the news of her enlisting with a sort of bemused surprise; she'd been vocal enough in resisting the notion at first, she supposed. Her mother, Ellen, had been sorrowfully supportive, recalling her own days during the first war.

"Of course I would never keep you from doing your duty," she'd said, "as I did mine, but war—it's a terrible thing, Rosie. We haven't seen it yet, not properly, this time. I know it can feel far away, but one day it won't be." Her face had been overcome with sadness as she'd continued, "One day the papers will be full of battles that have been fought—won or lost, there will always be losses. I hate to think of you in the thick of it all."

"I'm likely to be somewhere far away from the actual battles," Rosie had replied, giving her mother a quick hug. "You don't need to worry on that account, I'm sure I'll probably be out in Alberta or somewhere! But you're right—the war has felt far away. I don't like to think of it coming any closer." And yet perhaps it would be, or at least feel as if it was, once she enlisted.

Her father had been as supportive, but also cautious. "You don't have to do this for my sake, you know," he had ventured once, when Rosie had come home from university halls for Sunday supper. "Your studies are important, Rosie. I've always felt that."

"And so is serving," Rosie had flashed back. Ever since their discussion back in August, she'd felt prickly around her father, choosing to be snappish rather than show her hurt. It wasn't, she knew, a particularly helpful or mature reaction, but she still struggled to keep herself from it.

He'd sighed and shaken his head. "As long as you're doing it for the right reason."

"I am," she'd replied firmly, although she still wasn't entirely sure. In any case, it didn't really matter; once she'd signed that form, she'd committed to basic training, at the very least. Besides, the last thing she wanted to do was quit and somehow prove her father right, that she'd been foolish to join up.

They'd had a farewell party in early January, with both Violet's and Rosie's families, along with her Aunt Gracie and her husband Will, and their two children, and dear old Granny Rose, who lived with her other cousin Sarah in Gananoque. It had been a determinedly festive occasion, despite the ever-present ominousness of the war; the attack on Pearl Harbor had happened mere weeks ago, and the United States had finally entered the war—a fact which generated both jubilation and fear, for it surely brought the war closer to their shores, just as Rosie's mother had said, and it might even get closer still.

All through December, over two thousand Canadian soldiers had joined in the Battle of Hong Kong; they had been expecting guard duty and had instead faced a relentless invading force. Two boys in the year above Rosie were listed as missing, presumed dead. They were the first casualties she'd actually known, and it had given her some much-needed conviction that she'd been right to leave the ivory tower of Queen's and serve her country, however that looked.

And how *would* it look, she wondered, as the train finally

rumbled to a stop, with a long, slow exhalation of steam, the night outside impenetrably black, the barest hint of moon glinting briefly on drifts of hard-crusted snow. The girls on the train exchanged nervous looks and giggles as they waited for whatever came next, and, in truth, Rosie suspected none of them had any idea.

There had been remarkably little information given to the recruits so far, beyond being told they'd been accepted and to wait for their orders to attend basic training. What that meant was anyone's guess—there had been rumors flying around of having to crawl on your belly under barbed wire, or even learn how to shoot a gun, or maybe just marching and drilling, as well as the usual typing and other aptitude tests—and, of course, cleaning. For women, Rosie thought, would never be without a scrub brush.

But now they were about to find out.

The door to their train car opened and, after a few taut seconds, a woman, wrapped up in a greatcoat and muffler, came onto the train. "Attention, recruits!" she bellowed, making more than a few of them jump; there were one or two titters, quickly stifled. "Rise, please, and follow me. A bus will take you to the base, where you will be processed."

Women rose in a flurry, grabbing suitcases and hats, wrapping coats more firmly around them, for the wind coming from outside was bitter indeed. Then, as the officer marched off the train, they followed in a tremulous shuffle, the glib and gleeful bravado of their journey fading into an uncertain silence as a silent and wintry, night-cloaked tundra greeted them, the only sight a few buses waiting to take them on the rest of their jolting journey. Rosie glanced at Violet, who gave her a bracing look back.

A driver threw their cases in the hold underneath as they all scrambled onto the bus, shooting each other anxious glances, no one quite daring to say anything.

After they'd all been seated, the officer came onto the bus, gave them a quelling look, which made someone giggle before she quickly suppressed it, and then sat down. With a weary huff of exhaust and a coughing rattle of the engine, the bus started off down a track through the snow.

The best part of an exhausting hour later, the sight of several barracks squatting in the snow greeted them, not a person in sight, the whole place looking, Rosie thought, a bit dreary in the darkness.

"I hope we'll at least get something to eat," Violet whispered to Rosie as they followed the officer in an untidy line toward a tin-roofed hall. "I'm absolutely starving. Goodness, this place really does look depressing, doesn't it? Maybe it's better in the daylight."

"We can hope," Rosie agreed, for she thought there was certainly something dispiriting about the endlessly dark sky, the utilitarian barracks lined up underneath it like soldiers, empty fields of snow stretching in every direction, the wind sweeping across them and cutting right through her wool coat. She shivered, hunching her shoulders against the bone-chilling cold as her boots crunched across the frozen snow. It had to be hovering near zero, her breath coming out in frosty puffs, her nose and lips already starting to go numb.

In a hall empty of anything but a table and chair, they gave their names to another woman in uniform, this one just as stern-looking and decidedly taciturn, and then dropped off their suit-cases in a heap before being herded into an empty canteen, where all that was waiting for them to eat was, improbably, a pot of over-boiled macaroni and a tureen of gravy.

"What on earth!" Violet exclaimed, wrinkling her nose as she gazed down at her plate of food. "Whoever heard of maca-roni and *gravy*?"

"At least it's hot," Vera replied, scooping up a forkful. "That'll do me." She'd sat with them all the way on the train

from Kingston, full of good cheer and excitement, her enthusiasm unflagging despite the cold and discomfort, and now, the
unusual menu.

"It *is* hot," Rosie replied, blowing on her own forkful. "And
not a bad combination, actually, although I admit, I never would
have thought of it!" She smiled at Vera, who smiled back, but
Violet wasn't paying attention.

Rosie glanced around the canteen, full of tables of women
like her, their faces pale under the electric light, their shoulders
hunched, all of them seeming a bit shell-shocked by their
strange reception—near-silent officers, the unusual food, the
strange sense of emptiness and waiting.

"It's almost as if they didn't know we were coming," one
woman at their table remarked in a hushed whisper, as if afraid
to break the silence that hung over the room like a cold mist.

"Well, it did happen awfully fast, didn't it?" Rosie returned,
determined to see the best of things, for Violet's benefit as well
as her own. "They had only a few months to get everything
ready, didn't they? The barracks, the training, the uniform, all of
it. I suspect we'll get ourselves sorted out tomorrow." She tried
to give the girl a reassuring smile. "For now, at least we have a
hot meal and a bed."

Sure enough, they'd barely finished their macaroni when
another officer ordered them to rise, and they were all taken to
their barracks.

Rosie eyed the narrow cot with its regulation army blankets and a barracks box underneath for her few belongings
with some trepidation; there was precious little privacy or
comfort, compared to home. Of course, she'd *known* it would
be like that, and had said as much to Violet, who had insisted it
would be an adventure, but it felt lonelier now that she was
standing in a freezing-cold hut, small suitcase in hand, staring
at her uncomfortable-looking bed, a group of strangers milling
about her, looking just as lost as she felt. A wave of homesick-

ness rose in her like a tide, making her blink quickly and swallow hard.

"It's absolutely freezing in here," one woman exclaimed, crouching by the small, pot-bellied stove at one end of the room. "They haven't even lit the stove!"

"They're trying to weed out the wheat from the chaff," another woman said, in the self-important tone of someone who clearly thought she was wheat. "See who can stand it."

"What's the point of a stove if it's not lit?" the other woman returned irritably. "That's common sense, nothing more. It's well below freezing."

"Is there any kindling?"

Rosie watched, a wave of exhaustion crashing over her, as Violet and a few other women bustled around industriously, finding wood and kindling, matches and paper. Within a few minutes, they had a fire cheerily blazing in the little stove, and she could feel the warmth from where she stood, swaying on her feet, too tired to move.

With the problem of heating solved, the other women began to unpack their belongings and ready themselves for bed. Outside, the wind howled, making the windowpanes rattle.

Violet, toothbrush already in hand, glanced at Rosie in concern. "Aren't you going to get ready?"

"Yes..." Rosie realized she had been simply standing there, watching everyone else move busily around her. "Sorry."

She glanced at the woman who had talked about the wheat and the chaff; she had already put all her belongings away and changed into her flannel nightgown, her hair neatly braided as she climbed into bed and drew the covers up to her chin. Another woman was slipping into a threadbare and patched nightgown, its hem ragged. The latter was the woman Violet had been talking to on the train, who had all the little ones at home. She looked pale and exhausted and very young. Other women were getting ready for bed, too, and all the while, Rosie had simply been standing there, staring into space.

"Rosie," Violet called over with a laugh, as cheerful as ever, as she wriggled out of her skirt and blouse, nightgown in hand. "Get a move on!"

"Yes..." Rosie said again, blinking slowly. With her mind finally kicking into gear, she opened her suitcase and fumbled through her belongings for her nightgown, washcloth, and toothbrush.

All the other girls were already in bed by the time she managed to change and wash at a row of sinks, the toilet stalls behind not even possessing any doors. She'd heard they'd rushed to get the base at Kitchener turned into training facilities, and so it seemed.

Quickly, she put away her things and jumped beneath the covers. Even with the fire in the stove finally blazing away, the room was terribly cold.

The only sound in the barracks was the crackling of the fire and the wind rattling the panes, along with a bit of snuffling and shifting as everyone settled into bed. No one spoke.

Rosie huddled under the thin blankets, trying not to shiver. She should have put on a pair of socks and maybe even a sweater, but her mind had felt as if it were as frozen as her toes now were. She was, she realized with a lurch of alarm, very close to tears, and she wasn't even sure why.

She'd *expected* this. She knew she had. And yet, lying here, trying not to shiver, it felt so very different.

And worse than the homesickness that was threatening to sweep right over her was the fear. Violet had been right; she *was* scared. Scared of the unknown, but also scared of failing. What if she wasn't even able to pass her basic training and had to return to Kingston, shamed, a failure? What if this was too *hard*?

Rosie sniffed, and in the dark she heard the rustle of blan-

kets as Violet, in the bed next to her, moved, and then she felt
her cousin's hand fumbling for her own. Violet didn't say a
word, but her fingers clasped Rosie's tightly and for a few
moments the lump in her throat lessened and the tears
crowding behind her lids eased.

Violet squeezed her hand, and Rosie squeezed back.

CHAPTER THREE

"At-ten*tion!*"

Outside, the sky had not even begun to lighten as Rosie blinked sleep out of her eyes, the women in the cots next to her already scrambling from underneath their covers to stand to attention at their foot of their beds. A good few seconds behind even the last, Rosie jumped to her feet and half-stumbled to the end of her bed, throwing her shoulders back and lifting her chin.

Still half-asleep, she struggled to listen as the officer strolled briskly up and down the room, informing the new recruits what would happen that day—how they would have medicals, receive their inoculations and uniforms, and then take a series of aptitude tests—but first they needed to make their beds.

"Every morning will start at six, when you will make your bed and make sure your uniform is in immaculate condition. After breakfast, you will parade back to the square for marching and drilling before you attend your various classes in the afternoon." The officer stopped before Rosie, her cool gaze scanning the room, meeting each recruit's timid look in challenge before moving on. "I am not interested in fainting lilies who need their beauty sleep or a day in bed during a certain time of the month. You are here to serve, and I am here to weed out the wheat from the chaff. If you can't handle the pace, you don't belong here and you'd be better back at home, helping your mother in the kitchen." This was said matter-of-factly, and Rosie struggled not to look away when the officer's unyielding gaze briefly met hers.

"They really do want to weed out the wheat from the chaff," Violet whispered, eyes dancing, as they dressed, after the officer had left. Everyone was hurrying into their clothes as quickly as they could, as much because the room was freezing as the fact they only had fifteen minutes before they had to report for medicals, and they still had to have breakfast. "Just like Marjorie said."

Rosie glanced at the woman from last night, tall and strong-boned, her fair hair in a neat French roll, her bed made with the crispest corners she had ever seen. Her heart sank a little bit at the sight, because as much as she prided herself on being neat and practical, she knew she wasn't a patch on someone like Marjorie. She had to be in her late twenties, with the experienced air of someone just that much older, and, as she'd told all and sundry last night, she'd volunteered in an auxiliary service for three years already, and worked as a secretary for a bank in Ottawa. She seemed so very cool and competent, far more than Rosie felt, at any rate, only twenty years old with her hair half undone, her blouse buttoned up wrong before she quickly corrected it.

"I'm feeling very much like chaff at the minute," she told Violet as she stuck some pins in her hair.

Violet gave her a commiserating smile. "You and me both! You know I never even make my bed at home."

Rosie had to swallow a laugh as she glanced down at her cousin's decidedly rumpled covers. "Oh, Violet, you'll have to do better than that," she teased as she quickly tucked the corners in tightly. "If you're going to be sent home, don't have it be for not making your bed, of all things!"

"And that's just the start," Violet returned, her eyes sparkling. She seemed, as she always did, unrepentant about her own shortcomings. "Never mind. I'll get there, I know it. And it's still an adventure. I wonder what our uniforms will look like! I do hope they're smart." She pulled Rosie along, out of their barracks. "Come on, slowpoke, or we won't get anything to eat. Nancy told me the bread goes that fast."

In early dawn, Rosie thought, the camp was only a little more appealing than it had been in the dead of night. The sky seemed endless, a blanket of gray, with a few faint pink streaks on the horizon, snow stretching in every direction. The training facility was no more than a dozen or so barracks and a couple of halls, looking as if it had all been dropped down into a snowy field from a great hand above.

In the dining hall, a cheerful, red-faced woman gave Rosie her breakfast—a single, hard-boiled egg in the middle of a plate of thick white china.

"Well, I suppose we'll get thin in the army," Violet whispered as they headed back to their table. "Nancy said the cook told her not to take the top piece of bread—it's always cold."

By the time Rosie realized she meant the plate of piled bread in the center of the table, all of it save for the top piece was gone, and the butter too. She ate it dry and cold, along with the egg, her stomach roiling queasily, as Violet chatted easily to her neighbors and Rosie munched in silence, trying to bolster her already flagging spirits. She was doing her best to be as cheerful as the others, but everything felt so strange.

The rest of the day passed in a haze of activity—first was the shock of having to line up with a dozen other girls and strip off her clothes for her medical. She'd never been naked in front of

anyone before, and Rosie struggled not to blush with embarrassment as some girls shucked off their clothes with seeming abandon, strutting about, others shyer even than she was. She stood
there in her brassiere and pants, crossing her arms over her
chest and shivering in the cold, while the army doctor stood in
front of each one of them, eyeing them up and down, before
moving on without a word.

"I don't know what that was for," Vera remarked when they
were finally able to get back into their clothes. "They didn't do a
thing to us!"

"Besides look as if we were disappointing specimens?"
Rosie returned, trying for a smile. "That was enough for me."

"I suppose he wanted a right old look at us, the old geezer,"
one of the women in their barracks, Nancy—the one, Rosie
recalled, who had known about the bread—remarked with a
wink. "Must be the most exciting thing he does all day. Doesn't
do for him to get *too* excited, though, does it?"

Violet laughed and Rosie was also unable to stop herself
smiling a little, even though she felt acutely embarrassed by
such a remark. She certainly wasn't going to show it.

After the medical inspection, they had to have their inoculations—two jabs in each arm, done hard enough to make Rosie
wince and bite her lip. She told herself not to be such a ninny;
the training hadn't even started yet, and she'd certainly had
inoculations before. But everything felt unfamiliar—the officers'
voices so brisk and sharp, the rooms so cold, the other girls still
strangers.

Violet, she saw, had made friends with the cheery, fast-
talking Nancy, a cleaner from Hamilton, and Rosie watched
them laugh together, elbowing each other in fun, with a flicker
of jealousy she did her best to squash. Of course Violet would
find like-minded, high-spirited friends to pal around with. She
always had, first at school and then at Queen's.

After their inoculations, it was time to shed their civilian clothes for the promised uniform—a stiff cap, jacket, and skirt, all made of heavy barathea, in a drab, khaki color, along with stockings, greatcoat, waterproof, gloves and sturdy shoes of brown leather, a pullover, overalls, and a haversack and water bottle, all Army regulation.

"You will each be given an allowance of fifteen dollars to purchase necessary toiletries and undergarments," they were told by a stern-sounding officer. "And then three dollars quarterly thereafter. This is not to be used on any fripperies!"

Rosie changed into the uniform, grimacing at the stiff material, the attached collar of her blouse chafing her neck and hitting her chin. She also realized how much altering she would have to do to have it fit properly—their skirts were meant to be a regulation sixteen inches from the floor and hers was a good few inches below that; her jacket sleeves were too long, as well, hiding her hands. She'd always been pretty handy with a needle, but it would be a fair amount of work, on top of everything else.

"Come on, then, it's time for lunch," Violet said, linking arms with her and Nancy. "Don't we all look smart? I feel like I ought to go fly a plane or something."

The other girls chattered excitedly while they ate ham sandwiches washed down with mugs of coffee and Rosie tried to join in the fast-flying conversation, but barely managed to get in a word in edgewise, over the chatter and laughter.

After lunch, they were herded into yet another freezing hall for a series of aptitude tests. If Rosie had thought, thanks to Violet's encouragement, that she might have some success in this area of army life, the sheet given out to each recruit made her confidence falter indeed.

Accounting—candidates must have two years' experience at a reputable business, or have two years' education at a school of commerce.

Stenographers—candidates must be able to take dictation at the rate of one hundred words per minute, and type forty words per minute.

Dental Assistant—candidates must have experience assisting at the chair in a reputable dental office.

Drivers—candidates must have a recognized motor mechanics certificate and driver's license.

Hospital Assistant—candidates must hold a St. John Ambulance or Red Cross certificate.

Operators, telephone—candidates must have experience operating a switchboard.

She didn't qualify for any of these, Rosie realized with a flare of panic. As much as she'd once prided herself on her academic skills, her only work experience was in her father's office, pecking away at the typewriter, well below the required forty words a minute. She held no certificates besides her one of General Education, didn't know how to drive a car, didn't particularly enjoy the sight of blood, and had barely seen a switchboard.

She looked back down at the sheet, at the last trade listed. *Mess women—candidates must be of a suitable competency.* So maybe she would be slinging soup, after all.

Rosie glanced up from the sheet at the other women studying their own papers, many who seemed unfazed by the list of trades and their necessary qualifications. On the train to Kitchener, she'd overheard quite a few of the recruits talking about their work experience—some of them were secretaries and nurses, laboratory assistants or teachers, cleaners or waitresses, a few of them helped out at home or on the farm, but she, Violet, and Vera had been the only students.

Uncomfortably, Rosie realized she'd thought that her studies would have given her some sort of advantage, but it didn't feel that way right now. Right now, everyone, save her, was turning toward the test paper that had been slapped down in front of them and starting to work out the questions.

Swallowing hard, Rosie put the list of trades aside and turned to the test she'd been given—a jumbled mix of math, science, logic, and grammar. *You can do this*, she told herself. *This is what you're good at.*

She glanced at Violet, hoping for a reassuring smile, but her cousin was already concentrating on the test, her head bent over the paper. She might have struggled with her exams back at Queen's, but Violet clearly wanted to succeed at this.

Biting her lip, Rosie picked up her pencil and got to work.

That evening, the mood in their barracks was a mix of exhaustion and excitement. Some of the girls were in bed, having suffered after-effects from their jabs, while others were talking excitedly about everything they'd seen and done—their uniforms, the tests, the marching to and fro, the few men around the base, some of whom had smiled or winked at them as they'd sauntered past. Rosie was sitting on her bed, diligently hemming her skirt to its regulation length as she listened to the chatter fly.

"I'd love to be a driver. I don't have the mechanical cert, but I've driven my dad's tractor since I was fourteen. Do you think that counts?"

"I want to be a telephone operator. I have a nice speaking voice, don't I? My mother says I sound just like Rosalind Russell."

"Did you see that dishy airman, the one with the swagger?" This from Nancy, who was grinning.

Another woman rolled her eyes. "They all have a swagger!"

"Oh," one recruit wailed, "I've got *blisters!*"

"Isn't Corporal Jenkins an absolute dragon!" Evelyn, a particularly high-spirited girl from Napanee, exclaimed, shaking her head as she took off a shoe. "That face would as good as turn you to stone. I think she *wants* us to fail."

"Well, *some* of us must be the chaff, after all," Nancy remarked with a pointed look for Marjorie, who had, Rosie acknowledged, been something of a know-it-all all day, telling everyone how simple the tests had been, how her jabs hadn't hurt a bit, how *easy* it all was. Rosie certainly wasn't feeling as if any of it was easy, and it had barely begun. "Right, girls, so who's packing it in after day one?" Nancy glanced around in teasing challenge, eyebrows raised, hands planted on her hips.

There was silence, and then a woman in the corner bed, Josie, said quietly, "Eleanor's already gone."

"What!" Nancy's laughing expression turned shocked, and Rosie glanced at the bed next to Josie's, made from this morning, the barracks box underneath empty of belongings. "When did she go?"

"This afternoon, after the tests," Josie replied. "She just said it wasn't for her."

Nancy shook her head slowly. "Poor thing. She was a quiet one, wasn't she? She's got a strict father, and lots of little ones at home she's expected to care for. Can't be easy."

Several of the women exchanged uncomfortable glances, the mood of laughing excitement turned suddenly somber. With a jolt, Rosie realized Eleanor must have been the girl she and Violet had talked to on the train, who had sounded so grimly determined. And she'd already *gone?* How many more of them would be gone before the week was out, too frightened even to try? *Would she?*

"That's the point of this, you know," Marjorie said, a pompous pronouncement, and behind her back, Nancy rolled her eyes. A few girls stifled nervous titters. "We can't all make it to the end of training, you know," she continued in the same lofty tone. "The whole purpose is to see who can take it and who can't. Who has the stamina and the strength and the experience—"

"You do, obviously," one woman muttered under her breath.

Marjorie lifted her chin. "Eleanor didn't, at any rate. To quit after just one day! What a waste of our military's time and money. There's a war on, remember. This is no place for slackers coming just for a lark or a jaunt."

"Oh, for heaven's sake," someone muttered, and a prickly silence ensued. The mood in the room was starting to feel uncomfortable, even hostile. Marjorie, bristling with affront, began to fold her jacket very slowly and carefully, not looking at anyone else.

Rosie felt a bit badly for her, but more so for everyone else. "Why do we have to be pitted against one another," she remarked quietly to Violet. "There's already a war on, we don't need to make another one here."

Violet turned to give her a sudden, surprised look, before she nodded decisively. "You're right." She stood up by her bed, her hands on her hips. "Why can't we all make it?" she challenged everyone in a loud voice, her bright eyes blazing. "This doesn't have to be a competition, you know. There's plenty of war work for everyone. Maybe if we help each other along, instead of wondering who's ridiculous wheat and who's silly chaff, hoping someone else fails so you don't, we'll *all* graduate out."

Rosie smiled, glad for her cousin's courage, and wishing, only a little bit, that she'd been brave enough to speak up first.

Marjorie glanced at Violet, looking as if she wanted to argue, but she merely pressed her lips together and resumed folding her jacket, smoothing out the creases with painstaking care.

"I agree," Nancy stated, her voice rising as she stepped from behind Marjorie. "This is all going to be hard enough without us bringing each other down. I say we all resolve to give each other a helping hand, keep each other going. If one of us fails, we all fail."

"Yes, exactly," Violet exclaimed as she linked arms with

Nancy. Rosie watched, conscious of how bright and fierce they both looked, glancing around the room in determined challenge. "And that means covering for each other, too," Violet stated. "No ratting each other out or anything like that."

"What are you suggesting we might do that we could be *ratted out*?" Marjorie asked sourly.

"I'm sure *you* won't put a little toe out of line," Violet assured her sweetly, "but the rest of us aren't quite so accomplished yet, Marjorie. Clearly, we have a lot to learn from you, but all I'm saying is, lend a hand when you can. Keep your chin up, and help someone else keep up theirs. If today was anything to go by, it's going to be pretty darn hard."

"Hear, hear!" someone else shouted, followed by a few giggles and glances toward Marjorie, who was looking decidedly out of sorts.

"I'm hardly against helping anyone," she stated after a moment, since it seemed as if everyone had been waiting for her answer. "There is a war on, after all."

"So you've said," someone called from the back of the room, and quite suddenly everyone erupted into great guffaws of laughter. Rosie found herself laughing a little, and even Marjorie managed a twitchy little smile.

A girl who had suffered from the inoculations let out a wretched moan from where she was curled up on her cot. "All I want is to feel a little less like death warmed up on a plate," she mumbled, her eyes scrunched closed. "Can anyone help me with that?"

"No, but I can give you an aspirin," Violet told her cheerfully. "And a glass of cold water. How does that sound?"

The girl smiled faintly, her eyes still closed. "Marvelous."

"So it's settled, then?" Violet said as she fished a bottle of aspirin out of her locker. "We're all in this together? All for one and one for all and all that jazz?"

Each of the women looked around at the others, their

expressions varying from hopeful, to shy, to apprehensive, everyone seeming to wait for someone else to speak first.

"Yes," Nancy sang out firmly as she took Violet's hand and shook it. "We are."

"The eleven musketeers of Barracks Five, that's us!" Violet pronounced with a firm nod, her eyes gleaming.

Rosie thought of how just a few weeks ago they'd been the two musketeers. Well, she supposed as she smiled round at the group, the more, the merrier.

A little while later, as everyone was getting ready for bed, Rosie found Violet in the laundry that was attached to the barracks on the other side, rinsing out her blouse in the sink.

"I spilled tea on the cuff at supper," she told her with a shake of her head. "Can't have that at roll call tomorrow, can I? It might be enough to get me sent home." She kept scrubbing the stain, her lips pursed.

"I'm glad you got everyone together," Rosie said. "You've always been good at that, Violet."

"Well, it was your idea, wasn't it," Violet replied briskly. "And, in any case, we're all in the same boat, aren't we? And some of the girls are really nice. Funny, too." She gave Rosie a knowing, and somewhat stern, look from beneath her lashes. "You should try to get to know them a bit better, Rosie."

"I am," Rosie protested. She'd spent the evening helping Evelyn and Josie alter their uniforms, while Violet and Nancy had been chatting away, but it didn't seem right to point it out now.

"Frankly, I admire a girl who can come here and take it all on, without an education to back her up. Nancy only just scraped her Grade Eight Gen Ed, and she can barely read, yet she did her best with those tests."

"I'm—I'm glad for her," Rosie replied. Why was Violet

acting as if she wasn't? Despite claiming to want to be like musketeers, Violet didn't seem to be acting like one now.

"Are you?" Violet said skeptically. "It's just you're so quiet, Rosie, and I know you don't mean to, but sometimes it seems as if you're looking down your nose on everybody. A few of them have been talking among themselves, wondering what's made you so snooty."

"*What?*" Rosie stared at her cousin in shock. She hadn't got that sense from the other girls. "Who?"

"Oh, it doesn't matter," Violet replied, and Rosie wondered if it was just Nancy who was gossiping about her. She wasn't sure that her cousin's new pal liked her very much, for whatever reason, but the other girls had been friendly enough, and she, Evelyn, and Josie had laughed and chatted while they'd sewed. She couldn't help but feel Violet was being rather unfair.

"Well, I'm certainly not gossiping about anyone," she said, her tone turning a little cool, to hide her hurt.

"It's not gossip," Violet protested. "They're just wondering why you're so quiet and—well, cold, I suppose."

"*Cold!* Who's saying that?" she demanded, now unable to hide her hurt. "Nancy?"

Violet's eyes flashed. "What if it is Nancy?"

Rosie just shook her head. She wasn't going to play these schoolgirl games. "So much for being the eleven musketeers," she said, her voice choking a little, before she turned on her heel and walked away.

Back in the dormitory, girls were chatting as they got ready for bed, but a silence fell upon the room as Rosie came into it, making her flush with both humiliation and hurt. Was Violet right, and they had all been gossiping about her? Or had they overheard her conversation with her cousin? Either way, she wasn't brave enough to confront anyone now, as much as she longed to.

Yet, later, as she lay in bed, utterly unable to sleep despite her exhaustion, Rosie forced herself to consider if Violet actually had a point, as unpalatable as it seemed. She knew she was shy rather than standoffish, but if it came across that way to anyone—Nancy included—she knew she needed to make more of an effort. The earthy gossip and life experience of some of the girls might have taken her a bit by surprise, but that didn't mean she thought she was better than they were. In fact, she'd been feeling the opposite—less accomplished and experienced in so many ways.

Tomorrow she'd try a bit harder, she told herself. She might never be the bright butterfly that Violet was, but she could shine in other ways, and she could certainly lend a helping hand when needed. All for one and one for all, she reminded herself, if they really were going to be the eleven musketeers.

CHAPTER FOUR

The next couple of weeks passed in a blur of activity, a haze of exhaustion. Roll call every morning at six, making their beds, gulping down breakfast, marching and drilling, often for hours at a time, no matter the weather—rain, snow, or the occasional weak sunshine breaking through dank gray cloud. Sometimes, they were left standing for an hour or more in the freezing cold, fingers and toes going numb, waiting for the officer in charge to allow them to be at ease. In the afternoon, there were lessons—how to put on a gas mask, basic first aid, self-defense, map reading, even weapons training, although they were assured they would neither be expected nor allowed to use the rifles that were put into their hands.

And then, in every other waking moment, there were the duties, endless mundane tasks, just as Rosie had suspected, yet was now determined to do to the best of her ability. She was not going to be a quitter, not on top of everything else. Girls like Nancy might have continued to look at her askance for being as quiet as she was, but they would have no other cause to criticize her, she vowed.

But the duties did take their toll. There was mess duty, fire duty, orderly duty... When she wasn't marching, drilling, or learning something new, she was sweeping, scrubbing, or stoking fires, peeling mountains of potatoes or chopping piles of onions, her eyes streaming.

Every three days, they had night duty of some sort, and yet were expected to report to roll call at 6 a.m. as if they'd had a full night's sleep. By the end of the first two weeks, Rosie was tottering on her feet, too exhausted even to feel dispirited by all the work, or jealous that Violet now seemed to be best friends with Nancy, who had definitely taken a dislike to her.

Rosie had at least found a quiet camaraderie with some of the other girls, chatting over a mountain of potatoes, or commiserating after a long, hard march.

Violet, naturally, was right in the thick of every chattering circle; she was the one who figured out how to toast bread nicked from the mess hall on a wire hanger in the wood stove, slathering it with purloined butter for a midnight feast. She arranged an impromptu pretend wedding when Nancy was asked out by a lance corporal, putting a lace slip on her head for a veil and whistling the bridal march as, in fits of giggles, Nancy processed between the beds, down the center of their dormitory. Violet was also the one who made sure to remind everyone of their pledge; when Evelyn was too tired to get up for roll call one morning, Violet enlisted Vera's help in dragging her out by the arms, and she managed to make it to the end of her freshly made bed, in uniform, with seconds to spare. When Josie struggled to finish the endless washing up after supper, Violet and Rosie worked alongside her, and cheerfully chivvied her along.

Violet was, Rosie acknowledged, the unofficial den mother of their little group, the one everyone looked to for guidance and encouragement.

By the end of two weeks, Rosie felt as if she'd been at Kitchener for months, not a mere fourteen days. She thought with nostalgia of the lovely limestone buildings of Queen's, the library where she'd often studied, the quads she'd strolled across, the hot supper her mother would have waiting for her, the laughter and conversation around their kitchen table, a few rubbers of bridge to round off a contented evening, and it all seemed as if it had happened to someone else, a million years ago.

And while life at Kitchener—the grinding duty, the complete lack of privacy, every minute of every day spoken for —still felt strange, the past and what she'd once known, and taken for granted, felt stranger still. And as hard as she found it all, Rosie already knew there would be no going back. She was not going to quit, and prove the doubters right—her father, her family, maybe even some of the recruits she worked alongside here at the base. She'd keep going, she told herself, and show everybody she was made of sterner stuff than they'd thought.

That Saturday night, the recruits were finally given a late pass, although Rosie's only hopes for the evening were to write some letters and then go to bed early. Such modest aspirations fell to the ground when Violet informed her that Nancy had roped her lance corporal into driving them into Kitchener in a military truck.

"Into Kitchener?" She had never even considered going into the nearest town; sometimes it felt as if they'd landed on the moon. "Why?"

"To have some fun, of course!" Violet wagged a warning finger at her before Rosie had said a word. "And don't worry, it's all perfectly respectable. We're going to the Walper Hotel for a drink, and there's a public telephone so we can all call home if we want to."

The officers had drilled into them, along with so much else, the importance of propriety. Among the long list of behavior that was considered questionable was "holding hands while walking out with airmen" and "habitually visiting public

beverage rooms," both of which Rosie suspected Nancy antici-
pated breaking that night, and with glee.

"I don't know..." Rosie began, shaking her head. As much as
she was trying to join in the camaraderie of Barracks Five, she
didn't want to feel like a fifth wheel when everyone was out and
about, determined to have a good time. She'd much rather be
tucked up in bed, perhaps even with the luxury of a hot-water
bottle.

"Well, *I* know," Violet replied, "and you're coming, no ands,
ifs, buts about it! I am not going to let you be a wet blanket,
Rosie Lyman. Even Marjorie has agreed to come along, and you
know what she can be like. We've worked darned hard," she
continued, "and we all deserve a break. And it will be *fun*,
which is something you certainly need more of!"

"But you know how I am at parties," Rosie protested, and
Violet shook her head.

"Not this time. I'm not going to let you sit in the corner
looking sour, let me tell you. You'll be the life of the party
whether you want to be or not!"

And so, with little choice in the matter, and wanting to
prove her cousin wrong at least a little, Rosie let herself be
jollied along.

They'd all had to package up their civilian clothes and send
them home on the first day of training, but there were plenty of
other ways to primp, as the women of Barracks Five brought out
their lipstick and curlers. Rosie found herself having Elizabeth
Arden's Montezuma Red slicked on her lips—a color created
specifically for women in the armed forces.

"The Americans get it issued with their uniforms, along
with a matching cream rouge and nail polish," Evelyn told her
with a grin. "Too bad for us, eh?"

"I don't normally wear lipstick," Rosie confessed with a
smile, and Evelyn's grin widened.

"Yes, I know," she said, and she gave her own lips an extra slick of the bright red lipstick.

The mood was exuberant as the women tumbled out of the barracks, and then picked their way through the snowy landscape, to the waiting truck, where Nancy's date, Sam, a lance corporal from Barrie, was leaning against the driver's door.

"Your chariot awaits, ladies," he proclaimed with a wink as he opened the tailgate of the truck's bed and helped them clamber up.

Rosie glanced at the truck, taken aback. They were going to be sitting in the bed of the truck, in the open air, in the dead of winter? They'd all freeze to death!

"We'd better huddle together for warmth," she told Violet. "Otherwise we're going to catch our death of cold."

"We'll be fine, I'm sure," Violet dismissed, rolling her eyes at the other girls, as if Rosie was being ridiculous for worrying. She took the hand of the lance corporal, winking back at him as she clambered up into the truck, and then laughing when she landed in a heap.

Rosie hesitated, and Sam gave her a smile. "It's not too bad. Like you said, you can huddle together to keep warm."

"I suppose we'll have to," Rosie replied, doing her best to rally, and she took his hand as she followed Violet into the truck.

Even huddled together cheek by jowl, it was absolutely freezing as they started off, away from the base toward downtown Kitchener. Everyone was in high spirits, belting out songs as they jolted along, and Rosie did her best to hum along to the rousing rendition of Jimmy Dorsey's "Green Eyes" as Sam drove them to the Walper Hotel in downtown Kitchener. The sky above was scattered with stars, the moonlight glinting off the snowbanks as they bumped their way into the city, burrowing deeper into their coats to avoid the cutting wind. Even so, Rosie's eyes streamed with cold, and her nose and lips were numb, her fingers and toes too, as the truck pulled up to the hotel, blazing with lights.

"Now we need a drink," Vera announced, jumping off the truck with alacrity.

The other women followed suit, Nancy linking arms with her corporal, and as they headed into the hotel, Rosie noticed with a frisson of surprise the pursed lips and narrowed eyes of an older couple who were also entering the building, the man in a suit and the woman in furs, their expressions decidedly disdainful.

The officers had warned them all that their behavior had to be absolutely exemplary, as so many in the public, as well as plenty in the military, assumed that the women serving in the CWAC were loose or fast. There had been rumors flying around that the army had taken their recruits from brothels, and even one that many of the CWACs had syphilis. Rosie had heard that plenty of people considered them as little more than camp followers, one step up from prostitutes, but tucked away on the base, she hadn't seen any evidence of that kind of opinion, until tonight.

Now, as she walked into the hotel, she felt the cold gaze of the woman swathed in mink, and tried not to flush. She felt almost as if she'd done something wrong; she shrank into herself a little. The woman in fur swept by without a word.

"Oh, don't start with that," Violet told her when Rosie ventured to say that they really should be on their best behavior, considering how they were being watched. They'd commandeered two tables in a corner of the bar, pushing them together with a lot of squeaking and screeching while others looked on, nonplussed. "We deserve to have a good time. We've been working like dogs since we got here."

"I know," Rosie replied placatingly, "and I agree with you, really, but we're on display here, and it seems like people are just waiting for us to put a toe out of line. I wouldn't want any of us to be put on charge for bad behavior—"

"I intend to put a whole *foot* out of line," Vera pronounced as she put down a tray of glasses of beer, some of it slopping out onto the table. "Maybe even two!"

This was met with cheers, and Rosie subsided, knowing her concerns would fall on deaf ears. Violet clearly thought she was being a goody two shoes, and maybe she was, but surely part of their musketeer pledge was making sure none of them got into trouble, or, heaven forbid, discharged from service?

"Try not to worry so much," Violet told her, a touch of impatience to her voice. "Who cares what a couple of old biddies think? They'd disapprove of us no matter what we did, because they didn't want us CWACs around in the first place. We might as well enjoy it." She handed Rosie a glass of beer while the other women hoisted theirs up in a toast.

"Bottoms up, girls," Vera called out merrily, and among the clinking of glasses, they all drank.

Rosie took a small sip as the chat and gossip flew around her. She'd never been much of a drinker, and she certainly wanted to keep her head tonight, although she suspected many of her new friends were keen to lose theirs. But maybe Violet was right and she was being overly cautious. They'd all worked darned hard, as she'd said, and they did deserve a bit of a break.

Taking another sip of her beer, Rosie caught the eye of the woman she'd seen at the entrance of the hotel—an old biddy, just as Violet had said. She ventured a smile, and the woman looked away with a haughty sniff.

"What are you hoping to go for, with trade?" Josie was asking everyone, and Rosie sat and listened, sipping her beer, as they talked about the different options. At the end of their basic training, she knew, they would all be posted onward for several months of further training in one of the trades; she was hoping to be a stenographer or typist, although she already knew, despite her work in her father's office, that her dictation and typing speeds were not up to what was required, unlike some of the other girls, who had already worked as secretaries.

"I want to be a driver," Nancy declared. "I have my license, but I'm afraid they'll put me in mess because I was a cleaner, and I only just got my Grade Eight." She glanced at Rosie in a way that didn't seem entirely friendly. "I'm not a smarty, like you," she said, making it almost sound like an insult, and Rosie flushed. She'd always suspected Nancy didn't like her, but surely there was no need to single her out in such a way, when both Violet and Vera had also been students at Queen's. But then Violet and Vera had both got into the thick of things immediately, and neither of them had ever had much interest in their studies.

"I'm not really..." Rosie began in protest, but no one was listening. Evelyn was talking about wanting to be a telephone operator, and Marjorie admitted, taking everyone's ribbing good-naturedly, that she wanted to go on to officer's training; only a few would be selected.

"Of course you'd make a good officer," Nancy had told her with a laugh. "As long as none of us is under you!"

A little while later, Nancy bought the second round of drinks, although this time Rosie discovered there wasn't one for her.

"You barely finished your first," Nancy told her with a shrug, "and you seem a bit teetotal, to tell you the truth."

"That's fine," Rosie told her, trying to smile. "I didn't want anything, anyway."

Nancy smirked a little bit in response, and Rosie looked away, telling herself not to be so hurt. She was just playing into the other woman's opinion of her, she realized; the more Nancy teased and smirked, the more Rosie retreated into herself. She watched as Vera drained her glass and then winked at an RCAF airman from the nearby base at Guelph, who sprang to attention, to buy her another drink.

A few other servicemen followed suit, and soon their table was surrounded by soldiers of varying stripes, the mood turning rather raucous. Rosie understood why everyone was high-spirited, and part of her really did wish she could join in, at least a little bit. Bat her eyelashes and tilt her head the way Violet did, snag some handsome man's attention, laugh her way through the evening, link arms with the other girls and sing merrily along to the song on the radio, but she just *couldn't*. It felt as if it were all physically impossible: a lump in her throat that kept her from speaking, and arms and legs like blocks of concrete, unable to move. The innate caution and shyness of her childhood rose up to strangle her, and as much as she resented its suffocating hold, she found she could not break it. She wouldn't even know how to flirt or be fun, and she suspected she'd look ridiculous if she tried. Besides, more likely than not, they wouldn't see any of these servicemen ever again, so what was the point of getting to know them in the first place?

Nancy was now sitting in her lance corporal's lap, her arms twined around his neck. The couple seated at a table nearby were eyeing her with obvious disdain in a way that annoyed Rosie, but also made her squirm in discomfort. She'd always considered herself a liberated thinker, but she particularly felt the narrowness of her own prejudices—and experience—now.

"I think I'm going to call home," she told Violet. "That's why we came here, isn't it?"

"Is it?" Violet tossed back with a glint in her eye, and Rosie managed a smile.

"Well, it is for me." She was looking forward to talking to her family, even as she feared it might make her homesickness all the more acute. It felt like a long time since she'd heard their voices.

She excused herself from the table and headed out into the

hotel's hall, where a wooden telephone box was located. Taking a deep breath, she opened the door and picked up the receiver, realizing she needed to steel herself for the conversation ahead. Hearing her mother's tender concern would be, she feared, just as hard as speaking to her father properly for the first time since she'd enlisted. They hadn't had a proper conversation since he'd told her not to enlist for his sake, and she knew, whether it was justified or not, she was still hurt by how he had not embraced her ambition to join him in his practice. The memory of just how regretful yet firm he'd been, insisting that those stuck-in-the-mud farmers wouldn't be able to stomach her, stung, now more than ever, when she was feeling like such a misfit. She might have joined the CWAC in little more than a fit of pique, but she was determined to prove to her father, and everybody else, that she was up for it—and more. She just hoped she actually was.

"Rosie!" her mother exclaimed when the call went through and the operator had stated who was calling. "Oh, Rosie. How we've been thinking of you, and wondering what you've been up to. How are you, darling?"

"Tired, mostly," Rosie managed a laugh. The homesickness she'd been just about keeping at bay rose up suddenly to engulf her, making it difficult to speak past the lump in her throat. "They keep us busy here, that's for certain."

"I'm sure they do," Ellen returned. "Are you learning all sorts of amazing things?"

"I suppose," Rosie said after a moment as she thought of the marching and drilling, scrubbing and sweeping. She had learned how to dress a wound, and read a map, and even the basics of semaphore. "Yes, I'm learning a lot," she said more firmly, determined to be as upbeat as she could. She didn't want her mother to worry about her, along with Jamie. "I'll learn even more in a few weeks, when they tell me my trade and I go on to further training."

"Your trade! Oh, how exciting."

"Yes, it really is," Rosie said in that same firm tone. She still wasn't at all sure she wouldn't be consigned to the kitchen for the next few years as a mess woman, perhaps with Nancy. Maybe then they'd finally learn to get along.

"I am proud of you," her mother said, and then added more quietly, "and your father is, too."

"Is he?" Rosie returned, a bit spikily. "Well, maybe he now realizes that women can do all sorts of things." Even if she wasn't actually doing them yet.

"Oh, Rosie..."

"Never mind," she said quickly, not wanting to get into all that. She felt too raw already, as it was. "How's Jamie? Can I speak to him?" She glanced outside the box and saw a young serviceman in the uniform of the First Canadian Army waiting to use the telephone. "I'll have to be quick, someone's waiting to make a call."

"Rosie!" Jamie sounded jubilant, making her laugh and want to cry all at once. She blinked rapidly as she managed a greeting. "Are you doing anything with planes?" her brother asked eagerly. "Or trucks—"

"No, not yet, but some of the women in training will become transport drivers. I'll most likely end up as a stenographer, or maybe a mess woman."

"Oh." Jamie couldn't keep the disappointment from his voice and Rosie managed a laugh.

"Sorry it's not more exciting," she told him. "Mostly I'm peeling potatoes and scrubbing pots and pans, among other things. But there are bits that are interesting—map reading and semaphore and things like that. It's hard to keep it all straight in my head, to be honest." She glanced again at the soldier waiting outside. He looked affable enough, but she was conscious of the time passing, as well as the expense of the call for her parents. "I should go—"

"Dad's here, he can say hello—"

"No, no, I really do need to go," Rosie replied hurriedly. "Tell him I said hello, and I'll try to call next week." She hung up before her brother could reply, her eyes now definitely stinging.

Why hadn't she wanted to say hello to her father? She feared the distance would make the strain between them worse, not better, especially if she refused to speak to him like she'd just done. And yet she knew she wouldn't have been able to, not without making some sharp retort, the way she had with her mother, and that certainly wouldn't have gone over well at all. Besides, she was already feeling lonely and out of sorts. An argument with her father might send her into an even deeper funk.

She took a deep breath and then wiped her eyes as discreetly as she could before exiting the box. "Sorry," she murmured to the soldier. "All yours now."

He smiled at her in wry sympathy and then, to her surprise, handed her a handkerchief.

"Oh—"

"Looked like you might need it. Calling home for the first time?"

Wordlessly, she nodded, dabbing at her eyes.

"It gets to you, especially at first. It will get better, though. Are you one of the CWACs?"

"Yes, we're doing our basic training at the base outside town." She folded the now damp handkerchief and handed it back to him. "Thank you for this."

"My pleasure." He tucked it into his breast pocket. "I hope you're managing all right."

"Yes, just about," Rosie replied, thankful for his kind interest, especially after having felt ignored and rebuffed for most of the evening. "Thanks again."

She was just about to return to the bar when, with a

drunken giggle, Nancy stumbled into the hall, followed by the lance corporal, Sam. Rosie watched as Nancy turned to Sam and wound her arms his neck before he pulled her in for an uncomfortably long and passionate kiss. Rosie felt her cheeks heat as she and the serviceman stood there uncomfortably; Nancy and Sam had blocked the entrance back to the bar.

"Well, they do say the CWACs know how to have a good time," the serviceman said after a moment, with a wry laugh. "I didn't believe all the rumors, but..." He shrugged, spreading his hands.

Still blushing, Rosie moved past him, as Sam pulled Nancy, laughing and half-stumbling, down the hall.

Back in the bar, the party thankfully seemed to be winding down; there was no more money for beer, and several of the women looked decidedly worse for wear.

"Why are you looking so spooked?" Violet asked as she buttoned up her coat.

Rosie shook her head, not wanting to explain. "I just want to go back."

"Did you call home?" Violet asked, and Rosie nodded. Her cousin's expression softened. "Was it hard? I'm sorry—"

"It's not that," Rosie said, although it had been, at least at first. "It's just... I don't know. Everyone's been looking at us here—"

"Oh not that again, Rosie!" Violet exclaimed, shaking her head. "Anyway, I think it's probably time to call it a night. Let's round everyone up." She looked around, a bit blearily. "Where's Sam?"

"I think he's occupied elsewhere," Rosie replied, and Violet raised her eyebrows.

"With Nancy?"

Rosie nodded, and Violet laughed.

"Oh, Rosie! No wonder you were blushing."

A few minutes later, they all headed outside into the still

night, the air sharp and cold. "Where's Nancy?" someone called, a bit grumpily, from the bed of the truck. "And Sam? We need to get back to the base before lights out or we'll all be on charge. Besides, I'm freezing my tits off back here."

"Now, now," Violet replied affably. "Huddle together and you won't freeze off any of your bits. Besides, you've drunk enough booze to keep you nice and toasty, I should say!"

"I saw Sam and Nancy canoodling in the hall," someone else said. "Looked like they wanted to rent a room."

"Well, they'd better not have, because we need a driver," someone else called back.

"If they don't come soon, we'll really be in it."

A glum silence followed, and then someone yawned hugely. "I just want to go to bed. My head won't stop spinning."

No one seemed inclined to do anything, and Rosie realized that if they didn't hurry up, they really would get in trouble. "I'll look for her," she announced, and Violet looked surprised before she nodded.

"I'll come with you."

They hurried into the hotel, which had emptied out of most of its customers. "She was in the hallway a few moments ago," Rosie said, looking around, and Violet pursed her lips, her hands on her hips.

"She isn't now. Maybe they did get a room."

"They wouldn't..." Rosie began uncertainly. Nancy could be discharged for such behavior, she knew, and that would be a huge disappointment to her. Whatever Violet insisted about having fun and not getting the other girls down, Rosie wished she'd exerted a bit more of a restricting influence on Nancy. She'd be so cross with herself if she was discharged.

"We can ask at reception, I suppose," Violet said dubiously, but when they did, they were given a humiliating dressing-down, to presume that an establishment such as the Walper Hotel would rent rooms to unmarried couples.

"I've heard about you camp followers," the concierge told them in a tone of icy disapproval. "I didn't want to believe it, but it seems it was right to be suspicious. Women have no place in the army."

"Oh, stuff it," Violet muttered as she turned away. "We're all really going to be in hot water if we don't do something quick!"

"Well, then," Rosie replied, "we'd better do something quick. If they didn't get a room, they're somewhere down here, most likely somewhere at least a little private. If you take one side of the hotel, I'll take the other."

Violet gave her a quick, grateful look. "Right, good idea. Let's go."

As Rosie started searching through the various hallways and reception rooms, she was glad that she was doing something practical to help. She might not always be up for joining in their singalongs or escapades, but she still had something to offer.

Yet, as time passed and she couldn't find Nancy and Sam, she started to worry. What if they all got in trouble for coming back late? They might all get discharged, to set an example, which would be a disaster.

In that moment, Rosie realized just how much she didn't want to give up on her training, or have it give up on her. No matter how difficult or dispiriting she found it at times, she wasn't going to be a quitter. And she wasn't going to let Nancy get her, or any of them, into trouble.

Ten long minutes later, she found Sam and Nancy emerging from a broom closet, looking red-faced and rumpled as they buttoned up their clothes. Rosie kept her expression as unfazed as she could as she said briskly, "There you two are. We need to leave immediately if we want to get back to the base without any trouble."

Sam glanced at his watch and swore softly. "Sorry," he said sheepishly. "Lost track of time."

"Clearly," Rosie returned, but softened her reply with a smile. "Here comes Violet. Let's go."

"I suppose you're going to rat me out to the sergeant," Nancy muttered under her breath as they headed back to the truck.

Rosie looked at her in mingled sympathy and exasperation. "That's not part of the musketeers' pledge, is it?" she replied, before adding quietly, "I don't know why you've decided to make me your enemy, Nancy, but I'm really not."

And without waiting for a reply, she swung herself up into the truck for the cold, bumpy journey back to the base.

CHAPTER FIVE

MARCH 1942

"Can you see? Can you see?"

Rosie stood on her tiptoes to peer past the women clamoring to learn of their trades from the list that had just been posted.

"I can't see a thing," she told Violet. "We'll just have to wait."

"Fingers crossed I'm for stenography," Violet said. "Or clerical work. I haven't the brains or guts for anything else, I know I haven't."

"Yes, fingers crossed." Rosie gave Violet a quick, hopeful smile; over the last four weeks, as they'd continued with their training, their friendship had remained steadfast, if not, she knew, completely what it once was. The other girls had eventually accepted Rosie for being quiet, and although she'd certainly tried to make more of an effort to be involved, she knew she would never be like Violet, who had continued to shine as their unofficial den mother, friend to everyone, always cheerfully chivvying them along.

Two more women had left Barracks Five—Josie, who had feared all along she wasn't up to the job, and dear old Vera, who had had to return home after her father had fallen ill.

Rosie was more than half-amazed that she was still standing, along with Violet, who had her moments, as they all had, fighting homesickness and wondering what on earth it was all for. And now they were about to learn what would happen to them next.

"Budge *up*," someone called irritably to a woman standing right in front of the list. "We can't see."

The woman grudgingly took herself off, and Violet pushed forward, scanning the list of trades and postings for all the cadets graduating out. "I'm going to Hamilton," she squealed. "To train as a stenographer!"

"Oh, Violet!" Rosie squeezed between two cadets to get closer to the list. "What am I doing? Am I in stenography, too?" She hoped so, for both her and Violet's sakes. Maybe if they trained together, they could renew their friendship, make it stronger. And Rosie would get a second chance at making friends with the other CWACs with whom she served.

Violet was silent for a second, and Rosie's heart swooped. She was a mess woman, after all, she *must* be, somewhere far away and all alone, and Violet didn't know how to tell her.

"You're going to Quebec," Violet said after a moment, her voice strangely restrained. "To Sainte-Anne-de-Bellevue, for their officer training school."

"Officer..." Rosie gaped at her cousin in disbelief. She'd been selected to train as an *officer*? Only a handful had been, from basic training. Most would be taken later, from their training in trades. How could they have possibly chosen her— and why? She'd barely said boo to any of her commanding officers, wanting only to keep her head down and get through the training, quiet, barely noticeable, unlike so many other girls, unlike *Violet*...

"You must have impressed someone," Violet said, injecting some enthusiasm into her voice as she smiled determinedly at Rosie. "Well done, you. You'll go higher still, I'm sure. The sky's the limit!" Violet's bright smile dimmed for a second before she turned it up all the more, her eyes positively glittering. "You must be so proud."

"Violet..." Even though her cousin wasn't saying as much, Rosie had the distinct sense she was hurt or perhaps just envious that Rosie had been selected to become an officer, and she hadn't. But Rosie obviously hadn't had any say in it. She would have rather, she realized despondently, been a stenographer, or even a mess woman.

Violet was far more officer material than she was—organizing the girls, keeping their spirits up, mucking in. Rosie had kept her head down and gone about her work without any fuss or notice... or so she'd thought.

"Congratulations," Violet said again, and moved past her, back to the barracks.

Feeling dismayed, as well as still reeling from the news, Rosie followed her. By the time she went inside, Violet was already packing.

"We ship out this very afternoon," she told Rosie without looking at her. "They certainly don't let the grass grow under our feet, do they?"

"I don't even want to be an officer, Violet," Rosie blurted.

Her cousin paused, and then straightened up, one hand on her hip as she gave Rosie a rather appraising look. "Don't you?" she returned coolly. "I would have thought this was exactly what you wanted, Rosie. No more scrubbing and sweeping for you. No more mucking in with the hoi polloi—or not, as it happened."

Rosie felt herself flush. "That's not fair," she said quietly. "I know you think I was standoffish, especially in the beginning, but I have tried, Violet. I've changed, too, and I thought—"

"Well, you ought to be pleased," Violet cut her off. "Officer training! You'll be with all the well-to-do ladies, all the university students and finishing-school girls, with cut-glass voices and their noses stuck in the air. My mother will be *so* impressed. I've heard they take you to all sorts of parties at that school, to hobnob with the gentlemen, entertain visiting dignitaries, all that sort of thing. You learn how to laugh at their dull jokes and ask interesting questions." Her voice turned uncharacteristically spiteful. "Maybe you'll finally learn how to flirt!"

"Violet," Rosie said quietly, unable to hide the hurt from her voice. She thought they'd moved past all that in the last few weeks, all of them working together, accepting each other as they were. She'd hoped things had improved, that *she* had. Had it all been wishful thinking?

With a sigh, Violet sank onto her bed. "I'm sorry," she said after a moment, her head bowed. "I'm being a complete cow, I know I am. It's just... joining up was *my* idea." She looked up at Rosie with tears in her eyes; Rosie couldn't tell if she was angry or sad. Perhaps both. "You wouldn't have even done it," she said like an accusation, "if it weren't for me."

"I know that full well—" Rosie began, only to be cut off once more.

"And," Violet interjected, her voice rising a little, "I'm the one who has kept everyone together. *I* made us into the eleven musketeers at the start, *I* did my best to keep us all going, I mucked in—"

"I know you did," Rosie returned in a whisper. Violet had been so good-humored all along, the anchor of their little group, its cheerful, smiling center, around which they had all revolved. "Violet, I really don't know why they sent me to officer training school. Maybe it's a mistake—"

"No, it isn't," Violet replied tiredly. She stood up and resumed packing. "You're smart and quiet and contained, and you haven't got into scrapes the way the rest of us have. Kept your nose clean, didn't you? Made sure of it."

There was a waspish note in her voice that made Rosie blink. It was true, she hadn't got up to the high-spirited jinks the other cadets did—only last week they'd all snuck out and stolen a military truck for a joyride—but was that her *fault*? Violet had never been so cold with her before. Even when her cousin had been criticizing her, Rosie had believed it had been meant for her own good. Now it felt different.

"I can't help who I am," she protested quietly. "I've said that all along."

"I'm happy for you," Violet told her, sounding anything but. "Truly. And the truth is, I'm not surprised they didn't think I was officer material. I'm not. I could never be so serious, standing above everyone else, wagging your finger and giving orders. I don't suppose you'll have any trouble."

"*Violet—*"

Violet didn't look at her as she closed up her kit bag. "Write me from Quebec, won't you?" she asked, her tone so very cool, and Rosie watched, in a terrible mix of dismay and disbelief, as her cousin slung her bag over her shoulder and then marched out of the barracks without another word.

Rosie stood there, gaping for a moment, reeling with both hurt and shock, before she took a shuddering breath and went to the bathroom to tidy her hair and compose herself. She couldn't believe Violet had been so sharp, so dismissive, with her. She hadn't expected to be put up for officer training, and Violet *knew* that. Besides, they wouldn't be seeing each other for months now, with their separate postings. Was Violet really going to end the friendship they'd had since they were children over a silly spat about training?

A sound like a sob came from one of the toilet stalls—they still didn't have doors—and Rosie turned around in surprise to see Nancy slumped on a toilet seat, her head in her hands.

"Nancy!" She pressed one hand to her chest. Had Nancy overheard her argument with Violet? "I didn't see you there. Are you all right? I thought you'd be over at the hall, looking at the postings."

"There's no point now, is there?" Nancy replied dully, her head still bowed, her hair half undone.

Rosie regarded her uncertainly. Something was clearly wrong, but she had no idea what it could be. What could have happened, now that their training was over? They'd all passed; they'd all received postings. "Are you ill?" she asked. "I could call for the nurse—"

"No, I'm not ill," Nancy returned with a sniff, "unless being up the duff counts as an illness."

Rosie drew her breath in sharply and Nancy looked up with a grim smile, her hair hanging in tangles about her face.

"That's shocked you good and proper, hasn't it?"

"Oh, Nancy..." Rosie regarded her helplessly. Yes, she was a little bit shocked, but not as much as Nancy seemed to think. Over the last six weeks, they'd had enough lectures on "being sensible" and avoiding VD that Rosie didn't think much could shock her anymore, not like at the beginning, when she'd been so quick to blush. "I'm sorry," she said quietly. "Does Sam know?" He and Nancy had been stepping out—and more, obviously—ever since the first week.

"How can I tell him? I know I was just a bit of fun for him. It wasn't supposed to mean anything."

Rosie frowned. "Did he say that to you?"

Nancy shrugged. "He didn't have to."

Rosie hesitated, unsure how to reply. She'd thought Sam a decent sort of fellow, but she had no idea how he would respond to the news he was going to become a father, especially with a war on. He was hoping to be shipped over to England any day now. "You should still tell him," she advised Nancy. "He's as responsible for your condition as you are, if not more so. They're always lecturing the soldiers about being careful about that sort of thing, and using, you know, protection." It seemed she could still be put to the blush, Rosie thought wryly, but she managed to keep her tone practical.

Nancy let out a tired laugh. "Listen to you, Miss Know-it-All," she said, but for once without spite. "I didn't think you had much experience with the birds and bees."

"Not directly, no," Rosie replied honestly. She'd never even been kissed. "But I have heard things—everyone has, here. Or did you miss one of the many lectures on avoiding VD?"

Nancy let out another laugh and Rosie took a step toward her, longing to help.

"Really, Nancy, you should tell him," she said quietly. "Who knows, he might be pleased."

"Well, I'm not pleased," Nancy retorted on a sigh. "I wanted to train to be a transport driver. I haven't even looked at my posting—I couldn't bear it if I got what I wanted, only to have to turn it down." She shook her head. "Now it will be back home for me, hanging my head in shame. My dad is going to kill me, and that's if my ma doesn't do it first. I don't even know if they'll let me stay with them, with the shame of it as well as another mouth to feed. They haven't got much."

Rosie had learned a little bit about Nancy's background—strict, hardworking, poor. "What will you do, then?" she asked after a moment.

"What else can I do?" Nancy replied. "Go home and manage as best as I can and hope my parents don't kick me out. I know some girls might think about getting rid of it, but I couldn't do that." She gave a little shudder. "And you hear stories about it going so terribly wrong..."

"No, no, you mustn't think of anything like that," Rosie cut her off quickly. The idea was awful. "Listen," she said impulsively, "if you find yourself in a fix, write to me at Sainte-Anne-de-Bellevue. My parents are in Kingston and they have plenty of room going spare with just my brother at home. You might be able to stay there, at least until the baby is born."

Nancy looked up at her, her mouth agape. "Do you really mean that?"

"Yes, I do." Her parents might be a bit taken aback by the offer, Rosie knew, but she hoped they would be welcoming. Her cousin, Gracie, had had a pregnancy out of wedlock, after all, over ten years ago now, long before she'd met and married her husband, Will. The baby had died before it had even been born, but Gracie had told Rosie about it a year or two ago, her usually laughing expression shadowed with remembered grief. If her parents had accepted Gracie, wouldn't they accept Nancy, especially if Rosie asked them to?

Even if she still hadn't spoken to her father, despite having called home twice more during her training. But her mother surely would, at least. They both would, Rosie thought. She was certain of it.

"They wouldn't mind the shame of it?" Nancy asked, looking dubious. "I don't know if I could stay with strangers, especially if they were looking at me all disapproving like."

"They are good, kind people," Rosie said firmly. "And if I vouch for you, they'll be happy to have you stay." She'd write to them as soon as she could and let them know what might be happening.

Nancy shook her head slowly. "Why would you vouch for me, Rosie? I know I haven't been much of a friend to you here."

"Well, I know I might have seemed a bit... well, standoffish at first," Rosie admitted. "I've always been quiet, I'm afraid. That's just the way I am. But, anyway, that's all past now." Even if Violet had just walked out on her without a single kind word.

"You weren't all that stuck up, really," Nancy said. "I was just jealous about you being so close with Violet. Seems silly, now, with us all going our own ways."

"And I was a bit jealous of you for the same reason," Rosie returned with a small, sad laugh. She wished they'd been able to sort out their differences before now. "But never mind that now," she told Nancy. "I really do think you need to tell Sam about the baby. Even if he's not pleased, he has a right to know

—and a responsibility to you, and your child. You shouldn't let him get away with not being responsible about it. At the very least, he should give you some money. Remember it's his child as much as it is yours."

Nancy's mouth quirked in a small smile. "You sound like a right old crusader."

"I am," Rosie told her firmly. "Women bear enough burdens as it is. They shouldn't have to bear the one of children alone, especially since, as the captain says, it takes two to tango!"

Nancy let out a grudging laugh. "I think she was saying that because we're meant to keep both feet on the floor and not *tango* at all."

Rosie smiled, determined. "Even so."

Nancy gave a shuddering breath as she started to tuck up her hair. "Did you really mean what you said, about your family?"

"Yes," Rosie said without hesitation. She really would have to write to her mother as soon as possible.

Nancy stood up and held out a hand. "Thank you for that. It means a lot. And I'm sorry I misjudged you, Rosie Lyman. You're all right."

CHAPTER SIX

JUNE 1942

Sainte-Anne-de-Bellevue, Quebec

"Captain wants to see you, Private."

Rosie glanced at Anne, her fellow-officer-in-training and roommate, standing in the doorway of their dormitory. She'd been at the training program at MacDonald College, in Sainte-Anne-de-Bellevue, Quebec, for over two months now and she and her several dozen co-officers-in-training were all about to go on to their new posts. Rosie was looking forward to finding out where—and what—hers was.

She'd come to Sainte-Anne-de-Bellevue with some trepidation, away from Violet and the other women she'd gotten to know at basic training; even though there had certainly been difficulties, especially at the beginning, the musketeers of Barracks Five had become familiar, and by the end, Rosie liked to think she had come to develop a certain camaraderie with them all, even, unexpectedly, Nancy, who had written to tell her she was back at home and her mum, at least, seemed almost pleased about a baby, although her father wasn't speaking to her. *Mum says Dad will come round, but I'm not sure. Least-ways, I'm allowed to stay for now, but thanks again for your offer. It was real kind of you, and I'll write if I need to take you up on it, after all.*

Nancy hadn't told Sam about the baby, but Rosie had written back, encouraging her to do so, and assuring her that her parents were happy to welcome her to their home in Kingston should the need arise. She felt a surprising warmth for Nancy, a closeness with her she hadn't expected but was grateful for.

When Rosie had arrived at Saint-Anne-de-Bellevue, she hadn't been sure she'd had it in her to try all over again with another lot of new girls. In any case, she soon learned that she didn't need to, because officer training wasn't the barrel of laughs basic training had been in comparison. There was little camaraderie or recreational time, and certainly no pranks or parties. Their schedule was packed with activities and lessons, and what little free time they had was spent studying or sleeping. It felt, Rosie sometimes thought, like a somewhat dour finishing school, with a fair bit of army training thrown in. The women who had been selected all seemed determined to shine the brightest, and so a sense of competition and rivalry had sprung up, sometimes making even the simplest of exchanges feel rather loaded and tense. Rosie had missed Violet and her sense of fun more than ever as she'd gone about her duties, wondering the whole while why she'd been chosen.

Each day started at six-thirty, with morning reveille, followed by twenty minutes of intensive physical training parade, and then lessons in all sorts of things Rosie had had no idea about. She'd learned about Corps administration, organization of the army, military law, army filing, allowances and pay, anti-gas precautions, first aid, and proper correspondence. More tediously, she'd had lessons on all the military protocols—

whether a rider of a motorcycle had to salute while in motion, or if three servicewomen walking down the street together had to all salute to an officer, or just the one on the right—and all the many, many rules and regulations of army life.

All the officers-in-training were required to hold themselves to the highest standard in terms of dress and behavior; Rosie learned she was never to carry a bag, umbrella, or cane, and she must always hold her gloves in her left hand. She could wear no jewelry, save for a wedding or small engagement ring—neither of which she possessed, of course. Moreover, she could not engage in any of the high-spirited antics that the girls had gotten up to in basic training; it was simply not to be thought of.

When she'd received a late pass, Rosie had done nothing more than take a walk about the neighborhood when the weather was fine, and then return to her room to write letters home. She'd written her mother every week, and Violet twice, light and chatty letters, describing some of her dragon-like teachers, and making fun of the useless bits of knowledge she'd had to learn. She liked to think of Violet laughing at the ridiculousness of it all; she felt sure, had they been there together, they would have. She certainly hadn't mentioned any of the officers' lectures on how the women there had been selected for 'a higher calling', or that such women were expected to behave to a higher standard than ordinary recruits. In any case, it didn't seem to matter what she wrote, because Violet did not write back.

Rosie had hoped her cousin's hurt and anger might have dissipated with the help of both distance and time, but her silence seemed to suggest otherwise. She wondered when she would see Violet again, and how they would treat each other when they did. She hated to think their friendship had been wrecked forever, and yet Rosie was afraid it might have been, as well as angry that Violet had let something so silly come between them. She'd thought their friendship had been stronger that that; it seemed she'd been wrong, and that hurt most of all.

"The captain wants to see me?" she asked Anne now in surprise, turning from the window. "I wonder why." Tomorrow was their passing-out parade, where they would all receive the King's Commission, and then go on to their new postings. Many were hoping to be posted to Military Headquarters in Ottawa, where CWACs were assigned as drivers, hostesses, and secretaries—a large part of their role would be entertaining high-ranking officers at the kind of parties Violet had mentioned, back in Kitchener. Rosie could think of little worse than such enforced socializing.

"Who knows?" Anne replied with a shrug. She was in her mid-twenties, married, and had worked as a schoolteacher before enlisting. Her husband was in the RCAF, and she'd been friendly enough with Rosie, but a bit restrained, focused on doing a good job and moving on, as all the other women there were. "But you'd better hop to it."

Rosie quickly straightened her uniform and tidied her hair before reporting to the captain's office on the ground floor of the administration building. The captain was a petite, steely-eyed woman who made many of the officers-in-training quake, despite her small stature. Rosie's mind raced as she tried to think of something that might have gotten her in trouble at such a late stage in her training. Had her shoes not been polished enough? Her skirt not the regulation sixteen inches from the floor? She'd tried to be so careful, but there were so very many regulations to remember, so many rules to keep, and as much as she prided herself on a quick mind and good memory, the minutiae of it all sometimes felt overwhelming.

"Officer Cadet Lyman." Captain Smith gave a brisk nod as Rosie stood to attention, her heart thundering in her chest. She hadn't been summoned to see the captain or any other superior officer since she'd arrived at Sainte-Anne-de-Bellevue. Just like at Kitchener, she'd done her best to keep her head down and go about her work.

"Captain," she said as she saluted.

"You've done decent work here at Sainte-Anne-de-Bellevue," she said, and Rosie found herself breathing a bit easier. Surely she wasn't in trouble, then. "You're quiet and studious and sensible," the captain continued, reminding Rosie of when Violet had said the same things, but almost as insults.

"Thank you, Captain."

"I am tasked with the responsibility of recommending some of my cadets to positions overseas," she continued, and Rosie blinked. *Overseas...* "CMHQ in London is asking for four hundred recruits from the Canadian Women's Army Corps. You will mainly be performing clerical duties at CMHQ, at which you have been proficient, although some further training would certainly be needed. They are looking for officers like you, quiet and contained, who can show our fellow subjects of the King that Canadian women are respectable and hard-working."

She paused significantly, and Rosie managed a whispered, "Yes, Ma'am."

"All those recommended to go overseas will be going with the rank of private," the captain explained. "So if you agree to this posting, you will parade out tomorrow as a second lieutenant, and then take the pips off your shoulder as soon as you get on the train!" She smiled briefly, and Rosie managed a smile back. She didn't care about being a lieutenant, or any kind of officer. She never had. "There are plenty of young women who are eager to go overseas, so therefore I am only recommending those who wish to go," the captain continued. "But I'm afraid you don't have much time to think about it, as I intend to pass on my list of recommended names this afternoon. CWACs are required to have had eight months in the Corps before going overseas, but I don't see that as problem as they won't be ready to sail at least until autumn." She glanced down at the papers on her desk. "They also must be twenty-one years of age, but as your birthday is in the summer, that shouldn't be a problem, either. Therefore, if you agree to this posting, I will recommend you for four months' further training before heading to London sometime in the autumn."

Another pause, and Rosie realized she was meant to think about it—and decide—right there and then. Did she want to go all the way to England? she wondered, her head spinning with the new idea. She knew plenty of girls, Violet included, were desperate for the chance of such an incredible adventure. And yet Rosie had been insisting all along that she wasn't interested in adventures—and to go so far from home, for who knew how long...

"Well, Officer Cadet?" the captain barked. "Will I be putting your name on my list?"

Rosie's mind raced. What was the alternative? To entertain officers in Ottawa at a bunch of boring parties, or possibly be posted to some remote military base and chivvy girls along... She and the other officers-in-training had already been warned about how they would have to keep themselves apart from the lower ranks; it could be a lonely life, being the one who had to have a restraining hand. She'd had a small taste of that already, back in Kitchener, and she didn't think she wanted it again.

And *London*. A chance to see the world, do something different. As the war had gone on, women had been learning all sorts of new trades, far more than the original nine they'd been offered just a few months ago. And Rosie had heard that women in Britain were allowed to do even more than their Canadian counterparts. Some of them were even doing top-secret work, or operating wirelesses, or flying planes... Who knew what she might be asked to do? Already, without any real effort on her part, she'd been recommended for both officer training *and* an overseas posting. Maybe she would do something exciting, even something secret or important... who knew? Who could possibly say?

"Yes, Captain," she said, as firmly as she could. "I am honored to be recommended for an overseas posting."

Two days later, Rosie found herself back home in Kingston. She had what was known as a "forty-eight"—a two-day pass before she was due to report for further training in typing and stenography, and then await her orders to ship out.

The day before, she'd had her passing-out parade; just as the captain had said, she'd had to remove the white tapes on the shoulders of her uniform as soon as the ceremony had finished. She was back to being a private, and heading off to Hamilton for secretarial training. Rosie wondered if she'd see Violet there; she had no idea how big the base was, or whether Violet would have been moved on to a further, more permanent posting.

Sometimes it seemed as if the whole country had been turned into one enormous transit station, with both men and woman constantly coming and going, a sea of uniforms in every train and bus station, as more and more bases and training centers were set up across the country.

Rosie didn't know how she felt about seeing Violet again. As much as she longed to be friends, the way they'd parted—and the ensuing months of silence—still stung. Did Violet hold a grudge? *Did she?*

"Rosie, oh Rosie!" Ellen Lyman rushed to the door and put her arms around her daughter before Rosie had even let go of the kit bag slung over her shoulders.

"Hello, Mum." She dropped the bag on the floor to hug her mother properly.

"Goodness, don't you look smart." Ellen stepped back, her

hands on Rosie's shoulders, as she surveyed her in her uniform. "So very official. And you're a second lieutenant now?"

"Actually, I'm back to being a private." There had been no time for a telephone call to explain what had happened. "They had to reduce my rank because..." She paused, wondering how her mum would take the news. "Because I'm going to be posted overseas."

"*What*..." Her mother looked at her in a mix of surprise and dismay. "You mean to England? Oh, Rosie, but it's so far away... and so dangerous. You hear about the air raids, the bombs dropping over London..."

Rosie realized she hadn't even considered the dangers when she'd accepted the posting. According to the newspapers, London was being bombed most nights, with many people having to spend the night in air-raid shelters, buildings being damaged, lives being lost. Even though the war had now been going on for three years, it had all felt rather far away. Now she would be in the thick of it, close to the action, feeling a bit more of the urgency and necessity that had sometimes been lacking, all the way over here in Canada. Even though she felt nervous about it all, Rosie realized she was looking forward to being more involved, having a greater sense of purpose.

"Well, it's not like it's France, at any rate," she told her mother with a smile. "Or anywhere else in Europe. And I'm sure CMHQ must have a very good air-raid shelter!"

"I certainly hope so." Her mother hugged her again, tightly. "It's so good to see you, darling. And I'm so proud of you. Your father and Jamie will be thrilled to bits you're back."

"Only for forty-eight hours," Rosie told her. "Then I'm off to Hamilton. I won't be shipping out to England until the fall."

"Violet just came from Hamilton! She was training as a stenographer, I think. She seems to be enjoying it immensely, but, of course, you'll know that. I'm sure you've been writing each other letters."

Rosie gave her mother a brief smile, not wanting to get into all of that.

"You've only just missed her, unfortunately," her mother continued as she went to fill the kettle. "She had three days' leave, and now she's been posted out to a base in Manitoba. I think she was a bit disappointed by that, although she didn't say as much. But I have a feeling she would much rather be going to London, like you."

Yet another thing to keep her and Violet apart, Rosie thought with a sigh. Well, there was nothing she could do about it, and she was unlikely to see her cousin anyway, whether she wanted to or not. She thought about how all those months ago she'd joked to Violet about being posted to somewhere like Manitoba, out in the middle of nowhere, among the cornfields. Was her cousin really disappointed by the new position? Rosie felt an uncomfortable mixture of sorrow and relief that she wouldn't see Violet while she was in Kingston. She had no idea what her reception would have been, but she still hoped they could reconcile at some point. Although who knew when their paths would cross again, if Violet was now in Manitoba and she would soon be going to England?

And meanwhile she had to think about how to handle her father, whom she hadn't talked to properly since she'd left for basic training back in February. Would things be tense between the two of them, still?

In the end, though, it wasn't nearly as hard as Rosie had feared. When her father came home from work to see Rosie sitting at the kitchen table, his face lit up and he held out his arms. "Rosie! Rosie, my girl!"

Rosie stood up and, without a thought, she rushed into his arms, just as she'd done as a small child. As her father's arms closed around her, she remembered how much she loved him, how he had always encouraged and supported her. Yes, his refusal to consider her for his law practice still stung, but perhaps she'd been foolish, or at least foolishly optimistic, suggesting such things as a young fresher at Queen's, only twenty years old. Just six months later, on the eve of her twenty-first birthday, she felt far wiser and older. As she stepped back from her father's embrace, she was able to let go of that old hurt and disappointment... mostly.

"Aren't you looking smart!" her father exclaimed, and Rosie let out a little laugh.

"That's what Mum said. It's just the uniform, really. I'm still the same." Although, she wondered, was she? She really did feel different.

"Still, an officer! How long are you with us for? And where are you going next?"

As he joined her and her mother at the kitchen table, Rosie explained about losing her officer rank as soon as she'd even got it, and her posting overseas.

"Overseas! Well, won't that be an adventure. Of course, we'll worry." The smile her father gave her was tinged with sorrow, and Rosie thought she saw a bit more gray in his hair, a few more lines on his face. A lump formed in her throat. How long would she be in England? When would she her family again?

"I'll write," Rosie promised. "Every week. And I'm off to Hamilton first, to learn how to type faster and that sort of thing, so I won't be as far away as all that for quite a while. I'm sure I'll get some leave before we ship out, across the pond, so this isn't as long a goodbye as you might think."

"I certainly hope not," her father replied. He sat back in his chair, shaking his head. "Look at you! So grown up and so very smart. I'm proud of you, Rosie. Truly."

Rosie smiled briefly before looking away.

When Jamie returned that evening from school, he was admiring and envious in equal measure. "England! Blimey!" he exclaimed in a mock British accent. "You're going to be right where the action is."

"I don't know how much fighting there is in London," Rosie returned with a smile. "I hope there won't be any! And I've already been warned that I'll be doing dull stuff—typing, filing, that sort of thing." Inadvertently, she glanced at her father, who gave her a small, apologetic smile.

"Still, it beats kicking around here," Jamie replied, and Rosie gave him a quick, searching glance. Something in his tone made her wonder how much longer her brother would be kicking around Kingston, at all.

He told her his plans later that evening, after their parents had gone to bed. Rosie, exhausted yet unable to sleep due to all the excitement, her mind seething with thoughts of both Hamilton and London, had come downstairs to warm up some milk, stopping in surprise at the sight of her brother at the kitchen table, filling out a form.

"What are you doing down here, Jamie, at this time of night?"

"Nothing," he said, covering the form with his hand and reminding her of when he'd been about six, hiding the truth about one of the innumerable scrapes he'd gotten into. Even with his poor health, he'd been irrepressible, chomping at the bit to do things in a way Rosie never, ever had.

"You're clearly not doing nothing," she remarked mildly as she took a pint of milk from the icebox. "So why so secretive?"

He hesitated and then said a bit flatly, "I'm filling out an application to apply as a mechanic at the Collins Bay airfield. I'm eighteen next month, and they'd be willing to train me."

"A mechanic!" She wasn't at all surprised, Rosie realized, and yet at the same time she was. "But what about your chest...?"

"I'm not an invalid," Jamie answered irritably. "I had a medical a month ago and they said I'm fit to serve."

"They did?"

Jamie jerked his head in a nod and Rosie managed a smile.

"That's wonderful news for you, I'm sure. But do Mum and Dad know about this?" she asked, already suspecting they didn't.

"No, they don't," her brother confirmed, "and I'm not going to tell them till the whole thing is done and dusted. You won't either, I hope." He gave her a meaningful look.

"I won't," Rosie promised, although she wished her brother would give her parents a bit more warning.

"Besides," he continued, "I won't be all that far away, and I won't be getting into any danger."

"But if you enlist in the RCAF," Rosie said slowly, "even as a mechanic... you could be posted overseas, Jamie. All the military will, most likely, one day, once there's a proper invasion." Already, there was talk about the day the Allied Forces would regain Europe after the heroic disaster of Dunkirk.

"So?" her brother challenged. "You're going overseas a lot sooner than I might ever do."

"Yes, but just to London!"

"Where bombs are falling like rain, or so the papers like to say. You'll be in as much danger as I might be one day, if not more, Rosie. I don't even know if they'll accept me yet, or if they'll post me abroad. I might be stuck in Collins Bay for the whole war."

Not if he could help it, Rosie thought, judging by his belligerent tone. Her parents would be devastated that Jamie was thinking of doing such a thing, her mother especially. She doubted such a possibility had even crossed their minds, because of his ill health of the past.

"Why not serve in home defense?" she asked, already knowing what her brother's response would be. "They need good men—"

"To do what? March about the block with a broomstick? They're just playing soldiers, Rosie, you know that."

"Still..." How could she argue with her brother, when she had already agreed to an overseas posting, and without consulting her parents? "They'll worry for you, Jamie."

"They'll worry for you, as well."

Yes, but not in the same way, Rosie knew. Jamie, with his childhood brushes with death, bouts of pneumonia and fits of coughing, had always been more of a worry to her parents than she ever had. She'd never begrudged him the extra attention—at least she didn't think she had—but it remained a simple fact that her parents would be more concerned about Jamie serving than they would be about her, and understandably so.

"When are you going to tell them?" she asked, and he shrugged.

"Like I said, when it's done and dusted. I'm going to enlist as soon as I'm eighteen and hope they accept me for training as a mechanic."

"But they might not," Rosie pointed out. A healthy eighteen-year-old, as Jamie was now, no matter the weak chest of his childhood? They might put him on the front line.

"They won't have me fly," Jamie stated, as if reading her thoughts. "I may be fit to serve, but I'm not that top-notch. But I don't care. I just want to *do* something, the same as you are. Can't you understand that?"

"Yes, I can," Rosie said after a moment. She might have joined the CWAC five months ago because she'd felt frustrated and disappointed, but her desire to work and serve had grown since then. She was proud of the uniform she wore, the opportunities she'd had and the successes she'd achieved. Could she really deny her brother the same? "You should tell them sooner," she advised. "So they have time to adjust to it. They won't stand in your way, Jamie, if you're really certain."

"You don't think?" he retorted wryly. "Mum had me taken

off the football team last year. She thought I wasn't fit enough for it. It was humiliating, let me tell you."

"Oh, Jamie." Rosie hadn't realized that. "She just wants to protect you."

"And I want to protect our country," her brother returned staunchly. "And I'm going to do it, no matter what anyone says about it. Just like you are."

CHAPTER SEVEN

OCTOBER 1942

Halifax, Nova Scotia

Rosie had never seen such an enormous ship, or such a crowded one. Every single bit of floor space was covered—with personnel, with kits bags, and, both alarmingly and reassuringly, with guns. The huge and majestic *Queen Elizabeth* had been a passenger ship, the pride of the Cunard Line, before it had been requisitioned by the army for military transport, its gracious rooms turned into mess halls and barracks, its decks now bristling with ack-ack guns.

Rosie stood on the sundeck, which had been reserved for CWACs, officers, and nursing sisters, to catch the last sight of Canada as the ship moved away from the coastline, accompanied by Lysanders and Catalano flying boats until they were farther out to sea. Since the ship was considered fast and armed to the teeth with American gun crews, there would be no convoy to escort them until they reached the coast of Iceland, where they would be met by several destroyers and escorted the rest of the way.

But before that, Rosie knew, there would be five days of cruising through the cold, submarine-infested waters of the north Atlantic. Lifeboat drills were to be practiced twice a day, and they'd been advised to wear their clothes even to bed, and always carry their life belt and water bottle with them.

So far, the CWACs on board had not passed their drills satisfactorily; they were meant to assemble from their barracks to the main deck in three minutes, and, as they'd rushed about their cramped cabin, bumping into each other as they grabbed their greatcoats and strapped on life belts, it had taken, to the great displeasure of their commanding officer, a whole fifteen. Rosie had been warned there would be a drill in the middle of the night several times during the journey, and she suspected it would be even more of a frantic commotion then.

Still, despite the dangers as well as the crowded conditions —eight to a tiny cabin, with some even having to share a berth— the mood aboard the *Queen Elizabeth* seemed almost jolly with expectation. There were twenty-two thousand personnel aboard, and every one of them was eager to get to England. As they'd marched up the gangplank in formation yesterday, the CWACs wearing their greatcoats, steel helmets, anti-gas capes, and respirators, there had been a terrific ovation, people whistling and clapping and cheering. Rosie had found herself grinning, shoulders thrown back, chin lifted with pride. For all the gossip about the "fast women" in the Canadian Women's Army Corps, they were being feted today, and she was glad.

There were only about a hundred CWACS on board the *Queen Elizabeth*, along with a handful of officers and a few dozen nursing sisters. Even at the base in Hamilton, Rosie had never seen so many men in uniform as she did on the ship— smoking on deck, playing poker or bridge in the lounges, voices rising rowdily in the mess hall. Men everywhere, chatting, smiling, winking. Men brushing shoulders as they moved past, or giving someone's waist a little squeeze. It was a bit disconcerting, but Rosie hoped she'd get used to it. It was only five days, after all, that they'd be on board, living cheek by jowl.

As she gazed out at the placid sea, as smooth as a millpond, she wondered what the next five days would hold, as well as the months and maybe even years after that. She'd been granted forty-eight hours' leave to say goodbye to her family before reporting to Ottawa, and the farewell had felt more poignant than ever, with the future so uncertain.

"I will write," Rosie had promised, hugging her mother and father in turn. Jamie had been accepted as a trainee mechanic at Collins Bay in July, and so she would have to say goodbye to him separately, later that day, on the base.

"As will we," her mother had returned, "although I've heard it can take ages for letters to get through. Oh, Rosie." She'd shaken her head, looking near tears. "You're doing the same as I did, all those years ago, when I nursed on the Front, but I never considered how Aunt Rose must have felt, having me go so far away. I'd already said goodbye to go to art school in Glasgow, I suppose, but it wasn't the same."

"We've all got to do our bit," Rosie had replied bracingly. She had felt a lot wiser and more experienced than even when she'd returned home in Kingston four months ago, thinking she'd already learned so much. Four months of further training in Hamilton had toughened her up considerably, but also given her the gift of the kind of camaraderie she'd once feared had been beyond her, back in Kitchener. She'd made good friends on her course, women who, like her, had been learning clerical skills. She was the only one of them, however, who was being posted overseas. They'd all had a tearful goodbye a week ago now, before Rosie had gone on leave before reporting to Glebe Barracks in Ottawa, and then on to Halifax.

"Just think, there won't be any drilling and marching in London, you lucky thing," one of them had said, squeezing her tightly. "When you walk about CMHQ in your smart heels, with no bunions or blisters, think of me with my poor, aching feet!"

"I certainly will," Rosie had promised with a laugh. At Hamilton, they'd had three-to-ten-mile marches nearly every day, in addition to the endless inspections, parades, and drilling, and all their clerical classes. Most evenings, they'd fallen into bed exhausted, although there had been time enough for recreation—Rosie had joined the base's tennis team, and enjoyed watching several amateur theatricals. It had all been a busy and challenging yet fun time—there had even been a number of station dances, which had always been popular, and because there were so many more men than women on the base, Rosie had been asked—and accepted—to dance more than she ever had before in her life.

A few of the other girls had gone out with soldiers, but Rosie had held herself back. There was no point getting attached to anyone, she'd felt, since she knew she was bound overseas in just a few months, and, in any case, she wouldn't even know how to begin with such a thing. No matter what Violet had once said in spite, she still hadn't learned to flirt. Her dancing might have improved somewhat—she was careful not to step on anyone's feet—but men remained a mystery.

In any case, she'd told herself, it was just as well. She had a job to do, a country to serve, and her determination to do so had increased over the last few months, especially after the terrible and shocking news of the failed amphibious assault at Dieppe in August. Of the six thousand mostly Canadian soldiers, three thousand had died or been injured. It had been hailed as a complete disaster for the Allied forces, although Rosie had heard some say that the lessons learned at Dieppe would serve them well later in the war. Still, it was cold comfort indeed for the families of the three thousand Canadian boys who wouldn't be coming home.

"Goodness, we're properly out to sea, now, aren't we?"

Another CWAC came to join Rosie at the railing. She had yet to get to know anyone well; the noisy crowdedness of the ship had the converse effect of making it hard to chat. Meals were eaten quickly, and recreational opportunities were limited. "I'm Beth," the woman said, sticking out a hand. "I trained as a switchboard operator in Montreal, but I still feel like a bit of a greenhorn, to tell you the truth. What about you?"

"I'm Rosie." She shook the other woman's hand, liking the frank openness of her expression, her ready smile. Beth had hair the color and consistency of straw, pulled back into a bushy bun, and a liberal sprinkling of freckles on her nose and cheeks. "I did clerical training at Hamilton." No need to mention the two months at Sainte-Anne-de-Bellevue; she wasn't an officer anymore, and she didn't mind a bit.

Beth surveyed the calm sea. "Hard to believe it might be heaving with U-boats under there," she remarked with a shake of her head. "Here's hoping the *Queen Elizabeth* is as quick as they say she is, and those ack-ack guns really do the trick if they're needed."

"I don't know why they wouldn't," Rosie replied with a smile. "With so many personnel on board, they're going to want us to be properly defended. At least that's what I've been telling myself!" She smiled to soften her words, in case Beth worried she was rebuking her.

"I suppose you're right," Beth replied with a laugh. "I've never seen a ship this big, at any rate—the biggest boat I'd ever been in before this was the Longueuil ferry in Montreal. What about you?"

Rosie nodded in agreement. "I'm the same, really. Before this, the only boat I'd been on was the ferry to Amherst Island, where I used to live, near Kingston. It was just a little tug. This feels absolutely enormous in comparison."

"I got lost trying to make it to the mess hall," Beth

confessed. "And by the time I arrived, most of the food had gone! I hope I don't starve before we get to Old Blighty."

"I know how to get to the mess all right, I think. We can go together, if you like," Rosie offered, smiling when she saw the look of hope and gratitude on the other woman's face.

"Can we? That would be swell."

"Of course. Shall we see if we can find a cup of tea? I think they're serving it in the officers' lounge—the one that's been reserved for the CWACs."

Rosie led the way from the deck to the lounge, glad that she was able to be of help to her new friend. It felt like a long time ago indeed since she'd felt so homesick and overwhelmed back in Barracks Five at Kitchener, wondering how to get on with everyone.

The five days of their journey passed with blessed uneventfulness; no alarms or attacks, although, on occasion, the engines were cut, and in the sudden, unnerving stillness, everyone went quiet, wary, as the crew listened for U-boat signals. Artillerymen had taken shifts relieving the American gun crews at their posts, and Rosie had gotten used to the sight of them standing to attention, endlessly scanning the smooth horizon. She was grateful that despite their unwavering attention, they hadn't actually seen anything.

The mood of jollity had waned, a bit, as everyone began to get fed up with how crowded the ship was; Rosie had become used to stepping over sprawled legs, or sharing a seat with Beth, who had become a good friend.

One evening, she and Beth were sitting in one of the lounges, squashed together on an armchair, four Scottish pilots perched on the floor beside them, playing a rather vicious game of bridge. Rosie found her attention drawn to the pilot in front of her, whose hand she could see. She hadn't played a rubber of bridge since university; not many people had been interested in the game at Hamilton, and there had been no time at Sainte-Anne-de-Bellevue. Her interest sharpened when he won the bid, with five hearts; she leaned forward, barely aware of what she was doing, avidly watching how the hand played out.

Beth, who wasn't a bridge player, watched her in bemusement. "Rosie, what on earth..."

"Just a moment," she whispered. "I want to see if he..." She drew her breath sharply as the pilot played one of his hearts. She hadn't realized quite how noticeable her reaction had been until he looked behind him, an eyebrow arched.

"Do you want to play the hand?" he asked wryly, and Rosie blushed, abashed.

"No, no, I'm sorry, but..."

Now the pilot looked decidedly amused. "But?"

"You shouldn't have played your trump just then," she whispered, unable to keep herself from saying it, although she knew it would give away his hand. "If you'd deliberately lost that trick, you could have won back control with the queen, and then you would have been able to finesse the king and win the rest. You would have won all five of your heart tricks, but as it is, you'll lose either the queen or..." She trailed off, biting her lip, realizing belatedly just how presumptuous she was being, telling a stranger how to play.

Fortunately, the pilot wasn't offended by her unexpected plain speaking. He let out a sharp crack of laughter that had several heads turning and then returned to his hand, studying his cards. "By George," he said after a moment, "I think she's right! Should I have done that?"

He showed his hand to the other players, who, while Rosie watched nervously, agreed that she had played the hand correctly.

"Better than you, anyway," one of them laughed, slapping the pilot on the back.

"Sorry." Rosie ducked her head. "I didn't mean to be nosy. I just couldn't help it."

The pilot glanced at her appraisingly. "That was a pretty display of quick, critical thinking," he remarked, and Rosie shrugged.

"I just like bridge."

"You play a lot?"

"I used to, at university, before I joined up."

The pilot nodded slowly. "What's your name?" he asked.

"Rosie Lyman," she replied, wondering why he wanted to know. Then, in a moment of uncharacteristic boldness, she asked, "What's yours?"

For some reason, this made all four pilots start to laugh.

"David McConnell," the pilot answered, holding out his hand for her to shake. "Nice to meet you, Rosie Lyman."

By the time several destroyers met them off the coast of Iceland to escort them to Scotland, where they would disembark and then take a train to London, everyone seemed ready to get off the crowded ship. A dense fog, apparently typical for that time of year, shrouded Scotland as the *Queen Elizabeth* anchored offshore; they would disembark the next morning.

Rosie stood on the sundeck in the chilly morning air, watching the sun rise, its rays burning through the dense mist that cloaked the harbor as well as the mainland in a soft, gray shroud. The air was cold and damp, but as the sun rose, the dampness dissipated and the sky turned a pearly, luminescent blue; the mist evaporated in ghostly shreds, revealing first the hills in the distance, gleaming in the sunlight and violet with heather, and then the harbor itself, the bulky shapes of warships emerging from the fog like enormous apparitions.

"There's so many," Beth, who had joined her at the deck,

breathed as she looked around the harbor, its choppy waters positively bristling with ships. "So *many...*"

In all her travels, from Kitchener to Quebec to Hamilton to here, Rosie had never seen so many ships—every kind of warship imaginable—destroyers, cruisers, minesweepers, escort carriers, battleships, frigates, and others she didn't recognize. They emerged from the fog like a vast, silent army, all of them somberly waiting and ready to be used. To be used in battle, to destroy or be destroyed, to win this war... or to lose it.

A shudder went through her as the understanding of all that was at stake swept over her in a chilling wave. Back in Canada, she realized, joining the Corps had all felt a bit like playacting, almost like dress-up. Yes, it had been grueling in its own way— the marches, the drilling, the discipline, the mess and orderly duty, the exhaustion—but even so, the stakes of what they were doing, the why of it, hadn't felt quite *real*.

When they'd learned of the casualties at Dieppe, the war had come that much closer, touching lives with its horror and grief, but still seeming far away. And even here, on the ship, all those airmen and soldiers, ready to disembark, to serve, to fight... even then it hadn't seemed quite real; more like a jolly party, everyone cheerful and laughing, waiting for their adventure to begin, despite the shadows that lengthened, the artillerymen standing sentry, scanning the horizon.

Despite all that, Rosie hadn't appreciated the enormity of the undertaking, and all that was at stake... until now, with the sight of all those silent ships before her... She felt a prickling on the back of her neck, and she had the odd sense of time both rushing past and standing still. She had an urge not to move on from this moment, even as she felt as if she had already passed it, as if she were looking back on herself from a long distance, old and gray and shaking her head, wondering at the young woman standing so still at the deck railing, with so much unknown ahead of her, both excitement and danger.

A whistle blew, and she and Beth both turned away from the deck.

"We'll have to get ready to disembark," Beth said. "I imagine it will take ages to get all of us off this tub! I've heard they're going to put on a good show to welcome us—a band and all sorts, down by the docks."

"How nice," Rosie murmured, but her mind was still on the sight of those ships, their gray hulls gleaming under the morning sun, the last of the mist having been burned away.

Just a few hours later, they disembarked to some fanfare, although not as much as Beth had hoped, for the planned reception had been canceled due to the fog. Still, as the CWACs marched abreast down the gangplank and then through a huge transport shed where hundreds, if not thousands, of navy men had assembled, a cheer went up through the crowd, even louder and more effusive than back at Halifax, and Rosie found herself smiling, the remnant of that odd, premonitory feeling finally fading away.

Men whistled and clapped as the CWACs marched by in their uniforms and greatcoats in perfect step, shoulders back, chins lifted, staring straight ahead. A fierce pride rushed through Rosie as she marched on, past the men and out of the shed, into the bright fall morning, and the new adventure ahead of her.

CHAPTER EIGHT

NOVEMBER 1942

CMHQ, London, England

"Drat this typewriter!" Rosie muttered under her breath as her sheet of paper got stuck for the second time that morning, smearing the ink. All around her, typewriters clacked busily as other CWACs bent their heads to their tasks at CMHQ, in the former Sun Life Assurance Building, off Trafalgar Square.

Their commanding officer, Major Eva Davis, walked by smartly, low heels clicking on the floor, her narrowed, assessing gaze surveying the "special detachment" of the Canadian Woman's Army Corps posted there, making sure, as always, that they were all hard at work.

In the three weeks since Rosie had arrived in England, the major had been eagle-eyed in ensuring every private under her authority was always industriously occupied and well-turned out, whether working at CMHQ or lining up for inspection back at their barracks on South Street, in Mayfair.

Already, they had been confined to barracks on several Monday evenings for having their shoes less than perfectly polished, or a stray hair on their collar, or a bed slightly rumpled. Standards were even higher than they'd been for the officers-in-training at Sainte-Anne-de-Bellevue, and they were told, over and over, how important it was for the CWACs to make a good impression on their fellow Commonwealth subjects.

Rosie carefully rolled the paper back into the typewriter and got back to work—typing out rather dreary correspondence about staffing requirements at different bases around the country, which is what she'd been doing since she had first reported to CMHQ the second week in November. All the other CWACs were doing much the same kind of work. Despite what she'd told Jamie about her job most likely being dull, Rosie knew she hadn't expected it to be *quite* as dull as it was, typing out list after list, filing each one in the wooden tray in the middle of the room before moving onto the next one with depressing regularity.

She had, she could now acknowledge with wry bemusement, secretly thought she might be doing something a *little* bit important to the war effort. Perhaps it was having been selected first for officer training and then to go overseas, but she'd begun to think, without even articulating or acknowledging it to herself, that she was someone just a little bit important. Someone who could *do* something important—a notion now which made her sigh, laugh, and shake her head all at once.

Violet would have told her what a ninny she was, putting on such airs and graces, she thought, missing her cousin all over again, even as the old hurt needled her, that Violet hadn't cared enough to write. It had been nearly nine months since she'd last seen or spoken to her cousin, and the absence—and silence— still tried her greatly.

Rosie had still had no letter from her, although she'd sent a letter to Violet as soon as she'd arrived in London, informing her of all her news, trying to keep it chatty and friendly and light, in what she suspected was a vain attempt to regain the easy camaraderie they'd once had.

The CWACs had been told that eight thousand bags of mail bound for Canadians overseas had been lost in a fire, so perhaps Violet's letter had gone missing then. Rosie hoped so; she hoped Violet had written, even if she hadn't received the letter. Perhaps she'd receive one soon, along with one from her parents. She had, happily, received a letter from Nancy, who had written that she'd told Sam about the baby, and they were getting married, the baby due very soon. Rosie was pleased for her, and now counted Nancy as a friend, even if she had no idea when—or even if—she'd ever see her again. As for Violet... Rosie hoped one day they might be able to reconcile, even if it was after she'd finished her work in London, or even when the war ended.

Despite the mundane nature of her work, Rosie still found living in London both exciting and strange. When they'd marched from ship to train three weeks ago, she had been taken aback by how *different* it all was. The Scottish accents of the warm-hearted ladies who had given them mugs of hot tea and homemade scones as they'd boarded the train had been near impenetrable, although, as Beth had said, a smile was the same in any language. The train they'd traveled on had been swift but incredibly dirty, as apparently there was no one left to clean them out anymore; unlike back home, just about everyone here was doing war work.

"It's all very shabby, isn't it," one of the CWACs had whispered as she'd sipped her tea, her eyes wide over the rim of her cup. "Did you notice, those ladies all had darns in their stockings, poor things!"

"Well, there is a war on, after all," someone else had replied a bit sharply. "They're bound to feel the lack in a way we haven't back home. Not yet, anyway."

It was true, Rosie thought, that the heavy price of the war

was felt here in a way it wasn't all the way across the Atlantic; whether it was through clothing coupons or ration books, the scarcity of such items as an egg or an orange. The thick blackout curtains that were drawn across the windows every night was another oddity the CWACs were unused to; there hadn't been an air raid yet, but they were all told to be prepared at any time, and bring their respirators wherever they went.

Despite all these seeming hardships, there had been plenty to take Rosie's and the other CWACs' interest. Their billet was the most amazingly grand house, right in the center of the city, with a huge staircase of black marble, and ornate fireplaces in every room. Apparently, it had been offered up when the war had started by some great lord or lady, and would be given back when it ended.

That first night, Rosie and Beth had tumbled into the first room they had found—a grand bedroom with a dais in the middle presumably once used for a four-poster, now filled with fifteen army regulation cots, barracks boxes underneath. The next morning, they'd had a conducted tour of the city, and they'd reported for duty to CMHQ in Trafalgar Square on Monday morning.

When they weren't working, there were plenty of options for entertainment; perhaps the CWACs were a novelty, but they were courted by both British and American soldiers alike. Rosie had never had so much male attention, and she still had no idea what to do with it. Although some of the girls accepted dates with alacrity, Rosie quickly decided she would only step out with someone within a group, when other people could do the talking—and flirting.

"My cousin once told me I couldn't flirt," she had told Beth after such an evening, when she'd struggled through dinner, making painful chitchat with an RAF pilot from somewhere up north. "And it seems she was right. No matter how much I try, I get completely tongue-tied in that type of situation. I can't for the life of me think of what to do or say, and to be honest, I think I'd rather just stay home."

"Just be yourself," Beth, who managed to chat to anyone with her simple, honest friendliness, had advised. "All they want is a bit of a laugh and a chat. They're quite funny, the British boys, aren't they, the way they suddenly crack into laughter? It makes me jump every time!"

"And me," Rosie had agreed. She hadn't quite become accustomed to the dry wit and sudden laughter of their British "cousins," although the CWACs had clearly taken London by storm; even the American army newspaper, *Stars and Stripes*, had effused about their "northern friends" who were so "smart and slim," advising their American counterparts to "watch out."

Rosie had no intention of making a splash with either the British or American servicemen; she was content simply to do her job, although on mornings like this, as she typed yet another list of names and duties, she really did wish it was a little more exciting.

When she ventured to say as much to Beth over lunch in the canteen, her friend was more philosophical. "I don't know that I've got the brains to do much more than I am, and I'd have never seen London, or any place other than home, if I hadn't joined up. Next leave some of the girls are going to Edinburgh. I'd fancy seeing that! There's a castle and everything. Do you want to go with us?"

"Yes, that sounds fun," Rosie said firmly, because she had decided at the beginning of her overseas adventure that she would say yes to everything—or at least as much as she could. "My mother is actually from Glasgow originally, which is a funny thing to think, because I've only known her back home in Canada, of course."

"Golly, so that makes you half-Scottish, doesn't it?" Beth exclaimed. "Although you don't have an accent!"

"Neither does my mum, anymore," Rosie returned with a

laugh. "She emigrated to North America when she was twelve, although she did go back to Glasgow for a few years, for art school. But she's been in good old Ontario for over twenty years now."

"Have you got any family still there in Scotland?" Beth asked. "Maybe you could see them while we were up that way."

Rosie was jolted by that thought. "You know," she said slowly, "I'm not sure. My mum's mother died when she was little, and her father emigrated with her and died before I was born. Her aunt and uncle emigrated, too." She considered the matter, which seemed novel, because her mother rarely talked about her years in Glasgow. "There must be someone still there, though," she added after a moment. "Someone who knew her, whether family or friend. I'll write my mum and ask—it might be fun, to meet someone from those days. And I could pass on their news to my mum."

"Sounds swell," Beth agreed. "Now, are you coming with us tonight? We're all going to see Jack Hulbert and Cicely Court-neidge in *Full Swing*. It's meant to be a real gas, and do you know, I've never been to the theater before! Apparently, they do it differently here—they drink and smoke between and even during the acts! I wouldn't know any different, to be honest, but it sounds fun."

"I might," Rosie said, not wanting to turn down an invitation, although, in truth, she was desperate for a quiet night at home. The other CWACs seemed happy to sally forth every evening—to the theater, to the Overseas Club, to various dance halls or restaurants. For a city in blackout and a country at war, a girl could still have a very good time in London.

By the time she got home that evening, Rosie was aching with tiredness—and, she feared, coming down with a cold. Apparently, everyone got one as soon as they'd arrived, or so they'd been told by one of their commanding officers.

"It's the weather," the officer had said knowledgeably. "And, of course, all the different germs."

The weather had indeed been dreadful almost since the day they'd arrived—cold and damp, with a dense, rolling fog that made it hard sometimes to see so much as your hand in front of your face. It also got dark terribly early—by four o'clock, people were drawing their blackout curtains, which made for a very long evening. Rosie was certainly used to cold, but she missed the crisp, bright snowy days of Ontario; this damp cold felt much worse, seeping right into her bones.

"We're going to have a bite to eat at a Lyons Corner House before we go out," Beth told her as she hurried upstairs to change and Rosie followed her more slowly. "You're coming, aren't you, Rosie?"

Rosie shed her coat and hung it on a hook in their dormitory as she tried not to shiver. "I would, honestly," she said, "but I'm starting to feel rather dreadful. I think I might have to stay back."

"Oh, you poor thing, you do look a bit peaky." Beth paused in her flurry of getting ready to gaze at her in concern. "Do you need anything? A cup of tea or a hot-water bottle? This place is always so darned cold, it's no wonder we're all coming down with the flu."

"Not you, though," Rosie said with a smile, and Beth gave a grimacing sort of grin.

"I'm as healthy as a horse, or so my mother always told me. I could never be one of those delicate, fainting sort of girls, even if I wanted to be."

"Better for you, all things considered. I remember my CO back at training warned us she wouldn't suffer any fainting lilies!"

"No, indeed." Beth grinned. "I'm in the right place, then. But what about you? Can I get you something?'

"I'll be all right," Rosie returned, grateful for her friend's kindness. "I'm going to tuck myself up in bed with tea and toast and feel comfy indeed. You'll have to tell me all about it afterward, and show me the program."

"Oh, we will!" Beth began to twist her hair up, groaning as her thick, straw-colored hair refused to cooperate. "Why do I even bother trying to look fancy?" she exclaimed. "I never can pull it off."

"What was that advice you gave me?" Rosie teased. "Be yourself?"

"But not with my hair," Beth returned, and brushed it out as a few of the CWACs called up the stairs for her. "Never mind, I'll just leave it. Stay warm, honey, and feel better."

Rosie took off her uniform slowly, her whole body aching. It would be rather dreadful to come down with a cold, she thought with a sigh, especially so far from home. From downstairs, she heard laughter as many of the CWACs in the house got ready to go out, eager to make the most of their evening before their 10:15 curfew.

When they'd finally left, in a flurry of last-minute changes and chatter, the house felt very quiet and still, so Rosie wondered if she was the only one left, except perhaps Major Davis, who usually spent the evenings in her room on the ground floor. She had heard there would be a second contingent of CWACs arriving from Canada any day, and while most of them would be billeted at another grand house farther out of the city, they'd been told that some might have to squeeze in with them here in Mayfair. As she swathed herself in her dressing gown and tucked herself up in bed, Rosie wondered if she'd know any of them from Kitchener or Hamilton or Sainte-Anne-de-Bellevue. She'd come to know a few of the girls here pretty well, but she looked forward to the thought of some potentially familiar faces.

It felt surprisingly cozy, tucked up in bed, the blackout curtains drawn against the cold night, the only light coming from a little lamp as Rosie wrote a letter to Jamie.

I don't know how you'd find London—it's a big city, far bigger than Kingston, and with so many different kinds of buildings. It can all be a bit gray and grimy, but the squares they have make it quite pleasant—rectangles of green amidst all the brick and stone. There are quite a few parks, as well, although they're used for all sorts of things now—growing vegetables, or air-raid shelters, or anti-aircraft guns. Someone told me that the railings in front of Kensington Gardens were melted down for munitions! Everyone here does their bit—it's quite nice, really, but it is very different to home.

We had a fire drill the other night, which I thought might be my last—we had to line up in front of the window in the pitch black, tie a rope under our shoulders, and then hang onto the sill and drop down into nothing! My heart was thundering away in my chest, but the rope actually lets you down quite gradually—all you have to is make sure you don't bump into the wall. It's called a Davy apparatus, and it will let us get out in a hurry in case of a fire, but I for one certainly hope we don't have to use it!

The sound of the door opening downstairs, and then being blown shut by a gust of wind, had Rosie pausing in writing her letter.

"Hello?" a woman called up the stairs. "Is anyone here?"

Rosie scrambled out of bed, belting her dressing gown more tightly about her waist. Maybe she was the only one left at South Street, she thought in bemusement. Or perhaps the other

CWACs left at barracks were tucked up in bed, as she'd been, and didn't want to come out to greet this new arrival.

"Hello?" the voice said again, echoing through the hallway as someone began walking slowly up the stairs. "Goodness, but it's as dark as if I've been shut up in a cupboard! *Hello...?*"

Was there something familiar about that voice? Rosie wondered as she hurried toward the door. Her ears were blocked with cold, but she thought she recognized something about it.

"Hello," she called back, squinting into the darkness as she opened the door. She stepped onto the landing and, with a gasp, almost crashed into the woman who was edging her way up the stairs in the dark.

For a second, they engaged in an awkward dance as they held onto each other's shoulders, trying to keep the other from falling down the marble staircase. Rosie had no inclination to break a leg—or her neck.

"Sorry," she said once they'd both regained their balance and let go of each other. "The lights are kept off because of the blackout and I don't think anyone's home but me at the moment. Come into the dormitory, where there's a light." She ushered the woman into her bedroom, surprised at the gasp that the newly arrived CWAC gave. Then she turned, and her mouth dropped open in stunned surprise. "Violet!"

CHAPTER NINE

Rosie stared at Violet in amazement, hardly able to believe her cousin was here. Violet was looking back at her in similar stupefaction, but then she started laughing.

"How funny!" she exclaimed. "What an absolute *hoot*! There we are, practically falling all about in each other's arms without knowing who we were! I can't believe I didn't recognize your voice!"

"I thought I recognized yours, but I wasn't sure exactly..." Rosie shook her head slowly. "I can't believe you're here."

Violet's laughter subsided and quite suddenly she dropped her gaze. "No, I don't suppose I can, either," she agreed. "It was all a bit of a rush—first I was going, then I wasn't, then I was. I'd put my name forward from the beginning—well, you know how I always wanted to go overseas."

"Yes," Rosie answered after a brief pause. After that first wave of delighted surprise, and Violet's sudden burst of laughter, a coolness was descending between them that reminded her painfully of their farewell back at Kitchener.

"Goodness," Violet said, looking around. "What a place this is!"

"It is rather grand, isn't it?" Rosie agreed quickly, glad to have something to talk about. "It feels a bit ridiculous, to be living in a place like this, but all the antiques and valuables have been taken out, of course, although someone said there were all sorts of fancy things here before—paintings and statues and the like, marble and gold and gilt and all that kind of thing. It's all standard military stuff now, very basic." Rosie stopped talking, realizing she was rabbiting on in her nervousness. She, nervous, with Violet! It made her feel both frustrated and sad. How had it come to this between them? And yet it had.

"Well, it beats the barracks back at Manitoba, that's for sure," Violet replied. "Do you know where I'm bunking?"

"I'm sorry, I don't." Rosie hated how stilted she seemed. "Look, you must be parched. I remember we were, when we first arrived. It was such a long train journey, and everyone was so tired. If you come down to the kitchen, I'll make you a cup of tea."

Violet looked surprised by the offer, and for an awful second Rosie thought she might refuse. Then she nodded, briefly. "Thank you," she said. "That would be wonderful."

The kitchen was in the cellar of the house—an enormous room used by the mess women to make breakfast and supper, although CWACs could help themselves to tea and toast when they wanted, without too much fuss.

Rosie filled up the big kettle and lugged it onto the stove, while Violet watched without speaking.

"You've changed," she remarked after a moment, and Rosie couldn't tell from her tone if that was a good thing or not.

"I suspect we both have," she replied as she busied herself with the tea. "The tea is quite good here, but I'm afraid lots of things are rationed. You'll find that quite different—from home, I mean. I haven't seen an orange since I've been here, and hardly an egg. They use powdered egg instead, which isn't too bad once you get used to it, and I've heard that we still eat better than the Brits." She was rabbiting on again, she realized. She really had to stop.

"How long have you been here?" Violet asked.

"Four weeks now. We arrived on the fifth of November. Guy Fawkes Day, it's called here." With nothing to do but wait for the kettle to boil, Rosie turned to face Violet, cringing a little under her cousin's impassive scrutiny. "How was your journey over?"

Violet shrugged. "It wasn't a pleasure cruise, that's for certain, but we didn't get torpedoed, so that was a good thing."

She looked very smart in her uniform, Rosie thought; she had tailored the jacket so it nipped in a bit at the waist, and even with a gas mask slung around her neck, Violet still managed to seem elegant.

"Where are the others?" Rosie asked, realizing belatedly that Violet had arrived on her own. "Surely you didn't come here by yourself."

"We were all sent to some place out in the suburbs," she answered. "A grand place like this, but there wasn't enough room, so they picked six of us to make our way here in the dark." She paused and then finished a bit diffidently, "The other girls wanted to have a look around before they were back on duty, since no one was actually expecting us. I just wanted to get to my bed."

"Really?" Rosie asked before she could think better of it. "I would have thought you would have been up for a bit of an explore, Violet!" She didn't mean it spitefully—at least she hoped she didn't—but her cousin's eyes flashed briefly as she pressed her lips together.

"Well," she replied, "as you said, we've both changed."

In opposite ways perhaps, Rosie thought but decided not to say. Despite her initial laughter, Violet certainly seemed more restrained now than she once had been, although perhaps that was simply how she was with Rosie.

They, who had once been as close as could be, arms around each other, laughing over nothing much at all, were now standing here like two strangers, struggling to make even the most desultory of conversation.

The kettle boiled, and, to Rosie's relief, she was able to busy herself making the tea, so she didn't have to think of a reply.

A few minutes later, however, they were both seated at the kitchen table, their cups of tea in front of them, and still not much to say.

"There isn't any sugar, I'm afraid," Rosie said as she took a sip of her tea. "We could have it, and some of the girls in the other billets do, but our CO is a real stickler for rules. She says if it's rationed for the Brits, so it should be for us."

"She sounds like a real laugh a minute, then," Violet replied in the same diffident tone she'd used before.

"She's pretty strict," Rosie agreed. "Everything's got to be absolutely top-notch—shoes shined, buttons polished, not a single stray hair on your collar! But, otherwise, she's all right."

"And how have you been finding it here?" Violet asked after a moment. "Is the work very interesting?"

Rosie hesitated and then admitted with a little laugh, "Not very. In fact, I'd say most of the girls find it pretty dull work, indeed. I suppose we thought we'd be doing something a bit more exciting than typing out lists and things—I work on staffing requirements, generally, but there are other jobs. Some girls work in the medical office in Piccadilly, and some are doing other things—drivers and cleaners and mess women and the like. And we get to go on parade sometimes, which can be a bit fun. Last weekend, we went on parade at an exhibition of a football game, of all things—two American teams were putting on a show for the English, in aid of the Red Cross. It was quite fun, although pretty cold." She stopped abruptly, realizing once again how she'd been chattering on, and took a sip of her tea.

"Goodness," Violet said, sipping her own tea.

They were both silent, the huge kitchen cold and cavernous all around them. Why couldn't she think of something to say?

"How have you been, anyway?" Rosie asked at last. "I knew from my mum you'd gone to Manitoba."

Violet shrugged. "Manitoba was... Manitoba, I suppose." She gave a small, wry smile that reminded Rosie just a little of the way her cousin used to be, full of sparkle and wit, before it faded. "About what you'd expect—endless prairie and as hot as Hades in the summer. I tried not to get freckles, but after a while I gave it up as a lost cause." She let out a little sigh. "As dull as could be, to be honest. I was so pleased to hear I was going overseas. Even if the work is just as dull, at least it's somewhere different."

"I think you'll like it," Rosie said quickly. "There are all sorts of things to do—some of the CWACs go out just about every night, when they're not on duty. They're at the theater now, actually. And the British and American servicemen seem to like us Canadian girls."

Violet's mouth twisted as her eyebrows rose. "What about the poor Canadian boys?"

"Well," Rosie shrugged, smiling, "I wouldn't really know. I still haven't learned how to flirt, I'm afraid. I'm really quite hopeless at it." She'd meant to sound light, but to her horrified surprise, Violet's eyes suddenly filled with tears.

"Oh, Rosie," she said on something close to a sob, "I can't tell you how badly I feel about all that."

Rosie stared at her dumbly for a few seconds. "You *do*..."

"I was so horrible to you," Violet continued, taking a handkerchief from her sleeve and dabbing at her eyes. "I knew I was, even as I was doing it, and yet I couldn't stop. I was just so *jealous*. It's awful, isn't it? So petty, that I hate to have to admit it, but there you are. That's all it was. Good old ugly envy."

"Officer training wasn't very exciting," Rosie told her after a moment, her mind still reeling from Violet's confession. "And the girls weren't all that friendly. Everyone was trying to impress our COs. I was relieved when I was asked to go overseas, because it meant I had to give up my rank. I hadn't wanted it, anyway."

"I know you didn't," Violet replied. "And, if I'm honest, I didn't, really, either."

"You didn't?" Rosie couldn't keep the skepticism from her voice. "What were you so envious of, then?"

"Oh, this is even worse to admit," Violet said in a low voice, twisting her handkerchief between her fingers. "The truth is, Rosie, I was used to being the one to shine. Oh, I know you were always going to be better than me in the books department, but that didn't bother me a bit, because in every other way..." She trailed off and Rosie felt her cheeks heat as she realized what Violet was saying.

"In every other way?" she prompted quietly.

"In every other way, I thought I was... well, I suppose I thought I was better," Violet finished in a miserable rush. "Oh, I know how it sounds, Rosie, believe me, I do. It makes me sound like a complete pill, a truly horrible person, and maybe I am." She dabbed her eyes again, weeping openly now, while Rosie simply sat there, stunned. "But it's true, that was how I thought. Not that I even realized it, at least not completely, until you were selected as an officer, and I was so very cross about it." She let out a shuddery breath. "That last conversation went round and round in my head for ages. I was trying to figure out why I had behaved so badly, and what I could do about it."

Rosie glanced down at the table. "Why didn't you write me, then?" she asked.

"I tried, honestly, I tried. I wrote a dozen different letters and then threw them all away. I just didn't know how to explain without..."

"Without sounding like a pill?" Rosie finished. She tried to smile but her voice came out a bit flat. Violet's admission had both surprised and hurt her.

Violet bit her lip, her eyes wide and luminous with tears. "Do you hate me now?" she asked.

"I don't hate you," Rosie replied slowly. "And, to be honest, Violet, you haven't really said anything I haven't thought myself, at one time or another. I think I've believed you were better than me in just about everything, except the books department, too. You've always been prettier, and friendlier, and far more full of fun. That isn't anything I wasn't aware of, but..." She swallowed, the realization filtering through her. "I suppose I didn't think *you* thought that way, as well, or that you would get your nose so out of joint because I happened to be chosen for the one thing that you weren't."

A tear slipped down Violet's cheek. "I know," she whispered. "I'm awful, truly."

"No." Rosie sighed and shook her head, reaching for her tea even though it was now cold. "You're not awful, and I'm glad you've been honest. I was worried that our friendship had been lost forever." Although, Rosie wondered, perhaps it had, in some way, changed.

Violet leaned eagerly across the table, reaching for Rosie's hand. "So you'll still be friends with me, even after the way I've behaved?"

"Ye-es," Rosie replied, and they both heard the hesitation in her voice. Violet's face fell. "I still love you dearly, Violet, of course I do. But all these months apart... I've realized how they've actually helped me, not to be in your shadow for a little while. I finally got to be my own person, in a way I never did before, and it's been... *good*," she said, realizing as she said the words how much she meant them. Even though there had been hard times, they had been good and helped her to grow. She had changed, without Violet. She'd had the freedom to. "I suppose," she said slowly, "I don't want to lose that. I don't want to be in your shadow again, the way I was before."

"Rosie, I don't want you to be anyone but yourself," Violet protested.

"Actually," Rosie replied, "I think you did. I think you kept trying to make me a version of yourself, only a little dimmer so I didn't outshine you, which, of course, I never did. Why else would you keep harping at me, back at Kitchener, to have *fun?*"

Violet hung her head. "Maybe, a little," she admitted, "but I was also trying to help you. At least, I thought I was. You've always needed pushing out a bit, Rosie, to do new things. You know you have."

"Well, I don't, anymore," Rosie replied staunchly. "I didn't, without you. I've moved all around and came overseas without any pushing at all from you, or anyone else, for that matter. And I suppose that's what I want to be different from now on—I'm not going to stay in your shadow, Violet, but I promise you, I won't outshine you, either. I just want to be myself, and have you like me for what I am, and accept me for what I'm not, and I'll do the same for you."

Violet sniffed and then blew her nose with a loud honk that made Rosie's lips twitch in a small smile. "That sounds like a very good idea," she stated firmly. "And I really am sorry for how I behaved. I'm so ashamed of myself."

"You don't need to be sorry any longer," Rosie replied. "Or ashamed. Let's move on from here as friends—new friends, in a way." She held out her hand for Violet to shake, and her cousin took it with a tremulous smile.

"Thank you, Rosie."

"Thank you," Rosie returned. "I am glad you pushed me into joining the CWACs, you know. You were right, I wouldn't have done it otherwise. Some of the work is as dull as I feared back at the beginning, but I'm seeing the world and doing new things, and most importantly, I'm serving my country. I have a lot to thank you for, Violet, even if it wasn't easy."

"And will you go back to Queen's, after?" Violet asked curiously. "Finish your degree?"

Rosie paused to consider the possibility. She hadn't given much thought to Queen's or her old life there; the present had enough interest and busyness. "I don't know," she admitted after a moment. "It seems like a lifetime ago, and I don't think the war is going to end anytime soon, even though we've had some victories in Africa. Like Winston Churchill said, this isn't the end, or even the beginning of the end, but maybe the end of the beginning." She gave a little sigh. "Who knows what you or I, or any of us, will do or even be by the end of this war? I already feel so changed. I can't imagine what I might be like a few years from now. Maybe I'll be raring to go back to Queen's —but maybe I won't."

"Yes, it is hard to know, I suppose," Violet answered. "I have no idea what I'm going to do, to be honest! I can't see myself becoming a student again."

They both lapsed into silence, but this one felt more comfortable than those before, if a little melancholy. The future stretched out in front of them, entirely unknown. Their friendship had been restored, but it had also been changed. It would never, Rosie knew, be what it once was, but perhaps, in time, it could become something better. Something stronger.

From upstairs, they heard the door open, and someone call out.

"That will be the other CWACs in my group," Violet said, rising from the table and taking their teacups to the sink. "They're a rowdy bunch, I don't mind saying. I'm almost certain they went out for a drink and not just an explore. They're certainly a bit scruffier than the first contingent, I think! But it sounds like your CO will shape them up in no time. Shall we go find out where we're all meant to sleep?"

She gave Rosie a friendly smile, eyes sparkling the way they used to, and Rosie was reminded, despite everything Violet had confessed and how far they'd drifted apart, how much she loved her cousin and best friend.

"Yes, let's find out," she said, smiling back, and together they left the kitchen.

"All right, you lot," Violet called up the stairs with her old, irrepressible humor. "We're coming! But you've missed having a cup of tea, I'm afraid, although I'm guessing you'll need it!"

CHAPTER TEN

JUNE 1943

London, England

The next few months passed happily enough for Rosie; there were plenty of things to occupy her outside of office hours, and having Violet back again, as her best friend, made everything that much jollier.

Violet had, as she always seemed to, fit in with the other CWACs at the grand house in Mayfair. She'd been right, in that the new CWACs *were* a bit scruffier, and less inclined to work as hard as Rosie's contingent did, and so were confined to barracks more evenings than they liked as a result. Still, there was plenty of time to go out and explore the city, and even the whole country; one weekend in March, they took the train down to Brighton, which was off limits to civilians, and walked along the boardwalk, looking out at the barbed wire and barricades that dotted the beach.

Over Christmas, they'd gone to Edinburgh, and Rosie had been enchanted by that beautiful city, the "Queen of the North." The train journey had been terribly crowded, with soldiers sleeping under tables and in the aisles. Violet, Beth, and Rosie had all had to squash into one seat, reminding her of the conditions on the *Queen Elizabeth*. When they had arrived at the station near Princes Street, however, Rosie forgot the discomfort of the journey as she took in the wide, gracious street with gardens alongside and a castle high above, the whole thing looking as if it had been hewn right out of the rock.

There was a concert in the gardens as they had walked by, with a group of children singing "Loch Lomond." Rosie had watched, enchanted, until Beth had pulled her along, warning her that the city was heaving with military on leave, and they'd be lucky if they got a room.

They did get a room, although it took hours to find; unlike the Americans, who had bought up a big hotel and made a supper club and rooms out of it, the Canadians had to make do with what they could find. Still, it was an enjoyable trip, and even better was when Rosie took a train to Glasgow the day after and had tea with one of her mother's old friends she'd mentioned in her last letter—Ruby McCallister.

"Your mother was so kind to us," Ruby had exclaimed as she insisted on Rosie cutting another slice of the Dundee cake she'd made for the occasion. "Taking us in the way she did, my brother and me. Dougie's been gone these five years past—his chest got him in the end, as I knew it would. You know this dear little house was hers, but then she gifted it to us?"

"She did?" Rosie had glanced around the neat little sitting room with its well-mended cushion covers, a porcelain shepherdess on the mantle; she'd had no idea that her mother had once owned a house in Glasgow, or that she had given it to anyone at all. Her mother rarely spoke of her time in this city, although she had regaled Rosie with a few tales of her childhood when she'd been younger.

"And she took us down to Windermere for a holiday, for poor Dougie's health," Ruby had continued. "That was when war was declared—what a time it was, and yet here we are again." She shook her head, smiling a little sadly; she had already told Rosie about her own life, the man she'd fallen in love with during the first war, who had died at the battle of the Somme. "Everyone lost someone," she'd said pragmatically. "I'm just afraid the whole thing is happening again."

The thought had made Rosie feel like shivering; she didn't want to lose someone. She thought of Jamie, still safely back at Collins Bay, at least for now; the boys she knew from Queen's, who had all joined up early or else been forced to enlist; the CWACs she'd come to know, some of whom might be one day posted to the continent, once the Allies invaded.

"But enough of that talk, anyway," Ruby had said. "You must tell me how your mother is. Aren't you the spit of her! Same hair and eyes."

"Mum's well, last time she wrote," Rosie had replied. "She keeps busy managing our home back in Kingston, and she also teaches art to some little ones."

"Ah, her art! She was that gifted, you know. She turned down a position right here in Glasgow, after the war."

"Yes, she's told me that before." Rosie had taken a bite of her cake and swallowed it down. "She never said why, though."

"I think she was drifting a bit, after the war," Ruby had remarked sagely. "We all were, in one way or another. It was such a strange time... there wasn't this jolliness, the way there is now, everyone pulling together, maybe because there wasn't someone like that awful Hitler to rally against, make you keep your chin up and all that. It all just felt so... pointless, I suppose, and so sad." She'd smiled abashedly. "But I wasn't going to talk about the gloomy bits! Your mam could have been a drawing instructor at the Glasgow School of Art, but she decided she needed to go home to Canada. Her island, she said. That was where she felt she truly belonged."

"Amherst Island," Rosie had replied, and felt a pang of

homesickness for the place that she too felt was her true home, even though she hadn't lived there for years. She'd been happy in Kingston, it was true, but dear little Amherst Island, the tiny jewel of Lake Ontario, held a part of her soul... and maybe her mother's, as well. "We don't live there anymore, I'm afraid. It was just too far for my father's work. But it is a dear place. Maybe you'll visit one day. I'd like to go back, when I can."

"Me!" Ruby had laughed, shaking her head. "I shouldn't think so. I'm an old woman, now," she'd added, although Rosie didn't think she could be much more than fifty. She looked care-worn, though, her face lined and her hair gray; life had been hard, even with her mother's help.

"You must keep in touch," Ruby had said when Rosie finally took her leave. "You're always welcome to come and visit, you know. And do write your mother for me—I'd write her myself, but my handwriting has never been so good. I do think of her, though. Often."

Rosie had hugged Ruby before leaving, touched by the older woman's kindness, and feeling a strange connectedness to her, to the past, even to dear old Amherst Island. She couldn't remember the last time she'd been back there; so many people had left, looking for work, that there was hardly anyone left to go and visit. Yet it really had been her home, the place where she'd felt the most safe and loved; she'd felt more *herself* on Amherst Island, Rosie realized, than anywhere else in the world. She resolved she'd return there after the war, if just to see what had become of the place, and discover if it still held its charm and magic.

In mid-June, when the weather was turning balmy and the evenings were light, Violet triumphantly secured invitations to a dance at the American Red Cross Club near Piccadilly Circus, known as Rainbow Corner. It had opened in November and was considered one of the hottest spots to go of an evening, thanks to the plentiful American food and terrific music.

"How did you get an invite?" Beth breathed, for only American servicemen and their guests were allowed to frequent the vaunted establishment.

"I happen to know someone," Violet replied mischievously. She'd stepped out with quite a few servicemen since arriving in London—British, American, and Canadian, but there wasn't anyone serious. Rosie wondered if there ever would be. "Artie Shaw's Navy band is playing, and it will be an absolute hoot," Violet stated grandly. "Hamburgers and Coca-Colas all round!"

The mood was one of giggling excitement as the girls got ready back at the big house in Mayfair; someone had turned the radio up, and Johnny Mercer's "That Old Black Magic" drifted through the rooms, the windows thrown open to the summer air and sunshine. Rosie found herself humming along as she tucked her hair in neatly. She'd wanted to see the famous Rainbow Corner since she'd first heard of it.

"Now, now," Violet said, wagging a finger playfully at her. "You don't need to look like you're on duty, Private Lyman! Why don't you do something different with your hair? It's such a pretty color, and you have a natural wave, lucky thing."

Rosie glanced ruefully at her reflection. "It's a plain old mousy brown and it doesn't have a wave, it has a strange kink in the middle," she told Violet. "But do what you will."

"It's got lovely auburn shades," Violet replied, "just like your mother's, and it does have a wave, whether you call it something else or not. But, yes, I will do what I will with it!"

Clearly, Violet took this as complete license, for half an hour later, Rosie found herself with bright red lips, extra-long lashes, and hair that curled about her face in a perfectly ironed wave.

"Don't you do wonders," she told Violet. It was funny, Rosie reflected, how accepting who she was—as well as who she wasn't—had finally allowed her to be a bit braver, sometimes even in a way that felt almost reckless. She certainly wouldn't have gone out with this face of makeup on back in Kingston—or Kitchener.

Rainbow Corner was hopping as the half-dozen CWACs came in, accompanied by Violet's "friend"—a handsome American GI from Ohio named Ray. He got them all Cokes from the fancy fountain machine, and they sat at a table, tapping their feet and sipping their sodas while Ray and Violet took to the floor.

Despite her hair and makeup, Rosie wasn't really expecting to be asked to dance—there were plenty of girls to ask, including professional, paid hostesses who could dance like a dream. The experience of simply being there was novelty enough, and she sat back in the deep booth, sipping her soda, content, as she often was, simply to watch the world go by.

A few other girls were asked to dance, but Rosie was deep enough in the booth that she didn't think she'd be asked even if someone wanted to, because they couldn't see her in the dim lighting. Then Violet slid in next to her, breathless and laughing.

"Goodness, what a whirl! I'm absolutely pooped. Ray's getting me a drink—I've asked him to get you one, too."

Rosie held up her glass. "I'm still drinking my Coke!"

Violet rolled her eyes. "That's all very well, but we can't stick with soda for the whole evening! I asked Ray for a pink gin." She took a cigarette out of her pocket and lit it; that was a habit she'd developed since Kitchener, Rosie knew, although many of the CWACs smoked. She'd never found it appealing. "So, are you hiding back here in this booth," Violet asked, blowing out a stream of smoke, "or are you just enjoying the music?"

"Enjoying the music," Rosie replied firmly.

Violet slid her a sideways glance. "It seems a shame to waste that face and hair, though. Nobody can even see you all the way back there."

"Maybe not," Rosie agreed, with only a twinge of regret. "But you know me, Violet—"

"Yes, I do. And I know I agreed to let you be you, and I *will*, but tell me honestly." She turned to face Rosie with that typically shrewd and direct look that made her instinctively tense. "Are you happy hiding in this booth, or would you like it if a GI asked you to dance?"

Rosie hesitated for the briefest of seconds, and Violet crowed in triumph.

"I knew it! Part of you wants to be out there on that floor, Rosie! I'm sure of it."

Thankfully, Ray returned with their pink gins, and so Rosie was saved from having to answer. She took a sip of her drink, nearly choking on it as she hardly ever had spirits. Violet downed hers in a couple of gulps, but she was chatting with Ray now and Rosie hoped she would drop the whole subject of GIs and dancing.

Did she want to dance with a GI? A little bit, perhaps, but more importantly, she did, she realized, want some romance in her life... one day. She just had no idea how she would go about finding it. She supposed she hoped that it would find her... but that wouldn't happen, she was pragmatic enough to acknowledge, if she kept hiding in booths or in the backs of rooms the way she had been doing.

Rosie took another sip of her gin, wincing a little as she swallowed it, although it went down easier this time. She was starting to feel pleasantly relaxed, as well as a tiny bit reckless. It was the drink, of course, but Rosie thought it was something else, as well. A desire to change, or maybe just try to, in at least one little way. She'd changed so much already, but not in this. Not with men.

"Well, Rosie." Violet turned back to her, the previous

subject of conversation clearly not forgotten, her expression positively beady. Ray was chatting to another GI who had stopped by their table. "Are you going to do anything about it?"

Rosie took another sip of her gin. "About what?"

"About getting up there and asking a man to dance!"

She nearly spit out her drink. "Violet, women don't ask men to dance!"

"Why not? You've always been going on about how women deserve to be treated the same as men, paid the same—"

"At least our basic pay went up to four-fifths of a man's pay, from two-thirds," Rosie interjected tartly.

"Well, why can't you be as good as a man in this? Four-fifths as good, even, and ask one to dance."

Rosie shook her head. She might be feeling reckless, but she knew she didn't have the courage to do that.

"Or at least ask a man to buy you a drink," Violet pressed. "Plenty of girls do that all the time!" She leaned forward, her eyes alight. "Ask the most handsome man in the room to buy you a drink!" she stated, like a dare.

Rosie opened her mouth to say she couldn't possibly, and then she promptly shut it. Why shouldn't she do as her cousin said? She had nothing to prove to Violet, she realized, or anyone else at Rainbow Corner, or even in the whole world. Just something to prove to herself.

"All right, very well," she said, and, only slightly unsteadily, rose from the table. "I will."

"You will!" Violet's jaw went slack, and Rosie felt a fierce dart of satisfaction that she had surprised her cousin, for once.

"Yes, I will," she said, and, recovering from her surprise, Violet's eyes gleamed as she swiveled in her seat.

"Who have you got in your sights, then?"

Rosie glanced around the crowded room. The dance floor was heaving with couples, and a dozen or so men were by the bar, leaning against it, chatting and smoking. Her gaze fastened on a man she'd noticed when she'd first come into the room, although she hadn't quite realized she had. He was tall and blond, with blue eyes and a cleft in his chin, one elbow propped on the bar as he sipped his beer. He looked like a movie star, she thought, but he didn't seem too stuck up; she thought he looked affable, and she liked his smile.

"That one," she told Violet, and her cousin followed her gaze.

"Oh, nicely done! He looks like a real catch. A bit like Cary Grant, but with blond hair." Violet grinned. "Go get 'im, girl!"

For a second, Rosie faltered. What on earth was she doing? This was so unlike her, and she had no idea how to approach a man, how to talk to him... Then she steeled her spine, along with her nerve, and marched forward.

Maybe it was the gin sloshing around in her innards that both gave her Dutch courage and made her a little queasy, but somehow she made it across the room and squeezed herself in next to the GI, her heart thundering, the blood rushing in her ears. He didn't even look at her—of *course* he didn't—and she had no idea how to capture his attention.

She glanced back at Violet, who gave her an encouraging smile and a thumbs up.

Oh, help. What should she do?

There was nothing for it, she decided after a few seconds had passed, she was going to have do something obvious.

Recklessly, she nudged his elbow, hard enough, unfortunately, to make his beer slosh out of its glass.

"Oh, I'm so sorry," Rosie said as he turned to her in surprise. "I'm trying to get the bartender's attention, but he's not looking at me at all."

"Can I help?" the man asked solicitously, and she smiled at him, hoping she wasn't betraying her utter nerves—and that she didn't have lipstick on her teeth.

"Well, if you don't mind." She thought about fluttering her

lashes, but remembering the last time she'd tried such a thing, wisely decided against it.

"What would you like?" the man asked.

Of course, her mind went completely blank. Rosie stared at him, her expression turning stricken while the man glanced at her, his turning amused. She knew she'd been rumbled, and in a moment of complete and uncharacteristic recklessness, she decided to brazen it out.

"Actually, I didn't come over here for a drink," she declared. "I came over here to—to flirt with you."

Why on earth had she said *that*? Rosie's cheeks went bright red, but somehow she managed to keep his gaze, a little defiantly, even.

"Oh, did you?" the man said, clearly bemused, his eyebrows raised. "Well, then, how is it going?"

Rosie choked back a laugh. "Not very well," she admitted. "I'm trying to learn, you see. I've never flirted before, and I told my cousin I would try."

"You haven't?" He quirked an eyebrow. "I couldn't tell."

To her surprise, Rosie burst out laughing. The man's smile deepened, revealing a dimple, as his eyes glinted. "Oh, I'm sure you could," she told him, and now, she realized, she did sound a little flirtatious. How strange.

"Well, maybe a little," the man allowed. "But tell me this. *Why* haven't you ever flirted before?"

"Well, I don't know," Rosie replied slowly. "I just haven't."

"Not ever?"

She gave him a solemn look, her lips pursed. "Not ever." She ruined the moment—or perhaps made it—by bursting into peals of laughter again.

The man grinned. "Well, in any case, can I buy you a drink, after all?"

"Yes," Rosie decided. "You may."

"What would you like?"

"A shandy, please," she said, deciding she'd had enough pink gin.

The man raised a hand to get the bartender's attention.

"And while I'm at it," he asked, "can I know your name?"

"Rosie Lyman, with the Canadian Women's Army Corps."

"Well, Rosie Lyman of the Canadian Women's Army Corps, I'm Lieutenant Thomas Crewe, of the 101st Airborne, and I'm very pleased to meet you."

CHAPTER ELEVEN

SEPTEMBER 1943

London, England

It had been a wonderful summer, full of new and exciting adventures... adventures Rosie had never even dreamed of having. And it was all because of Lieutenant Thomas Crewe.

Rosie hadn't expected more than a chat and a drink and maybe a bit of a laugh when she'd walked up to him so boldly at the bar at Rainbow Corner, buoyed by Dutch courage. When he'd seemed to like her artless honesty, she'd been further emboldened to accept his invitation to dance, even though she knew jitterbugging was quite beyond her.

And indeed it had been—despite the dances back in Hamilton, she'd felt as if she were all knees and elbows, tripping over her own feet, until Thomas took her in hand, whirling her about with easy expertise until Rosie was laughing and breathless. Thomas was a wonderful dancer, just as Rosie would have expected him to be, because he was so clearly wonderful at just about everything. He had that careless confidence of someone to whom life had come easily, thanks to his blond good looks and graceful, athletic prowess. But, he wasn't, Rosie thought, arrogant or vain, and she liked that he could make her laugh, and even better, that she could make him laugh.

After that breathless dance, Thomas had bought them another set of drinks—beer for him and a shandy for her, even though her head was already spinning—and found them a table tucked in the corner of the room. When Rosie had first started chatting to him, she'd been conscious of Violet watching from afar so avidly, but as they sat in the corner, she'd forgotten her cousin completely.

"So where do you hail from, Rosie Lyman?" Thomas had asked as he'd eyed her with a speculative smile over the rim of his glass.

"Kingston, Ontario. Have you heard of it?"

His smile had widened, white teeth gleaming. "That's on the east coast, isn't it?"

"Well, not as far as the Maritimes, but yes, more or less." She'd taken a sip of her shandy, amazed at how *alive* she felt, as if every single nerve was tingling to life, just sitting here with Thomas's gaze set upon her.

"Not far from where I come from, then. Greenwich, Connecticut," he'd told her. "A pretty small town just outside New York City. Do you know it?"

"No, but I actually lived in New York, when I was a little girl. My father was a lawyer there."

"Was he?" Thomas had raised his eyebrows, his smile deepening so once again he'd showed that intriguing dimple. "So is mine, as it happens. Thomas Crewe and Partners. He expects me to follow him one day. So what took your family up Kingston way, then?"

"My father's job," Rosie had said, not wanting to go into all the details about how her family had lost everything in the Crash, not when she didn't know him very well yet, at any rate. "He got a position up there, where he and my mother both grew up—although she was born in Scotland. We've stayed there ever since."

He'd nodded slowly. "And what did you do, before you became a CWAC? I read about you ladies in the army paper, you know. Except they called you Quacks, with a Q."

Rosie had let out a little laugh. "Yes, people have lots of fun with that. I think they expect us to ruffle our feathers or something!" He'd laughed and she'd smiled, glad she could amuse him. "Before all this, I was a student at Queen's University, studying history. What about you?" She was eager to know more about him.

"I'd just finished my degree," Thomas had told her. "I was at Yale, just like my old man. I was lined up to join him in the family business, but then I got called up in '41 and joined the 101st Airborne the year after. We landed in England a few weeks ago."

"So you're fresh off the boat," Rosie had teased. "I've been here since November."

"Then you're an old hand," he'd rejoined easily. "You'll have to show me the ropes."

Which sounded like an invitation, almost a promise. Rosie had smiled and sipped her shandy, trying not to blush.

They'd chatted some more, and then danced some more, and at the end of the evening, Thomas had asked if he could see her again.

"I'm based out in Wiltshire at the moment, but I'll have leave again in another two weeks, if you fancy getting a bite to eat somewhere, maybe?"

"I'd love that," Rosie had replied shyly.

"It's a date, then." He'd grinned, and Rosie had grinned back, and then she had practically floated all the way home, while Violet teased her about falling head over heels in the space of a single evening.

"Or, really, in the space of five minutes! I guess you learned how to flirt all right."

"I'm not sure I did," Rosie had replied, "and I haven't fallen in love. Not yet."

"Ooh, listen to her!" Beth had teased. "Not yet!"

Two weeks later, as good as his word, Thomas had taken her out to eat at a restaurant off Piccadilly, and again Rosie had found the conversation remarkably easy. She had told him about her family, and he'd told her about his—a kid sister in high school, and an older sister who was married with two children; her husband was fighting too, but out in the Pacific.

"Seems like it's pretty rough out there," he'd remarked, "although, I guess I'll get my turn soon enough."

"Will you be part of the invasion?" Rosie had asked. It was on everyone's mind, when the Allied forces would invade Europe and reclaim all that Hitler had taken.

"I certainly hope so," Thomas had replied, "but you probably know about as much as me. I just follow my orders and show up when I'm told."

"Same as I do, then," Rosie had replied with a laugh. "Except I'm stuck in front of a typewriter all day."

"Well," Thomas had said easily as he'd signaled for the bill, "we all have to do our bit."

The summer had passed in a hazy of happy days; Rosie saw Thomas every few weeks, when he came into London. They went to the theater and out to Turnham Green to look at the houseboats and have a picnic; Thomas gave her her first kiss in the long grass of the meadow by the lazily winding river, smiling at her afterwards, while Rosie blinked up at him in wonder.

He took her to the theater and the cinema, and back to

Rainbow Corner for a steak dinner. Rosie felt proud to be on his arm, noticing other women's envious looks, the way Thomas shook the other GIs' hands with firm friendliness.

She found it so easy to talk to him; he was always affable and interested, cocking his head and listening, nodding along to whatever she said, so she found herself telling him more perhaps than she intended to. Over their steaks at Rainbow Corner, she told him about her family, and Jamie's illness, and the months she spent in California as a child.

"It was wonderful out there, like a long summer vacation—days at the beach, touring Los Angeles... we even had a swimming pool in back of our bungalow! I remember loving it so much, but it's blurred in my mind because right after, of course, was the Crash."

She had fallen silent as Thomas had nodded in sober understanding and then Rosie had ventured hesitantly, deciding she would tell him about what had happened. "My father lost everything in the Crash. I only remember it in bits and pieces, but it was terrible."

"I'm sorry." He'd reached over to clasp her hand with his. "You must have only been a kid, then, too."

"I was eight years old." She'd swallowed past the sudden tightness in her throat. "What about you? How did your family fare?"

He'd shrugged. "It was hard on everyone, I guess, but my old man seemed to do okay. He was always very cautious with his investments. Not, of course, that your dad wasn't." He had smiled, and Rosie had managed a slightly shaky smile back.

"I don't know whether he was or wasn't. I never learned the details, and we never spoke about them later. All I remember is it felt as if one day I was in my home, in my school, and the next I wasn't. I know it can't have really been like that, but that was how it felt." She'd swallowed again, amazed at how telling all this now still had the power to affect her, that old sorrow and fear swirling through her stomach again, even though it had all happened nearly fifteen years ago. "I remember our furniture piled in the street—the old grandfather clock I loved so much, and the bed from my room, which had a wrought-iron bedstead, all fancy curlicues. I don't know why those two things stick in my mind so much."

"Oh, Rosie." Thomas had squeezed her hand, his face full of sympathy. "That sounds tough."

"Good things came out of it," Rosie had insisted, lifting her chin a little. "We moved to Amherst Island, which I loved. It's my favorite place in the world—a little jewel in the lake."

"Maybe I'll get to see it one day," Thomas had said with a small smile that made Rosie's stomach swirl with excitement instead.

"Maybe," she'd agreed, feeling daring by simply agreeing with him, and he'd laughed and squeezed her hand again before he summoned the waiter to refill their wine glasses.

In July, the CWACs had taken the train out to Morden, where they were met with army trucks to transport them to the nearby base to play in a baseball game with the First Signal Corps. It was quite a laugh, with the men and women on mixed teams, and dozens of villagers coming to watch and cheer.

"What is it exactly that you fellows do?" Violet had asked after the game, when the Signal Corps hosted them at their hut, with Spam sandwiches and beer.

"Top secret, doncha know?" one of the soldiers had replied, swiping the side of his nose with a wink. "I could tell you, but then I'd have to kill you."

Violet had let out a peal of laughter and the soldier next to him had elbowed the first in the ribs.

"He's joking with you, miss, at least mostly. We're communication specialists—we manage the radios, the telephone lines, that sort of thing." He'd given the first soldier a pointed look, which had made Rosie wonder what more they might do that really *was* top secret.

"There are all sorts of secret things, aren't there?" Beth had said when they were bouncing in the truck on the way home. "And plenty of girls get picked for those jobs, too. I was talking to a Wren at one of the art lectures they put on and she was saying they'd had to take a bunch of tests—doing crosswords and the like. Then a few of them disappeared and were never seen again."

"You don't think something *happened* to them?" another CWAC, Myra, had exclaimed, wide-eyed.

"No, you ninny, they've just been chosen for something hush-hush," Violet had replied with a laugh. "I've heard about it, too. Somewhere just outside London, I think. Who knows what they do. Maybe they're spies! Now, *that* would be romantic."

"That would be terrifying," Rosie had said with a shudder. She still half-hoped to do something more important—and more interesting—for the war effort, but she didn't fancy being dropped into France as a modern-day Mata Hari at all.

As the summer had stretched on, so hazy and golden, the sense of war came ever closer; there were more and more air raids, with the CWACs stumbling downstairs sleepily in dressing gowns, to wait out the raid in the house's cellar. Rosie had gotten used to hardly opening her eyes as she made her way downstairs, to doze leaning against the stone wall as planes shrieked overhead and bombs thudded down before the siren sounded the all-clear.

One evening on the way home from work, as the sky had darkened to a deep rose with the oncoming of twilight, Rosie,

Violet and Beth saw a hundred planes fly overhead, in perfect formation, their wings dark against the darkening sky.

"They look like Canadian geese," Beth had said in an awestruck whisper. "Only bigger. Where do you think they're going?"

"To France, I expect," Violet had returned quietly, and they were all silent for a second, as they envisioned what those planes—and pilots—would be facing, and how many would come back.

"When you see a plane over here," Rosie had mused, "it actually *means* something. Not like at home, when it's just a training exercise."

"The First Division have been sent somewhere," Beth had told them. "Have you noticed they're off the streets? I heard talk that they might have gone to Italy."

"Good luck to our Canadian boys," Violet had replied sadly. "I expect all the men will be gone from London one day. They'll all be in France."

Rosie had thought of Thomas with a lurch of fear; she knew he would be gone to France, perhaps one day soon. She'd seen him a week ago, and she never knew when he would get leave and she would be able to see him again. The last time, he'd hugged her tightly and kissed her soundly, and Rosie had clung to him, just a little, because with every day that passed, the hours they spent together felt both more precious and fleeting.

In early September, there was news of an Allied invasion of Italy, including the Canadian Army's First Division, just as they'd suspected. Around the same time, the CWACs had the honor of being inspected by Princess Mary. Major Davis, true to form, insisted on their uniforms being freshly pressed, buttons perfectly polished and shoes shined till they gleamed. They arrived at the parade an hour early, only, after they'd lined up, to have it pelt down with rain.

Rosie stood to attention with all the others, chin lifted, shoulders back, as the rain ran in rivulets down her cheeks, her brass buttons turned green, and her uniform became completely sodden, the rain pooling around her and the other CWACs' feet. By the time Princess Mary's car showed up, they all looked a complete fright; the CWACs who were wearing makeup had eyes like raccoons and pale patches where their face powder had washed off.

"I've heard Princess Mary usually looks a fright," Violet whispered, "so maybe she won't mind—or even notice!"

But when Princess Mary finally emerged from her car, she looked very smart in her ATS uniform, and despite the rain, she inspected them all quite thoroughly. In order to increase the number of CWACs on parade, they'd brought in a laundry unit from Camp Borden, and afterwards Violet told Rosie they were a rough lot who had gotten in a fight in a country pub with a bunch of English ATS girls, and one of them had broken a girl's nose.

"Isn't it awful," she proclaimed with a shake of her head, "for CWACs to behave like that. They'll give us all a bad name."

"I can't see anyone looking at you and thinking you'll break somebody's nose," Rosie returned, her lips twitching at the realization of how prudish her cousin sounded—like she once had! "But it is true," she acknowledged fairly, "that we don't want to get a reputation. It's been nice having the Americans and the Brits be so encouraging—a far cry from back home, where they think we all have syphilis or something."

She made a face, and Beth laughed, while Violet smiled and shook her head.

. . .

In mid-September, Rosie saw Thomas for the last time in quite a while; he was being sent somewhere further north, although he couldn't say where.

Instead of flowers, he'd brought her a dozen eggs, fashioned into a cardboard bouquet and even tied with ribbon, which made her laugh.

"These are worth their weight in gold, and far better than roses! Where on earth did you get them?"

"I traded them for a dozen Hershey bars and some cigarettes," he replied with a grin. "I thought you'd rather have eggs than chocolate or flowers. I know my girl."

My girl. Rosie's heart felt as if it were fizzing.

"Oh, I would, I would," she replied as she put them away. "I'll share them with the other girls. If I was going to see you again soon, I would have baked you a cake with them. Chocolate, because I know what *you* like." She gave him a pert look and he snuck his arm around her waist to give her cheek a smacking kiss.

"Something to look forward to, one day, for sure," Thomas proclaimed. "I hope you mean it."

"I do," she promised, and he caught her hand in his as they walked through a square toward Shaftesbury Avenue and Rainbow Corner, where he'd promised her champagne and dancing. "It's such a strange time," Rosie mused as they walked along. "The Canadian boys have all gone. I think they must be in Italy. And now you're going to go soon, and so many others."

"Well, it's good news, isn't it," Thomas replied cheerfully. "It means things are finally happening. I'd rather that than wait around on my—well, you know what." He gave her a sheepish grin. "We're all getting a little restless, I think. It's time to do something."

"It might be a while yet, though," Rosie replied thoughtfully. "They won't invade in winter, certainly." She sighed as she looked down at their clasped hands. "I think part of me thought we'd go on forever as we were. I almost want to. I've always been afraid of change. Now that I've got used to life like this, I'm not sure I want it any other way." She bit her lip, afraid she'd admitted too much. She hadn't told Thomas how much she cared, but she thought he probably guessed. How could a girl not fall in love with a man like him, so charming and handsome and, well, *wonderful*? "What I mean is," she added hurriedly, "I don't know what civilian life will look like anymore."

"Well, I know what mine will look like," Thomas replied meaningfully as he squeezed her hand. "At least I know what I want it to look like." Something in his tone made Rosie's heart skip a beat even as she tried to keep her expression alert and only mildly interested, just in case. "I want to live in Connecticut," he continued, glancing at her sideways, a smile lurking about his mouth, "in a white house with a picket fence, just like in the movies. I want a dog, maybe a black Lab or a golden retriever, the kind of dog who will fetch a ball when you ask it to."

Rosie let out an unsteady laugh because she could picture it all so clearly—and she wasn't sure if he was telling her for a reason, or if he was simply sharing his distant dream. "That sounds reasonable," she said after a moment, her tone deliberately cautious.

"And I'd like a couple of kids, too," Thomas continued, and she was glad the oncoming dusk hid her blush. Now she really didn't know if he was talking about her! *But if he was, oh, if he was...* "Maybe a boy and a girl, although I know you can't choose, of course." He paused, his fingers, long and dry and strong, twined thrillingly with hers. "And, of course, most important of all," he finished, his voice full of meaning, "I'd like a wife. A wonderful, loving wife to come home to every night."

"And fetch your slippers?" Rosie replied before she could help it, only to bite her lip in mortification. He'd think her a shrew...! Why on earth had she said such a thing? It had slipped out before she'd thought.

Thomas laughed softly, seemingly undeterred. "No, I reckon I can fetch them myself." He turned to face her, tugging on her hand so they were very close. Rosie could see the specks of gold in his blue eyes, the serious intentness of his expression, and her heart seemed to still in her chest as she breathed in the spicy scent of his Pinaud aftershave, her head swimming. "What do you think to my dream, Rosie?" he asked, his voice dropping to a low, lazy murmur. "Do you think it sounds nice?"

"Yes..." Rosie managed, trying not to sound too over-whelmed, too *hopeful*, because what if Thomas wasn't talking about her at all, but some other woman, in the distant future? But then he was kissing her passionately, his arms wrapped around her, his body tight against hers, as her mind blanked and a thousand wonderful sensations ran through her like fireworks, lighting up everything inside.

"Get a room, you two," someone shouted, "or at least a dark corner somewhere, for heaven's sake!"

Thomas let out a low chuckle as he reluctantly let her go, so their fingers were only loosely interlaced, and Rosie pressed her other hand to her buzzing lips. He'd kissed her before, but never like *that*.

"I'm glad you like the sound of my dream," he told her, a smile in his voice, and Rosie could only nod dumbly before they kept walking.

The rest of the evening passed in a haze. All Rosie could think about was what Thomas had said—*a white house, a dog, a boy and a girl... and a wife*. A wife! Could he have possibly been meaning her? She still wasn't sure enough to assume, or brave enough to ask, and yet she still hoped. She hoped quite a lot, because of that kiss, that wonderful kiss...!

Still, she cautioned herself, they'd been stepping out together for only three months, which really wasn't very long, but as Violet had once said, "with a war on, it's a lifetime." Maybe it was long enough to know...

Right then, it felt long enough for Rosie to know, at any rate.

It was dark as they walked home, the sky starless, their hands entwined as they felt their way along the street and then through one of London's many squares, at one point tripping over a set of tangled legs stretching out over the pavement.

"Watch it, buster!" a woman called from where she was lying with a GI, on the ground, and a very male chuckle followed.

Rosie was glad for the cover of darkness, for she knew her face must have been scarlet—now that her eyes had adjusted to the darkness, she could see a dozen or more couples lying together on the grass of the square, bodies entangled and writhing. Mortification rooted her to the spot before she forced herself to keep walking. Had they no shame at all? She hurried through the square, and now it was Thomas who was chuckling, a low, intimate sound.

"I suppose it's hard to get a room these days," he remarked once they'd left the square, "and a lot of GIs are shipping out soon. Everyone's feeling the urgency."

"Well, yes, I suppose," Rosie managed in a strangled voice. It was all too embarrassing for words.

They were reaching the house on South Street, and Thomas's steps slowed as they came closer to the door.

"Will you write me, Rosie," he asked, "when I'm gone?"

"Yes, of course I will," she replied automatically. Asking her to write didn't seem like much to ask at all, and she wasn't sure if she felt disappointed or not by such a simple request. "Will you write me too?"

"I certainly will, at least once a week." He tugged her around to face him so he could look at her seriously, although she could barely make out his expression in the darkness. "But I mean really write me... you know, as my girl."

"Your girl?" she repeated stupidly, for he'd said it before, but lightly, almost as if he hadn't quite meant it. But now...

Thomas laughed softly. "Yes, my girl. I'm asking you to be my girl, my one and only girl. Will you write me and only me—"

"I don't even know any other GIs," Rosie protested, and Thomas laughed again.

"I'm very glad to hear that. I don't know when I'll next be able to get away, but when I do, it will be to see you, if you'll let me."

"Of course I'll let you," Rosie exclaimed, too thrilled to be her usual cautious self, to keep her words close and her feelings even closer.

Thomas pulled her toward him. "Good," he said, and then he kissed her again, even more passionately than before, his arms around her, her body fit snugly against his, so Rosie's head swam and she thought about those couples in the park with less embarrassment and more longing.

A few minutes later, having said goodbye, she tottered into the house at South Street and upstairs, the silliest of grins on her face.

"*Well,*" Violet said when she saw her coming into their dormitory; she'd swapped with another CWAC so she and Rosie could be together. "You look as if you've just been kissed senseless, if I do so say myself."

"And then some," Rosie agreed, still grinning, and Violet let out a shriek of laughter.

"Oh, Rosie, I never would have thought it of you! Did you give your GI a proper goodbye, then?"

"Well, not that proper," Rosie said quickly. "But he asked me to be his girl, and I... I said yes."

"Are you in love?" Violet asked, her tone turning serious. "Properly, I mean?"

Slowly, Rosie hung her coat on the hook, thinking about Thomas—the bright blue of his eyes, the way his mouth quirked in a wry grin, the way he always listened when she spoke, and how he could make her laugh, and how she felt when he kissed her. She felt *seen* by him, understood and accepted in a way she didn't think she ever had before. When she was with him, her whole body—her whole self—came singing to life in a way she didn't even know could happen.

"Do you know," she said, turning around to face Violet, her tone turning wondering, "I think I actually might be."

CHAPTER TWELVE

NOVEMBER 1943

London, England

"You are to report to Room 101 immediately."

Rosie hadn't even taken off her hat, dripping with rain, when Major Davis addressed her. She'd just arrived at CMHQ, running through an icy downpour, and now she blinked the rain droplets out of her eyes as she took in her CO's stern expression.

"Room 101?" she repeated blankly.

"On the first floor. Immediately."

Major Davis turned around and walked smartly away, leaving Rosie gaping after her, her stomach swirling with apprehension. For the last few months, she'd gone about her job contentedly enough, living for the letters Thomas wrote regularly. Occasionally, she went out with Violet or Beth, or some of the other CWACs, to the theater or for a meal, but she no longer felt the need to chase after every entertainment simply to prove she was sociable. Surely she'd proved that already... with Thomas.

"You've found your own happiness," Violet had said pragmatically, "so I don't suppose you need to search for it the way we all do."

"Happiness shouldn't be found in a man," Rosie protested, because she did truly believe that, but her cousin merely scoffed.

"Says you, with a soppy smile on your face and a letter from Lieutenant Crewe once a week!"

Rosie had blushed, too happy to argue the point. Being in love, she thought more than once, was the best feeling in the world. Like floating and singing and laughing all at once. She could type any number of dull letters, sit sleepily through innumerable air raids, and she'd still be smiling at the end of the day... simply because of Thomas Crewe.

Not that she was brave or confident enough to let him know as much in *quite* as many words, and so she kept her letters newsy and interesting but hardly, as Violet had said after reading one over her shoulder, "dripping with lovelorn phrases and poetry." Thomas's letters came as regular as clockwork, and while Rosie enjoyed each and every one, they were not, it had to be said, written by a lovesick poet, either, more matter-of-fact descriptions of life at the base, although always with assurances, at least, that she was still his girl. Rosie didn't think it would matter what he wrote; she was thrilled that he simply wrote at all, that he kept writing.

She found herself thinking of him, wondering what he was doing, in the middle of typing a letter, and she'd lose her train of thought until a girl next to her would tell her to get a move on, and heaven forbid Major Davis notice she was slacking.

But why was she now wanted in room 101?

Rosie found out soon enough, or at least an inkling, as she stepped into the room, still somewhat sodden, patting her hair into place. Half a dozen other CWACs stood in there, looking as uncertain and apprehensive as she was. There was no officer about, and they stood around in uneasy silence for a few minutes before Rosie whispered to the woman next to her, "Do you know why we're here?"

The CWAC shook her head. "I just hope we're not in trouble."

She'd never been in trouble when she'd been summoned before, Rosie decided, so there was no reason to think that was the case now. As far as she knew, she hadn't broken any rules, and her work had been the same as it had always been.

Another few minutes passed as the CWACs fidgeted and shifted from foot to foot before an officer Rosie didn't recognize, a gruff-looking man, came into the room, shutting the door firmly behind him.

"Take a seat, ladies," he commanded. "You'll be taking an aptitude test." Already he was distributing papers on the tables as they hurried to take their seats. "You have sixty minutes, starting now."

Rosie grabbed a pencil, her mind racing as she scanned the questions on the typed sheet. She'd taken any number of tests before, and she'd become used to them, but this one—why, this one was *fun*, she thought in surprise—an intriguing mixture of crossword clues, logic puzzles, code words, even hands of cards. The problems were tricky—certainly, trickier than the kinds of crosswords and puzzles she did with Jamie sometimes—but this was the kind of challenge Rosie enjoyed.

The room and its occupants fell away as she immersed herself in the puzzles and problems, looking up in surprise only when the officer told them to put down their pencils. An entire hour had passed in the blink of an eye; Rosie was on the very last problem.

She glanced around the room and saw a variety of expressions on the other CWACs' faces—unease, satisfaction, disappointment, hope.

The officer collected their papers and told them to go to the canteen for a tea break before returning to their desks, with no other explanation given.

As they filed out of the room, one CWAC shook her head. "I didn't understand heads or tails of that. I don't suppose I'll get a special posting."

"Is that what it was for?" Rosie asked curiously. "A special posting? Where?"

"Who knows." Another CWAC shrugged. "It's not like they tell us anything here, is it?"

As they drank their tea in the canteen, the conversation turned to more immediate matters—the church parade they would be going on that weekend, plans for the next forty-eight. A few of the CWACs were going up to Lincolnshire, where one of them had a distant relation; Rosie was still hoping Thomas might get his own leave to come back to London. Last night, Violet had, rather tartly, accused her of "doing nothing but waiting around for Lieutenant Crewe", and feeling chastened, Rosie had agreed to go away for the weekend with her on their next leave... if Thomas didn't write first, telling her when he was able to come into town.

"I haven't seen him since September," she'd protested. "If he can come to London, you know I need to see him."

"You don't *need* to do anything," Violet had replied a bit sourly. "Who would have ever thunk it, Miss Liberated herself, dropping everything for a man!"

"I'm not," Rosie had protested, because Thomas hadn't had any leave yet, so there had been nothing to drop. Was it wrong to be putting him first, the man she might one day marry? The thought of it gave her a thrill of incredulous wonder, wary hope. It wasn't as if he'd actually asked her, and yet... he *almost* had. Well, only sort of, she'd acknowledged with a pang of doubt. She still wasn't sure whether it was foolish of her to pin so many hopes on a single conversation, and one that had been in the abstract.

Besides, what if things were different between them when he finally was able to get some leave and see her? They'd had only a few months together, after all, a handful of dates. After several months of not seeing him at all, it didn't feel as significant as it once had, even if she knew she still cared just as much. Rosie was pragmatic enough to realize that a man going off to war might imbue a romantic relationship with more meaning than it actually possessed in the cold, hard light of day.

She knew she would be bitterly disappointed, but not really surprised, if, when she saw Thomas next, things felt changed, cooled, simply because he realized he hadn't known her nearly as well as he thought he had. And maybe, Rosie had allowed, she didn't know him as well, either, although she couldn't quite make herself believe that. She *felt* as if she knew him. She felt as if she knew him very well, indeed.

In any case, Rosie wasn't given the opportunity either to go on leave or stay in town in the hope of a visit from Thomas. A week after she'd taken the aptitude test with the other CWACs, she was summoned to see Major Davis, who told her she'd be leaving for a special posting the very next morning.

"Tomorrow morning," Rosie repeated in surprise, as well as some dismay. "So soon?"

Major Davis, unimpressed by this outburst, arched an eyebrow. "Is there any reason to wait, Private Lyman?"

"No, no, that is..." She swallowed, flushing, and then stood a bit straighter. "I'm just surprised, because I don't even know how I was recommended for a special posting in the first place."

"Apparently a pilot in the RCAF, Captain McConnell, put your name forward some time ago," Major Davis replied with a small shrug.

"Captain McConnell!" Rosie realized it was the pilot who had played his bridge hand badly on the *Queen Elizabeth*—who would have ever thought her nosiness would have led her to this. She recalled how he'd been impressed by her bridge skills;

he'd even chatted with her about it a few days later, on the ship, had made some passing remarks that the war effort needed girls like her. Rosie hadn't paid it much mind at the time. "And do you know where it is I'm going?" she asked Major Davis.

"That is classified information," the major replied shortly. "You'll know when you get there."

Rosie went back to her desk in a haze of both excitement and anxiety, barely able to concentrate on her typing as she wondered where she was going—and what she would be doing. Would it be very far away? Would she be able to tell Thomas? She'd have to write him, she decided, and let him know she'd been posted elsewhere, and then write him again from wherever she ended up. Despite the potential interest of the work itself, the thought was dispiriting. She knew she was unlikely to see him for many months now, at the very least, and what if everything had changed between them when she finally did?

"A special posting!" Violet exclaimed when Rosie told her and Beth what had happened that evening, back at their barracks on South Street. She was packing her kit bag a bit dolefully, wondering how long she'd be gone, and how far away—from her friends, from Thomas, from everything and everyone she knew. Would she come back to London, to Mayfair, at all? "Why don't you look more pleased?" Violet asked, her eyes narrowing shrewdly. "You're finally doing something more important for the war effort."

"Maybe I am," Rosie replied. "I don't actually know what I'm going to be doing."

"Pish! Of course it's going to be more important, and more exciting, if they won't even tell you what it is."

"I suppose."

Violet rolled her eyes, her hands on her hips. "I don't understand you, Rosie Lyman! You didn't want to join the CWAC in the first place because you thought you wouldn't be doing something important, and now that you finally are, you're acting as if you're having a tooth pulled. There's no pleasing you, is there!"

Rosie managed a small, rueful smile of acknowledgement. "I suppose there isn't," she agreed. "I am pleased, really, and I know it could be a wonderful opportunity. It's just... I've been living here for a year, and I've become pretty settled. I'm not sure I want to go somewhere else, especially if it's somewhere remote, with lots of people I don't know..."

"You don't know what it will be like," Violet pointed out. "It could be on the other side of London for all you know."

"Some girls have had special postings just outside London," Beth put in helpfully. "Out in Buckinghamshire somewhere. They come into London on leave."

"That's true, but the way Major Davis talked about it," Rosie replied slowly, "it felt as if it might be quite far away."

"Major Davis doesn't give a thing away, ever," Violet replied, "and in any case, *she* might not know. She probably got the order from some other officer. I doubt she's more in the know than you are."

"I suppose..."

"If I were you, I'd be over the moon," Violet declared. "No more typing and filing! And who knows what sort of dishy officers might be there... although, of course, you're not looking, are you?" She pursed her lips. "Let me guess. You're reluctant to go because of a certain lieutenant who hasn't had any leave lately."

"It's true that I wish I could see Thomas before I left," Rosie admitted. "I don't think there's anything wrong with that."

"Of course not," Beth interjected, as loyal as ever. "I'd be the same, if I were in your shoes."

Violet shook her head slowly, undeterred. "What happened to your ambition, Rosie Lyman?" she demanded. "Before you joined up, you were determined to make something of yourself, get a fancy degree, change the world. What happened to all that?"

Rosie opened her mouth to object that she hadn't lost her ambition, only to close it as she realized that in some ways she had. "I don't know," she admitted. She sank onto her bed, her lips pursed in thought. "That feels like a long time ago, I suppose," she said after a moment. "And it was... almost two years ago now. And so much has happened, and changed... I've been moved around enough to make my head spin, and I suppose part of me just wanted to wait the war out right here, doing something useful but having a nice time of it, too." She ducked her head, embarrassed by the seeming smallness of her thoughts. "But you're right, really. I should be excited to do more for the war, and maybe I will, once I'm there and I've found my feet. It's the not knowing that's putting me off, I think. Not knowing where, or who with, or even what. They've given me no idea at all."

"Well, this time tomorrow you'll know," Violet replied with her usual indefatigable cheer. "You'll be there!"

That night, before she went to bed, Rosie wrote a long letter to Thomas, explaining the situation to him. He'd been writing her regularly, always hoping he'd have leave to go to London and then lamenting when he didn't, although there had been no further mention of the house with the white picket fence, the dog, the children, or most importantly, the wife.

Part of Rosie now felt a longing to tell him her true feelings, since she knew it would be months before she could possibly see him again. But what would he make of such an outpouring of an emotion? It went against every instinct, her very nature...

No, she couldn't do it, not as blatantly as that. Finally she put pen to paper.

I don't know where I'm going or what I'm doing, or any of it, and I don't suppose I'll be able to tell you even when I find out. These things seem to be awfully hush-hush. But I can at least write to you with my new address, so you'll be able to reach me there. Of course, this means I don't know when we'll see each other next, but I suppose that's the nature of wartime, isn't it? In any case, I look forward to hearing from you and telling you what I can about my own situation.

As ever,

Rosie.

The next morning Rosie reported to CMHQ in full uniform with her kit bag slung over one shoulder. There were three other girls waiting for orders, looking both excited and apprehensive, just as she was.

Now that she was ready to go—and she'd posted the letter to Thomas—she felt the first darts of excitement shooting through her, her old ambition reawakening. This was the kind of thing she'd wanted, she acknowledged, even if she didn't know yet what it was.

No explanations were forthcoming as they boarded a train heading north out of the city, the day gray and dank and getting only grayer and danker as they trundled north through a series of dreary-looking stations, their names covered up so Rosie couldn't even tell where they were. Not, of course, that she knew the country well at all, but it felt disconcerting to feel so ignorant, so utterly in the dark about everything.

"I reckon it's something pretty secret," one of the other CWACs, a pretty girl named Elsie, said in a confiding manner. "Since they're not telling us a darned thing. Although wouldn't it be typical if it's the fellows who get the interesting work, and we'll just be typing up their orders or what have you."

"I think women are getting to do more important things now," another CWAC, Kathleen, interjected. "You hear things, don't you? They're in factories, they're operating machinery, and those girls outside London are definitely doing something very hush-hush and important."

"But we're not going there, are we?" Elsie pointed out dryly.

The fourth CWAC who had come from CMHQ, Susan, looked up from the book she'd been reading, an annoyed expression on her face. "There's obviously no point speculating about it," she said crossly, "and making lots of useless chatter. If you want to show those in charge that you're capable of this kind of work, maybe you should be a bit quieter."

The other CWACs and Rosie exchanged startled glances, and then Elsie burst out laughing, making Kathleen and Rosie both smile a little.

"Well, aren't you going to be a barrel of laughs," Elsie told Susan dryly; the other CWAC did not respond, but merely turned the page of her book in a decidedly showy manner. Kathleen let out another laugh as she shook her head.

They did not arrive at their destination until well after nightfall, feeling tired and sore, dirty and hungry, as all they'd had to eat was a couple of sandwiches with a thin smear of meat paste and some wilted watercress, along with copious cups of tea, given to them by some kindly ladies on the platform when they finally stopped; one of the ladies told them it was Preston.

But even when they arrived at the last station, where they were all told to disembark the troop train, the evening wet and windy, cold and dark, it wasn't, Rosie discovered, the end of the journey. They still had to board a ferry that would cross the Irish Sea, to go to a training facility on the Isle of Man.

"I've never even heard of the place," Elsie exclaimed once they'd all found a seat on the ship that would take them across the rough and wild sea. Rosie's stomach was lurching alarmingly; this craft was a far cry from the enormous and steady *Queen Elizabeth* that had steamed through the north Atlantic waters with barely a ripple. This vessel, seaworthy though it was, pitched to and fro so she had to cling to her seat to stay upright, and the sandwich she'd had rose in her throat. "The Isle of Man, someone said! Is there an Isle of Woman, do you suppose?"

"Don't be ridiculous," Susan scoffed, and Elsie rolled her eyes.

"I was joking, you know," she informed Susan. "But maybe you don't know what a joke is."

Susan did not bother to reply, and Rosie hoped that relations between the four of them could get on a more even keel; it would be hard-going, working in this new place, if they couldn't all be chums. She wondered if she'd come across a bit like Susan back at Kitchener, her tone reproving, her manner censorious. She didn't think she'd been *quite* such a know-it-all, but it was humbling to remember just how stuck-up she'd once seemed, and all because she'd really been shy and lacking in confidence. Maybe Susan would find her way, along with the rest of them.

She didn't have much longer to think about it, because the ship lurched again, and Rosie soon found herself retching into a pail someone had helpfully provided. She wasn't the only one who was so miserably sick, but it was small comfort indeed as the journey seemed to go on and on with no end in sight.

"This is a particularly rough crossing," one kindly soldier, who had provided her with his handkerchief, said. "It's tough luck on your part, I'm afraid."

She glanced at the man's uniform, and saw it was of the Royal Corps of Signals. "Are you stationed on the Isle of Man?" she asked, before realizing what a foolish question it was. "Of course you are. Is that what we'll be doing? Something with signals?"

The soldier grinned. "Couldn't say, miss, but I reckon you'll find out soon enough."

An hour later, Rosie finally tottered off the ferry, along with the other CWACs, where they were met by a stern-looking officer in the ATS—the women's Auxiliary Territorial Service.

"I'll take you directly to your barracks," she told them, "and you'll report to duty at 8 a.m. sharp tomorrow morning."

Rosie could barely see anything of the seafront in the impenetrable darkness; there was no moon and the rain lashing her relentlessly made it hard to so much as make out her hand in front of her face, her shoulders hunched against the icy wind. She was grateful their accommodation was only a few minutes' walk away, in a terraced hotel facing the seafront. Their classrooms, the officer told them, would be downstairs, and they would be upstairs, sleeping two to a room. Elsie and Kathleen bunked up immediately, and so Rosie was left to make the best of it with Susan, who regarded her with a sniff before marching into their room.

"This is quite nice, actually," Rosie said as she dropped her kit bag at the foot of her bed. It was far nicer than the usual dormitory, with two twin beds, bureaus, and washstands, the window facing the street and the sea, the blackout curtains now drawn tightly against the view. "Better than barracks, at any rate."

"I suppose," Susan said, and began, with her back to Rosie, to undress.

Suppressing a sigh, Rosie did the same. As she lay in bed, huddled under the blankets, the rain spattering against the windowpane, she tried to hold onto the excitement she'd felt this morning, when she'd embarked on this journey, but fourteen hours later, tired, cold, and dispirited by her unfriendly roommate, it was hard not to give in to a little homesickness.

No, she wouldn't give in to it, Rosie told herself. She was finally doing something meaningful for the war effort—hopefully—and tomorrow she'd write to Thomas with her new address. A little discomfort and an unfriendly roommate were hardly the end of the world.

She snuggled deeper down under her blankets and felt the comforting lull of sleep pull at her consciousness. Tomorrow, she told herself as she drifted off, everything would surely seem better.

CHAPTER THIRTEEN

NOVEMBER, 1943

Douglas, Isle of Man

Things did seem better in the morning, Rosie decided as she drew the blackout blinds and gazed out at a fresh new day, the sky a pale, washed blue, the sea dancing and sparkling beneath it, stretching onward. She thought she could make out the mainland, a violet blur on the horizon, but she wasn't sure. The journey here had taken hours last night on a stormy sea, but today the water was calm, the sun shining.

Susan was already up and gone to breakfast, so Rosie had a few moments to herself before she reported downstairs. She craned her neck to inspect the street, a pleasant boulevard lined with terraced houses and hotels that faced the seafront, all behind neat iron railings, with a curved harbor visible in the distance, now filled with military craft.

Rosie knew nothing about the Isle of Man, or even where it was, besides somewhere up north, but she looked forward to finding out, along with her orders and duties. And, of course, she would write Thomas to let him know her new address as soon as possible.

Voices drifting in from the hall reminded Rosie that she needed to get downstairs sharpish, if she was going be on time to report for duty.

Breakfast was in the hotel's small dining room—some watery porridge, toast, and coffee. It was neither worse nor better than the fare in London, and Rosie ate it gladly; the last thing she'd had to eat had been a sad-looking sandwich back in Preston.

The other CWACs were eager to share the bits of gossip they'd gleaned; in addition to the four of them from CMHQ, there were six British girls from the ATS staying at the hotel and starting training that morning, and they'd all been chatting. No one seemed to know much of anything about what they'd be doing, although they knew more than Rosie at least.

"We'll be doing something with Morse code, I heard," one young woman in the ATS, with the same sort of pompous air as Susan, explained. "That's what the Royal Corps of Signals do, and they're stationed here."

"They do lots of things," Elsie returned in what Rosie was discovering was a quick and slightly sharp way. "They lay telephone lines, they manage wirelesses... you can't really know for certain that we'll be doing anything with Morse code."

The ATS girl tossed her head. "Well, that's what I heard."

"I suppose we'll find out soon enough," Rosie ventured placatingly. "It seems like a pleasant little town, from what I saw from my window, at least."

"A pleasant town full of Germans," Kathleen returned with something of a grimace.

Rosie turned to her in surprise. "Germans? What do you mean?"

"There are several internment camps here, for German residents of Great Britain," the girl in the ATS explained. "They've been here for ages—since the start of the war. Back then, they rounded anyone up who was of German descent. Austrian, too, I think. There were thousands."

Rosie had never heard about any of this. "And they put them in camps?" she said, unable to disguise her surprise and dismay.

Kathleen shrugged. "Well, it's wartime, isn't it?"

"Yes, but..." Rosie shook her head slowly. There were plenty of German immigrants in Canada, and to think of them being rounded up simply because of their ancestry seemed wrong. "It's not their fault they're German," she said, and Kathleen shrugged again.

"They've let a lot of them go, our landlady was telling me," Elsie chimed in. "And they're closing some of the camps down already. One of the ones here in Douglas is shutting down in the next few weeks."

"Why are they letting them go?" Rosie asked.

"They were obviously harmless, I suppose," Elsie replied as she sipped her coffee. "Some of them were even Jews."

"Jews..." Rosie looked at her in surprise. "But why would they intern Jews? Everybody knows Hitler hates the Jews." Not that she'd ever even met or seen a Jew. There were very few Jewish people in Kingston, and she'd yet to come across one in her time in England, although she supposed she wouldn't necessarily know it if she had. But, in any case, she'd certainly read about Hitler's relentless persecution of them in the papers—the yellow stars they had to wear, the utterly unjust laws that had been forced upon them. There had been rumors of even worse things, although Rosie wasn't sure what they were, but in any case, it was all part of the reason why they were at war with Germany, wasn't it? And yet the British government had put Jews in camps?

"It's wartime," Kathleen said again, a little flatly this time. "You've got to be sensible. And they are Germans."

"Our landlady said the camps were quite nice," Elsie offered, with a sympathetic smile. "They can take all sorts of classes, and they even have a sort of university or something. And there are lectures and plays—all in all, not a bad way to spend the war!"

"But a *camp*..." Rosie couldn't shake the feeling that the whole idea was, at its core, wrong and even repellent.

"You'd be better off not making too much noise about it," the ATS girl told Rosie in a warning tone. "Unless you want to be sent back to wherever you came from. This isn't the place to be making any sorts of protest."

Rosie nodded shortly, deciding discretion was the better part of valor. Judging from the conversation over breakfast, she had a feeling the motley mix of CWACs and ATS volunteers wouldn't become best friends; everyone was jostling for position, eager to prove themselves—and score a few petty points, perhaps, as well.

She didn't have much time to think about any of that, however, for she was still finishing her breakfast when they were told to assemble in the hall of the hotel; hastily she put down her cup of tea and hurried after the other women.

The first thing they were all required to do was sign the Official Secrets Act; one by one they were called into a room where a grave-looking officer drummed into them the importance of keeping entirely schtum, seeming to do his best to put the fear of God—or at least the Army—into them.

Rosie had an entirely inappropriate and Violet-like urge to laugh as she listened to him; fortunately, she kept her expression somber as she signed her name, swearing not to mention anything at all about her work to anyone, not even her family. All her letters would be read and censored, and if any information was found to be leaked, she could be prosecuted.

It all sounded dreadfully serious, and Rosie supposed it was, even if she still had no idea what she'd actually be doing.

She found out a short while later, when the ten of them were summoned to one of the reception rooms of the hotel that had been made into a sort of classroom, with plain deal tables and chairs. At the front of the room was a desk with a large wireless receiving set on it, unlike any Rosie had ever seen. An officer stood before it, his hands clasped behind his back, his expression stern.

"You've each been brought here because one of your commanding officers recommended you for this posting, and you must have done well enough on the tests to warrant being accepted into this training program. You'll be posted here for four months, after which, should you succeed at your training, you will receive a further posting." He paused, as if expecting questions, but no one so much as twitched. "While you're here," he resumed, "you'll be trained as cypher operators. You'll learn to distinguish Morse code"—at this, the ATS girl threw them all a triumphant look—"and German procedure signals. You'll write down what you hear and pass it on. That's it." He looked at them all sternly. "We don't need to have any clever clogs here, trying to crack a code or figure out what the messages mean. That's not your job. Your job is to listen, write it down, and pass it on. End of." He gave them all a forbidding look. "Any questions?"

No one said a word.

The rest of the morning was spent learning the rudiments of Morse code, which Rosie found easy enough to grasp the essentials of, but almost impossible to keep in her brain. By lunchtime, she was wondering why she'd been chosen, especially as she didn't speak German, and the messages they would be intercepting would, of course, be in that language.

"You must have impressed someone somewhere," Elsie told her, "to be recommended."

"I did, but not in the way you'd expect," Rosie replied, and told them about Captain McConnell and the hand of bridge, back on the *Queen Elizabeth*. "But that seems like such a small thing, and it has nothing to do with listening to Morse code. Back at CMHQ, no one took any notice of me at all."

"Well, obviously someone at CMHQ did," Kathleen returned in her flat way, "because you're here."

Rosie sighed, wishing there was a bit of camaraderie between all the girls, but they seemed determined to prove themselves, even if that meant elbowing others out of the way.

After a lunch of meat paste sandwiches and tea, they were back in their classrooms, with another officer giving them an introduction on how to operate the wireless. Then it was back to learning Morse, with a rudimentary listening test to see if they could write down simple words. The trick, Rosie soon realized, was differentiating one letter from another; adding a dash or stop to a certain letter would completely wreck the whole transmission. And, as they were told repeatedly, the ability of intelligence officers to successfully decode the message depended entirely on the reliability of the transmissions.

It was, Rosie thought, an awesome and intimidating responsibility, yet at its heart it was essentially doing what she'd done before, if in a more complex way—taking down someone else's words and passing them on. In essence, typing and filing, a prospect that was comforting and disappointing in equal measure.

That afternoon, they had some time off to take a stroll around Douglas, which seemed as pleasant a town as Rosie had viewed from the window, the violet hills rising above it and the sea sparkling all around. There were several streets of shops, and horse-drawn trams, which she found wonderfully quaint, and even though she felt very far from London and all that had become familiar, she decided it was not such a bad place to be, although she wished the company was a bit more congenial.

The ATS girls had gone off on their own, as had Kathleen and Elsie, which left Rosie to wander about with Susan, who seemed as sniffily dour as ever.

"Where do you hail from?" Rosie asked once they'd found a small teashop, where they shared a pot of tea and several currant buns.

"Selkirk, in Manitoba. It's on the Red River. It's not a particularly interesting place."

That was enough, along with Susan's dismissive tone, to keep Rosie from asking any more questions about it. "And your family?" she asked with an encouraging smile. "Have you any brothers or sisters?"

After a slight pause, Susan replied rather flatly, "No, I was an only child. My parents died when I was a baby, and I was raised by an aunt."

It sounded woefully grim, and it was clear Susan didn't want to talk about it, so Rosie nibbled her bun in silence for a few minutes before she ventured to change the subject.

"It's awfully tricky, the Morse code, isn't it?" she asked, keeping her voice low, for, of course, it was all meant to be top secret, although there were no other customers about. "And it feels as if so much is weighing on the transmissions—if we get a single letter wrong, it could all go pear-shaped, couldn't it?"

Susan made a dismissive sound as she sipped her tea. "There are so many radio transmissions to intercept, and most of them will be completely useless," she stated with an air of knowledge that Rosie wondered how she could possibly possess. "Shipping forecasts, weather conditions... nothing really of note. It may only be one transmission in ten thousand or more that could be of any use or interest, so I doubt we'll be doing anything actually important."

"Even so," Rosie replied, trying for a smile, a cheering tone.

"Something as simple as a weather forecast could be useful, if they're planning an attack or something. Anyway," she continued as Susan made another dismissive sound, "it's certainly more interesting and important than what I was doing before. What about you? Were you at CMHQ?"

"I was working in the medical office at Piccadilly, processing sick leaves."

"Well, this certainly sounds more interesting than that," Rosie said with feeling, and she was rewarded with the faintest flicker of a smile.

That evening, with the blackout curtains drawn and the wind starting up again, as she'd been told it often did at night, Rosie finally had time to write a letter to Thomas. She sat curled up on her bed, her notepaper on her lap, chewing the nib of her pen, her gaze distant and thoughtful. She couldn't tell him about her work; she didn't really want to mention the other girls, as she hadn't made friends with them yet, and wasn't sure she had the wherewithal to, anyway. So what was there to write about?

Rosie could almost picture Violet, rolling her eyes, hands on her hips as she shook her head. *You could write about how you feel, you know!* And Rosie would continue to shy away from such a thing, because the vulnerability of it made her nervous and frankly afraid—just as her cousin had told her, two years ago now, when she'd been reluctant to enlist. Well, here she was, having enlisted and moved over the world, conquered so many new challenges, except perhaps the last and most important one of her heart. Could she tell Thomas how she felt? Truly? Did she dare?

"I hope you're not going to be ages writing that letter," Susan said sourly as she came into the room, dressed for bed, having just been to the bathroom down the hall. "I'm exhausted and we have an early start, you know."

"Yes, I know," Rosie replied. "I'm almost finished," she added, even though she'd only written *Dear Thomas* so far. Susan huffed a bit, and Rosie started writing.

Dear Thomas,

I've landed at my posting and I'm afraid there's not much to write, because I can't tell you any of it! It does seem like it's going to be interesting work, if a bit intimidating. The air is very fresh here and I've enjoyed walking about a bit. But I do wish I could have seen you before I went—I don't know when we'll see each other next, what with me being here and you being wherever you are. But I hope that when we do see each other next, you'll be as glad to see me as I know I will be to see you. I've never been very good at expressing my feelings, and somehow it feels even harder in a letter, but I did want you to know how much I care.

Your girl,

Rosie.

"Are you done yet?" Susan asked from where she lay in bed, the covers pulled up all the way to her nose.

With her heart beating hard, Rosie folded the letter and slipped it into an envelope to post tomorrow, if she didn't chicken out. She'd never written so clearly about how she felt, and she had no idea how Thomas would take it. Still, she told herself, she was glad she'd done it—for her own sake as much as Thomas's.

"Yes, I'm done," she told Susan, and she turned out the light.

CHAPTER FOURTEEN

MARCH, 1944

Douglas, Isle of Man

"So, where are you posted?"

Elsie came up to Rosie in the hotel dining room, her eyes bright with excitement. "I'm going to somewhere in Bucking-hamshire. First, I've got forty-eight, though, and I'm spending them in London. What about you?"

"I'm somewhere in Leicestershire," Rosie replied, "Beau-manor Hall, it's called."

Elsie shook her head. "Haven't heard of the place."

"No, I haven't, either," Rosie replied. They'd all received their postings to various British signal intelligence collection sites, known as Y stations, around the country that morning, having finished the four months of training as intercept opera-tors. Rosie and Susan were going to Beaumanor Hall; the others to Buckinghamshire or the Isle of Wight. Rosie had been prag-matic about being paired with Susan, who was no less dour now than she'd been four months ago, but they'd learned to rub along together well enough, as long as Rosie made sure to turn the light out at a decent hour and didn't try to make too much chitchat.

The last few months had been full of hard work, learning to understand and transcribe Morse code, identifying letters, often from tinny, static-filled transmissions, trying not to get a single one wrong. When she went to Beaumanor Hall, she'd be working long shifts, either midnight to nine in the morning, or nine in the morning to four. As their training officer had warned, they would have to concentrate completely the whole time. Rosie imagined it would be utterly exhausting, but invigorating, too. Even in her training, she'd struggled not to try to make sense of the transmissions; as she'd been told often enough, her job was simply to transcribe, not to attempt to decode, but it was hard when she saw a string of letters not to want to figure out what they meant. Of course, not knowing German made it all the more difficult, although she'd tried to learn a bit in her free time. She'd gotten to chatting to a German woman, Ilse, who worked at a café in town, as many of the internment prisoners were allowed to work on various farms and in shops around the island. The other CWACs thought she was crazy for wanting to get to know a German, but Rosie found the woman quiet and kind; she'd lived in England for six years before being brought to the camp and could speak perfectly good English, as well as teaching Rosie a bit of German.

"She left Germany *because* of Hitler," Rosie had told the other CWACs one afternoon, after having had a long chat with Ilse. "It's ridiculous that she's been put in a camp."

"Well, they must have had a reason," Kathleen had replied staunchly, and Rosie knew she would not be convinced otherwise.

She'd said goodbye to Ilse yesterday, and they'd all be leaving that afternoon on a ferry to the mainland, and then a train down to London before reporting for duty two days later.

The last four months had been hard work, but there had been secret joys, as well. After posting her letter to Thomas with great trepidation, Rosie had received a reply just a few days later, a letter she now knew nearly by heart:

Dear Rosie, you dearest, darling girl!

Your letter made me smile all week. I don't mind not knowing what you're doing, although I wish I knew enough to imagine you someplace, but to know how you feel is a thousand times better! You do play your cards close to your chest, don't you, my darling? I'm glad you decided to reveal one or two, at least, and let me show you my whole hand—I'm in love with you, it's as simple as that. The other guys tease me about it, saying I must have it bad, and I do. I wish I could see you, but until I can, please be assured of my devotion.

Completely Yours,

Thomas.

Rosie had felt as if she were floating for weeks. There had been other letters since then, not quite so effusive, but still warm and affectionate, and she longed to see him with a yearning that sometimes felt like a physical pain. She still didn't know when she would; their leaves had never coincided and, in any case, the Isle of Man was too far to travel. She'd written him a few days ago to tell him when she'd be in London, but there had been no reply yet. Perhaps when she was at Beaumanor Hall, things would be better. She'd looked at a map and Leicestershire seemed quite central. In any case, Rosie knew there was nothing she could do about it, but continue to write—and hope.

· · ·

The journey across the Irish Sea was calmer this time, in late March, although the day was gray and the air still cold and damp, with barely a breath of spring in the air. It felt strange to be back on the mainland after four months in training, as if the world had changed, even if it hadn't. Everything was still the same, the deprivations of wartime pressing down on them all, with cups of weak tea and wilted sandwiches given to them at the Preston station just as before.

All the station signs remained blacked out, and the trains were full of servicemen and women, joking and jostling for space. That was what was different, Rosie decided; there was an energy about everyone, a sense of expectation.

"It's because the invasion will be soon," Susan, who was traveling down to London with her, said knowledgeably.

"How do you know?"

"Well, it's bound to be, isn't it? We've been waiting ages and, in spring, the weather will become fine—it's surely going to happen in the next few months."

Rosie felt a ripple of excitement at the thought, along with a shudder of apprehension. *Finally*... the end of the war glinted on the horizon, like a tantalizing promise. *And yet*... she knew Thomas was almost certainly going to be part of the force that went over to France, when the invasion did happen. Would she see him before then? Would she see him at *all*? Her heart lurched in her chest as she thought about how much was at stake... both for the whole world and her own heart.

When they arrived in London, all the CWACs went their separate ways; Elsie and Kathleen to a friend's in Clapham, while Rosie was eager to report back to South Street to see Violet and Beth. Susan, she saw, seemed to be uncharacteristically dithering at the entrance of the station. With Kathleen and Elsie having gone off, Rosie paused.

"Where are you going for your leave, Susan?" she asked, feeling guilty that she hadn't bothered to inquire before.

"Oh, I expect I shall find a room somewhere," Susan said with a poor attempt at airiness.

It took Rosie a few seconds to realize she didn't have anywhere to go, or anyone to see. "You won't go to your barracks?"

Susan managed a small, tight smile. "That's not much of a leave, is it?"

"But a room somewhere..." Rosie swallowed down the unhelpful observation that it sounded rather lonely. "Look, why don't you come back with me? I'm sure we can find you a spare bed, and even if it's barracks, it's a grand house, and my friends are wonderful." Susan looked unconvinced and, with sudden impulsiveness, Rosie reached for her hand. "Oh, do say you'll come, Susan. We're going to be working together, after all, and I'd like you to meet my friends."

"Would you?" Now, Susan most certainly sounded unconvinced, and Rosie could understand why. She wasn't the most fun to be around, it was true, but Rosie remembered when she'd been the damp squib of the party, and she wanted to be patient with Susan, maybe even help her to have fun, if just a little.

"Yes, I would," she said firmly. "And you'll ruin my leave if I have to think of you in some drafty boarding house, drinking weak tea and feeding a shilling in the gas meter all by yourself."

Susan's lips twitched. "When you put it like that..."

"Come with me," Rosie insisted. "We'll have a grand time."

After a second's pause, Susan nodded, somewhat reluctantly. "All right, then," she said without much grace. "If you insist."

It was early evening by the time Rosie arrived in Mayfair, the light turning dusky, and the blackout curtains already being drawn.

"Goodness, this place is grand," Susan remarked as they came into the entrance hall with its magnificent staircase of black marble. "I was staying way out of a town in a miserable little hotel. But then I came with the third contingent, and they were something of a sorry group, I have to say."

"Yes, I heard about them a while back," Rosie replied. "I heard they got in a fistfight with some ATS girls at a pub out near Morden."

"And more," Susan agreed. "They're pretty rough."

Which made Rosie understand all the more why Susan might not want to return to barracks for her leave.

"Hopefully somebody's in now," she told her as she headed upstairs. "Everyone's always going out somewhere, but—"

"Rosie!" Violet flew out from their dormitory to engulf Rosie in a tight hug. "I hoped you were coming today, but I couldn't tell from your letter. And the trains have been terrible, haven't they? So many delays..." She released her, her curious gaze moving past Rosie to Susan. "Hullo, who's this?"

"This is Susan, who was with me on the training course," Rosie said. "I invited her to stay with me, as we're both traveling out the day after tomorrow."

"Well, of course you're welcome." Violet's shrewd gaze seemed to take the measure of Susan in a matter of seconds. "But we can't stay here, we have to celebrate! Dump your bags and we'll go find somewhere to get a decent meal, my treat."

"Oh, I don't—" Susan began, but Violet cut her off with a firm shake of her head.

"None of that, please. I insist. It's not every day my cousin and best friend comes back, and with another friend, besides! A celebration is most certainly in order."

They dumped their kit bags as ordered, and then, with

Beth, headed outside to find something to eat. Violet linked arms with Rosie as they walked along, her head close to hers.

"I've missed you something terrible, you know. It's been so deadly dull here, just letters, letters, and more letters to type. But there's definitely something afoot—officers, real bigwigs, have been toing and froing between CMHQ and Southwick House."

"Southwick House?" Rosie repeated. She hadn't heard of it.

"It's the naval headquarters of the Allied forces, I think."

"They must be planning something soon, just like Susan said," Rosie mused, and Violet nodded.

"Yes, just about everyone is waiting, looking up at the sky, wondering when it's going to happen. But enough about that! Tell me how you've been."

"I've been all right." Rosie gave her an apologetic smile. "You know I can't talk about what I'm doing." She'd said as much in her letters.

"Yes, I know, and I'm not interested in any of that, anyway. What I want to know is—are you still in love with Thomas?"

"In love!" Rosie repeated, blushing. It was one thing to imply as much in a private letter, but for Violet to say it straight out, in company. She certainly hadn't said as much to Susan before, although she'd noticed all the letters.

"Yes, in love," Violet repeated impatiently. "Because he is certainly in love with you."

"What!" Rosie stopped in the street to stare at her cousin, amazed, abashed and hopeful all at once. "How could you possibly know something like that?"

"He was here last week, on leave," Beth explained, falling into step on her other side. "He was so sorry he missed you, but he left you a letter and a great big bar of Hershey's chocolate for whenever you came back."

"Did he..." Rosie's face warmed all the more. She felt a curious mix of wild elation and deep disappointment; she was glad—very glad—that he'd sought out her friends and left a letter, but to have missed him by only a few days...! It felt nothing short of tragic.

"And," Beth continued with an impish smile for Violet, "he brought a friend."

For a second, Rosie went cold. "A friend..."

"A male friend, silly!" Beth explained, reading her suddenly still expression perfectly. "Trust me, he's only got eyes for you! But there was another lieutenant from the 101st Airborne with him. Andrew Smith is his name. He was very quiet and shy, but Violet perked him up all right, I'd say."

"Beth," Violet scolded as Beth giggled, and now she was the one blushing.

Rosie sensed a good story and, with a smile for Susan, who had been walking a bit behind them, she told Violet, "You must tell us all about him." She didn't think she'd ever seen her cousin look so secretive—or so thrilled.

The story came out over a meal of ham pie and pear tart at a Lyons Corner House, the four of them gathered around a table by the window, a pot of tea in the center. Thomas had come to South Street to leave a letter for Rosie, knowing she wouldn't be there, and offered, with his friend Mr. Smith, to take Beth and Violet out on the town.

"It was clear Thomas was missing you dreadfully," Violet told her. "He spent the whole evening asking about you, what you'd said in your letters, how we thought you might be feeling. He even asked me for childhood stories—I told him about that time a stray dog chased you all the way down Princess Street and you ended up climbing a tree, except you couldn't."

"Oh, Violet, you didn't." Rosie let out a horrified laugh, although she was secretly thrilled Thomas had asked such questions, had wanted to know.

Violet turned to Susan. "Rosie tried to climb the tree, but she ended up hanging from a branch like a monkey, with the dog nipping at her ankles." She chuckled at the memory.

"It sounds dreadful," Susan said, and Rosie gave her a look of gratitude.

"It was, thank you very much! What a tale to tell him, Violet. I'm sure you could have thought of something a bit more complimentary."

"Oh, but why should I?" Violet replied airily, her eyes glinting with her usual impish humor.

Rosie just shook her head and smiled. "Tell me about Mr. Smith, then, since he seems to have caught your fancy."

"He's Thomas's opposite in every way," Beth told her. "Dark and small and quiet."

"Oh, Beth, you make him sound like a mouse!" Violet interjected. "He isn't at all. He's quite lovely. Thoughtful. Surprisingly witty. And you wouldn't know it to look at him, but he dances like a dream."

"You sound rather smitten," Rosie teased, only to stop in surprise when Violet looked at her quite seriously.

"Do you know," she said, lighting a cigarette, "I think I am. It's all a bit ridiculous, really—I don't know when, or even if, I'll see him again, and he's from Chicago, which is miles away, of course." She smiled dreamily, blowing out smoke, while Rosie exchanged a look with Beth.

"*Really* rather smitten," Rosie said, and Beth nodded her agreement.

"They're both out in Northampton now and I don't know when they'll next get leave," Violet continued. "Hardly any of the men are getting much leave these days, with things the way they are. You'll be lucky if you see Thomas at all."

Which was exactly what Rosie had feared. "We'll just have to make the best of it," she said as bravely as she could, but her heart sank to think of even more months passing without seeing him.

Later, back at the house in South Street, Rosie read Thomas's letter in private, blushing at his declarations of love, more ardent than any he'd made before. She still felt amazed that such a handsome, charming, interesting man had fallen in love with her—plain old Rosie Lyman, who hadn't been able to say boo to a goose for most of her childhood. She'd changed so much since joining the Canadian Women's Army Corps, she acknowledged, Thomas's letter pressed to her chest. She'd learned and grown and tried and failed and tried again. She'd dared—and loved! Would Thomas even have fallen in love with her if she hadn't changed and grown in the way that she had?

She supposed the question was unanswerable, but also essentially unimportant—she *had* fallen in love, and so had he. And all that now remained was a chance for them to see each other again, before the invasion happened and the war moved relentlessly on.

CHAPTER FIFTEEN

APRIL 1944

Beaumanor Hall, Leicestershire

Rosie and Susan arrived at Beaumanor Hall in the pouring rain, a downpour so relentless that they struggled even to see the great manor house that had been requisitioned by the government at the start of the war.

As they reported to reception, dripping in the front hall of the house, they were shown to their accommodation by a friendly ATS girl; they would be sharing a room on the top floor with a bunch of other ATS girls who acted as drivers.

"You're lucky, most of the listeners are billeted nearby, in Quorn or Woodhouse, but they've run out space," the girl said. "It's the drivers who are here, as well as some soldiers downstairs. They like to whistle when the girls come through the gates—and the girls whistle right back!"

"Good on them," Rosie replied, and the girl grinned.

The little attic room had two bedsteads crammed under the sloping ceiling, with a small chest at the end of each for their belongings, a washstand, and a couple of hooks on the wall. Over twelve hundred women worked at Beaumanor, they were told, along with three hundred men, although only a handful were lucky enough to be billeted in the house.

"This is quite nice, isn't it," Rosie said as she started to unpack her few belongings into the chest at the foot of her bed. They did not have to report to duty until the following morning.

"It'll be terribly hot in summer, all the way up here." As usual, Susan managed to find the least pleasing thing and remark upon it, Rosie thought with a sigh. And, as usual, she did not acknowledge the dispiriting remark.

"Shall we have a look around, after we unpack?" she suggested. "There are some gardens, I think."

Susan gave her a disbelieving glance. "I don't think we're meant to wander around, do you? Considering the state of the place."

"Yes, I suppose you're right." The whole estate was surrounded by barbed wire and patrolled by military police, and they'd been warned to only go where they were told. The huts where they would be working were somewhat disguised as stables or garden houses, although, even from a distance, Rosie thought they looked like exactly what they were—hastily constructed sheds meant for war work. Still, exploring was, she acknowledged, probably not a good idea. But what else could they do?

They ended up in the mess hall on the ground floor, in what Rosie thought must have been the original dining room, having a cup of tea while people bustled all around them. The place seemed to be a genuine hive of activity; there were a dozen or more huts in the parkland, which was bristling with aerial masts, and people seemed to be constantly rushing about, looking both hassled and important, while Rosie and Susan simply sat, sipping their tea, a bit morose.

A friendly-looking man in civilian clothes stopped by their table. "You look a little lost," he remarked on a laugh. "Are you new?"

"Arrived this morning," Rosie replied with a ready smile. "I wanted to have a wander around the gardens, but my friend here thought that wouldn't be a good idea."

"And she'd be right." Smiling easily in return, he sat down across from them. "It's all top-secret stuff, don't you know. You don't sound British, though?" He glanced at their uniforms. "Are you one of the Quacks? We've got a couple of you here already."

"Yes, we're in the Canadian Women's Army Corps," Rosie confirmed. "I'm Rosie, and this is Susan."

"Pleased to meet you." He shook both their hands. "I'm John Williams, ordinary civilian."

Rosie raised her eyebrows. "There are civilians serving here along with military?"

"Oh yes, most of the men here are civvies. It's the women who get to wear the uniform around this place." He smiled wryly, although Rosie thought she detected the slightest edge to his voice. "We've just been recruited for being—well, boffins, I suppose," he continued. "We tend to be amateur wireless enthusiasts who got a tap on the shoulder by someone important and so now we're here." He shrugged, smiling. "Not a bad place to spend the war, really."

Rosie wondered if, like the "zombies" back in Canada, who had chosen home defense over proper fighting, John Williams got some guff for not wearing a uniform. If he did, he must have made peace with it, because he had an open, friendly face Rosie liked the look of. It would be good to have a friend in this new place, she decided, considering she didn't feel terribly confident about what she'd be doing, or her own ability to do it.

After a few more minutes' chat, John Williams bid them

farewell, assuring them he'd most likely see them again soon and teasingly admonishing them not "to have a wander."

"Message received," Rosie replied with a mock salute. As she sipped the last of her tea, she looked forward to joining the busy people around her, contributing to the war effort, and maybe, finally doing something important.

When she and Susan reported to duty the next morning to J Hut, a cramped space filled with receiving sets placed on wooden tables, their CO, Captain Sillicoe, greeted them with a brisk manner that bordered on brusqueness.

"It's right to work, as there's not a moment to waste," he told them, pointing to two receiving sets that weren't being used. "Sit yourself down, clap on a pair of headphones, and find your frequency. We'll have one of the more experienced girls sitting beside you, to check your transcription till you get the hang of it."

He handed them each a list of wave bands they were to try, along with a pad of W/T red forms to record the signals in a grid of blocks of five letters. About a dozen girls were in the hut already, hard at work, twiddling the knobs of their wireless sets as they tried to find a frequency to tune into, and Captain Sillicoe directed two of them to sit next to Susan and Rosie, and listen in on their transmissions. Rosie was glad for the help; it felt daunting in the extreme, to start such essential work right away.

She slipped on the headphones, nerves swirling in her stomach as she twiddled the knob to find one of the bandwidths written on her sheet. The girl next to her smiled encouragingly as static filled Rosie's ears. If she thought she'd stumble on some-thing important, or even anything at all right away, she was mistaken; it was nearly an hour before she heard any Morse, and, at first, her mind went completely blank and she missed

the first few letters of the transmission before she quickly began
to copy it down.

There were hundreds of intercept operators at Beaumanor,
Rosie learned, and over one hundred Y stations across the country, with transmissions being listened to and transcribed every
moment of every hour. The trick, she soon discovered, was not
letting your mind drift, as you waited for a transmission to tune
into; hours could go by with nothing but static or snatches of
sound, twiddling the dial and trying to find something to hear.
Then, when the transmission finally came, her heart leaping in
her chest, her ears straining to catch every pause and dash and
transcribe it accurately, she felt both alert and exhausted,
desperate to get it right.

Transmissions were done in duplicate, with one copy to be
filed and another to be taken immediately to "Station X"—also
known simply as BP—by motorcycle dispatch rider, in case it
was something important. Rosie soon found a thrill in seeing the
transcriptions taken out immediately, although Susan reminded
her that almost all the transmissions they tuned into would be as
good as worthless. It was someone else's job, at the mysterious
BP, to figure out if there was any interesting information among
all the messages.

"Sometimes," Susan said darkly, "I think they might as well
as file it in the bin. I doubt it's anything important, and they
certainly wouldn't give us the interesting frequencies, when
we're so new."

They'd been at Beaumanor for two weeks, and had finally
been allowed to listen in by themselves, which had been both
a relief and a bit alarming. They had just got off a twelve-hour
night shift, aching and gritty-eyed with tiredness. They were
standing outside J Hut—the one used by newer operators—in
the gray, predawn light, with a few other girls who were

having a cigarette before they toddled off to breakfast and bed.

"You never know," Rosie said, trying to hold onto her optimism. "One of those transcriptions might be the key to everything."

"The key to the loo of some German submarine or something," one of the other operators sniffed. They'd been monitoring naval frequencies all evening, and at the end of their shift, their CO, Captain Sillicoe, had barely given their transcriptions a glance, deeming half of them unusable after the briefest of scans.

Rosie knew it would still all be bundled up and taken to Station X, where others would attempt to decode it—either that, she supposed, or deem it unusable, as the captain had claimed, and throw it in the bin. They'd all been taken to task for not making "clean" copies of transmissions that could be passed on and used in intelligence. Never mind that the weather conditions, the distance from the German transmitter, and a host of other considerations affected whether a transmission could be heard clearly or not.

"Right, cup of tea and toast and then bed," one of the other operators, a Wren named Isabel, said cheerfully as she stubbed out her cigarette. "And back at it again tomorrow."

Overall, Rosie had found the girls she worked with cheerful and friendly, without the sense of competition she'd encountered at Douglas. They were all in it together here, and it didn't help anyone if one of them faltered in a transmission. Rosie just hoped some of it helped to win the war.

She joined the other girls in the canteen for breakfast, barely listening to their chat about going into Loughborough, about four miles away. While it did not have the many entertainments of London, there was a picture house and a few restaurants and shops. Rosie hadn't gone yet, content to spend her free time reading or writing letters, or simply catching up on sleep. She'd taken John Williams at his word and not dared to explore the hall's parkland, most of which had been made off limits by barbed wire, anyway.

Even though Rose was tired after her shift, her mind was still buzzing with the sound of Morse code, the dits and dahs, which were the names for the quick and longer beeps that made up letters, which made up words, which made up sentences—whole paragraphs of potentially important intelligence, if only someone could figure out what it was. Even though she knew it wasn't her job, Rosie couldn't keep herself from sorting the sounds into patterns in her head, the same way she'd organize cards in a hand of bridge, wondering if there was a way to have them make sense.

"Your head is in the clouds today," Isabel remarked as Rosie blinked her into focus. "You look like you're away with the fairies, Rosie."

Rosie smiled and shook her head. "I was just thinking about what I heard on shift—"

"What you heard? I want that infernal racket out of my head as soon as I take off my headset! It keeps ringing in my ears... beep... beep beep... beep..."

"Don't you find it interesting," Rosie asked, leaning forward a little, "how there are sometimes patterns? Of sounds, I mean—or really letters?"

Isabel shrugged, unimpressed. "They're probably just using the same word for something," she said. "It hardly matters to us." She wagged her finger at Rosie. "That's not our job, you know!"

"Yes," Rosie replied on a sigh as she reached for her tea. "I know." But she still couldn't keep from thinking about it, from wondering.

. . .

Back in her room, Rosie fell almost immediately to sleep, despite the bright spring sunshine pouring in through the attic windows. When she woke a few hours later, she was dreadfully thirsty, groggy from both sleep and lack of it. It was midday, and she would be on duty again at eight o'clock that evening.

Susan had already gotten up, and so Rosie quickly dressed and washed her face before heading down to the mess hall for lunch—usually something vaguely inedible, but at least hot and filling. On the way down, she saw Isabel, who waved several envelopes at her.

"Post has arrived! Letters all around, I think!"

Rosie hurried to collect her own mail before heading to the mess hall, her heart lightening to see a letter from Thomas, another from Violet, and a third from her mother, all the way from Kingston. Her mother had done her best to write regularly, although the mail from Canada was not always reliable, and Rosie was always glad to receive a letter, with news from home.

After getting her lunch and pouring herself a cup of tea, Rosie sat at the end of a table by herself and opened her mother's letter first.

The first few paragraphs were the usual news—friendly gossip about family and neighbors—Gracie was driving an ambulance, and her Uncle Jed had volunteered for the Home Guard, even though he was over fifty. Violet's younger sister, Imogen, had enlisted as a CWAC when she'd turned eighteen, and was now serving somewhere out in Alberta.

Then, Rosie's heart seemed to stop, as she read her mother's next words:

And I am both sad and proud to tell you that Jamie has been shipped overseas. I knew it would happen, of course, because it's happening to all the boys, and he was absolutely thrilled to go. But it's still hard to have you both so far away. Jamie is hoping to go to France, but I can't help but pray that he is kept

safe in England. Perhaps you'll see him? I told him I'd forward
your new address when you have it, and he has his.

Slowly, Rosie lowered the letter to stare unseeingly out at
the manor's parkland, filled with huts and aerial masts, a sea of
industry. Jamie, here in England. Jamie, maybe even going to
France. A lump formed in her throat, and she swallowed it
down resolutely. It wasn't a surprise—of course it wasn't—and
yet still, somehow, she felt shocked. She'd let herself believe he'd
stay in Collins Bay, working on engines and never going
anywhere important, but, of course, that was never going to
happen. But, she told herself, at least as a mechanic, he had
some likelihood of staying in England. Or so she hoped.

"You look like you've seen a ghost."

Rosie blinked the world back into focus and saw John
Williams smiling down at her. She'd seen him a few times since
coming to Beaumanor, but only in passing or from afar. His
friendly gaze fell on the letter in her hand.

"Not bad news, I hope?"

"No, not exactly. My brother's been posted overseas—here
to England, I mean. He's a mechanic with the RCAF. He's only
nineteen." She hadn't seen him or any of her family for a year
and a half, she realized with a pang. It suddenly felt like an age.

"Bound to happen, I suppose," John replied with a grimace.
"Will you get to see him?"

"I hope so. I've written my mother with my address, and
he'll write to her with his, as well. Eventually, we'll be able to
write letters to one another, but by that time..." She trailed off,
and John nodded in understanding. Everyone knew the invasion would be soon. It was already April, the sky blue and clear,
the sun shining, the air warm. The perfect weather for an
amphibious assault, or so the whispers went. "Never mind."
Rosie folded her mother's letter and slid it back in the envelope.
"Like you said, it was bound to happen."

"Well, if you need cheering up, there's a dance in the Church Rooms in a village nearby—Quorn, it is—tonight. I think we could all do with a knees-up."

"Oh..." Rosie hesitated, unsure if he was asking her out on a date.

"A load of us are going," John continued in his easy way, as if he'd just read her mind, or at least understood the reason for her hesitation. "It'll be a laugh, I'm sure."

She hadn't ventured off the estate since she'd arrived, and after receiving her mother's letter with its news of her brother, Rosie realized she really was in need of some fun. She might not have enjoyed dancing back in Kingston, but since coming overseas she'd learned to kick up her heels almost as well as Violet.

"All right," she said with a nod and a smile. "Sounds swell."

About two dozen of them, Rosie and a reluctant Susan included, walked to the Church Rooms that evening through a soft, dusky light, the hedgerows lining the narrow country lane frothing with blackthorn, the drowsy air full of birdsong.

"You'd hardly know there was a war on," someone said, and for some reason this made everyone laugh.

It was a comfortably amiable group—mostly women, with only a handful of men; Beaumanor Hall was, Rosie had learned, staffed mainly by women, although all the officers were—as they so often were—men. The civilian men working there were similar to John—radio enthusiasts and university graduates who had been hand-picked for the war effort, working at various Y stations across the country, and some even out in the Pacific, along with a handful of soldiers to keep the place going.

By the time they got to the dance, the band was in full swing, and the hall was buzzing with dancers. Rosie instinctively sidled to the edge; there were far more women than men, so she didn't really expect to be asked to dance, at least not at first, but then John grabbed her hand and drew her out onto the dance floor.

"I'm not very good," Rosie warned him, "although I've managed to learn not to step on anyone's feet... Most of the time, anyway."

"I don't mind," he replied.

He wasn't that wonderful a dancer himself, which somehow made it funny, and with both of them doing their best not to step on each other's toes or crash into each other, Rosie enjoyed herself more than she'd expected.

When the band took a break from playing, John fetched her a glass of lemonade and they retreated to the side.

"So, a Quack," he said as he took a sip of his own drink. "How long have you been over here?"

"It will be two years in November... if the war hasn't been won by then."

His expression turned somber. "I doubt it will be."

His certainty made her falter a little. "But the invasion is going to be any day now—"

"And that won't be a stroll in the park," John replied. "It's a long way from the coast of France to Berlin, you know."

"I suppose it is." She hadn't really thought about that, Rosie realized, although, of course, it made sense. The invasion, whenever it came, was really just the beginning. The beginning of the end, perhaps, at last, as Churchill had said.

"Has some Canadian pilot stolen your heart, then?" John asked lightly. "I know how women take to a man in uniform. Blokes like me barely get a look-in." He sounded wry, but with that slight edge of bitterness Rosie had recognized from before that made her grimace in apology. He let out a dry laugh. "Ah, so, I'm right."

"Not Canadian, actually," she told him. "American. With the 101st Airborne."

"Stationed...?"

"Somewhere in Northamptonshire at the moment. But I haven't seen him in ages, because we've kept missing each other, what with my training and his work. I hope one day soon, though, before he goes." She still couldn't bear to think about that.

"Well, if it's been ages, then I'd say all's fair in love and war," John told her lightly. "Fancy another dance?"

Rosie hesitated, because after the conversation they'd just had, she didn't want to encourage him, but then John took her hand and she decided she'd made her situation clear, and a dance was just a dance, after all. It didn't have to mean anything.

As the weeks went by and April drifted into May, Rosie got into a rhythm, along with the other girls stationed at Beaumanor—a mixture of ATS girls and Wrens, with a sprinkling of CWACs and even a few Australians. Twelve-hour shifts, stumbling to bed, an occasional evening off to go for a drink in the country pub in the nearby villages of Woodhouse or Quorn, or venture the three and a half miles to sample the delights of Loughborough.

Violet would probably have gone stir-crazy, Rosie thought, in such an out-of-the-way place, but she didn't mind, and she'd come to enjoy her work, the sheer *focus* of it, as well as the fascinating allure of the mysterious messages that she transcribed as clearly as she could, without ever actually knowing what they meant, yet still trying to see and sift through the patterns.

In early May, she received forty-eight hours' leave and immediately wrote Thomas to let him know the dates, hoping he'd write back quickly so they could perhaps arrange to see each other. But when, much to her disappointment, no reply came, Rosie decided to go to London anyway, to see Violet and Beth. She'd asked Susan if she wanted to go, but she didn't have leave and didn't want to arrange a switch, so Rosie was on her own.

She hurried downstairs to catch the infrequent bus to Loughborough, run by a local firm called Barkus and having a timetable that nobody seemed to know, and then the train to London. She was looking forward to seeing Violet and Beth, but sorrow—and worse, a niggling worry—clouded her excitement. Why hadn't Thomas written? Had he not received her letter? Or was it that he simply hadn't cared? It had been so long since they'd seen each other; could she really be surprised if his affections went off the boil a bit?

She tried not to let the worry tax her too much; the train was crowded with servicemen and very slow, and Rosie told herself it would all look and feel better when she was back in Mayfair, with Violet and Beth. They'd ply her with cups of tea and talk perfect sense, which she knew she needed—*The mail has been so slow; most likely he didn't receive your letter, or you haven't yet had his. Only you, Rosie, can worry a man doesn't love you when he declares himself at least once a week!*

Just the thought of what Violet might say, hands on hips and eyes rolling, made Rosie feel at least a little better.

The platform was a crush of people as Rosie exited the train in London, but one head, with its peaked khaki-colored cap, stood above the others. One man wasn't striding down the platform intent on going somewhere; instead, he was scanning the crowded platform, as if he were looking for someone.

With a sense born of instinct, or maybe just hope, Rosie stopped right there on the platform, while people streamed around her, jostling her elbow, muttering under their breath at her sudden stillness.

The man turned, and she caught a glimpse of his face—the sweep of blond hair, the glint in his eyes, that cleft in his chin—

She started pushing her way through the crowd, and then

she was running—running toward the man she had been
longing to see, yet could hardly believe was here.

As she came toward him, he swept her up in his arms and
Rosie let out a trembling cry of joy.

"Thomas!"

CHAPTER SIXTEEN

MAY 1944

London, England

They were huddled at a corner table in a Lyons Corner House near the station, holding hands over the tabletop as they stared at each other in wonder and their tea turned lukewarm. At least, Rosie thought, *she* was staring in wonder; Thomas was grinning like a cat who had just licked up all the cream.

"I can't believe you're here," she said, for what had to be at least the third time.

His smile deepened, revealing his dimple. "I wanted to surprise you."

"I might have missed you!" This said almost, but not quite, like a scolding.

Thomas smiled and squeezed her hands. "Violet told me the time of your train."

"But I might have missed it, or changed my mind about coming to London, or not seen you..." She shuddered to think of all the things that could have happened so she may not have seen him; it could have been months *again*, or even longer.

"But you didn't," Thomas reminded her. "And it was worth it, to see the look on your face! Like you'd had all your Christmases and birthdays at once."

"That's what it felt like," Rosie admitted, unembarrassed to show the depth of her feeling, because he was *here*. He was finally here. "I've missed you, Thomas. It's been so *long*..."

He nodded. "I know, far too long. Seven months, and every day has felt like a year."

"For me, too." Rosie stared at him, content simply to drink in the sight of him—the blond hair brushed back from a high forehead, the bright blue eyes, the cleft chin, the ready smile. He was just as handsome, just as charming and laughing, and wry and *wonderful*, as she'd remembered. And he loved her! She could scarcely believe it, any of it—that he was here, that he loved her, that all of this was real.

"I can't believe you're here," she said again, and he laughed.

"I can't believe I'm here, either. I was going to surprise you at your posting, but I couldn't even find out where it was! No one would tell me."

All the letters to Beaumanor Hall, Rosie knew, were forwarded from a postal box in London. She wasn't allowed to tell anyone the location of where she worked, not even the county or postcode.

She grimaced now in apology. "I'm afraid it's all top secret."

"Yes, it must be very hush-hush indeed." He leaned back in his chair, his fingers still loosely twined with hers. "You must be doing something very important, for them to be secretive about it all, that I can't even know where you are."

Rosie considered his laughing remark seriously. "Yes," she said at last, "I think we are. Not every moment, of course, but still. The work is essential, and that feels... well, nice, I suppose. Like I'm finally doing something that matters."

"My goodness." He raised his eyebrows as he reached for his cigarettes, withdrawing the pack from his breast pocket.

Rosie had forgotten that he sometimes smoked, usually not around her. "It does sound serious."

"Well, let's not talk about all that." She smiled at him, wondering if she was imagining the slightly harder edge to him than she recalled from before; as laughing and light as he could be, there was a certain jadedness to him now, a slight cynicism that came through his tone and that she saw in the set of his mouth. Was that what war did to people? Perhaps it was always just a matter of time.

As if he had guessed the nature of her thoughts, Thomas stubbed out his cigarette as soon as he'd lit it and reached for both of her hands. "Sorry, I don't mean to sound—well, I don't even know what. Of course your work is serious, and important, and I'm so proud of you for doing it." He squeezed her hands. "You know that I believe that, don't you?"

"Yes, I do." She squeezed back, smiling at him, a little relieved that he'd addressed it—whatever "it" even was. She wasn't sure she could say. "What have you been doing, Thomas? Can you tell me?"

"Waiting around, mostly, for something to finally happen." He let go of her hands, sitting back in his chair. "It gets a guy on edge, let me tell you. Everybody seems ready to snap."

"It will happen soon, then, won't it?" she asked quietly.

"I think it has to, although I know about as much as you do. They said this would be my last leave for a while, though, so I guess that means something."

"For a while?" Rosie looked up, surprised, even though, just as with Jamie, she knew she shouldn't be. Of course things were starting to happen, to change. "Oh, Thomas." Her eyes smarted and she blinked rapidly, not wanting to spoil their time together with tears. "What shall we do, then?" she asked as cheerfully as she could. "I hadn't made any plans besides seeing Violet. I suppose I shall have to tell her I'll be busy—"

"She was in on the whole thing," Thomas replied with a

quick grin. "I doubt she'll be surprised. In any case, I've made plenty of plans. You didn't think I'd show up here with nothing to do, did you?"

"Well, I..." Her head had been spinning so much from seeing him again, she hadn't really thought about it at all. "What have you got planned?"

"Dinner at a slap-up restaurant, first of all," Thomas told her. "The best money can buy. And then dancing. There's a new club that plays the best tunes—they even have champagne."

Rosie smiled, her heart singing at the thought of a whole evening spent together, just the two of them. She didn't need dancing or champagne, she thought. She just needed Thomas. "It sounds wonderful," she told him, and Thomas signaled for the bill.

It *was* wonderful, eating roast lamb with mint sauce, followed by steamed fruit roll and custard, and then drinking champagne and dancing the night away to all the latest Glenn Miller tunes, until Rosie's feet were aching, her sides too from laughing so much as Thomas spun her around the floor until she was dizzy.

Toward the end of the evening, during a long, slow song, she danced with her arms wrapped around his shoulders, their cheeks pressed together, couples swaying silently together around them, everyone eking out the very last of the evening, for no one knew when such a time would come again. It felt painfully poignant, knowing these last moments were fading away, slipping from their fingers even as Rosie desperately tried to keep savoring them as much as she could.

Her eyes drifted shut as she confessed in a murmur, "I've had such a wonderful time, I can't bear for this evening to end." They'd have to leave soon, she realized, if she was going to catch a bus.

"You know it doesn't have to," Thomas replied, his voice as low and sleepy as hers, and Rosie opened her eyes, leaning back a little to look at him.

"Doesn't it?" She had assumed she would return to her former barracks in Mayfair, and Thomas would have made arrangements to stay somewhere in town, but she hadn't given it much thought beyond that.

Thomas drew back from her, then took her hand and led her off the dance floor, to the side of the room. He clasped both her hands in his, his expression endearingly earnest. "Rosie, you know that I love you, don't you?"

She stared at him in confusion, as well as surprised pleasure; he'd never said it in person to her before, although he had written it enough in his letters. "Well, yes..." she began.

"And that I'm going to marry you one day?"

She let out a pleased yet uncertain laugh, because he'd never actually made it quite as plain as that before, either, amidst all the declarations of love in his letters. "Was that a proposal?" she managed to tease.

Thomas hung his head in abashed admission before he looked up at her, eyes glinting with their old humor. "Well, not a real one, because one day I'm going to do it properly, with a ring and everything, down on one knee, the works. But maybe the first of two? A precursor, perhaps?"

She laughed again, shaking her head, too happy to care about how he did it. She didn't need a ring or a bended knee, candlelight or violins, or any of that nonsense. "All right, then," she told him. "This is my first acceptance, I suppose."

His eyes lit up and he drew her a little toward him. "You will marry me?"

She laughed again, this time a peal of pure happiness. "Yes—"

"You've made me the happiest man alive." He kissed her, quickly and firmly, before drawing back again. "You know it won't be long before we're heading overseas? Maybe a couple of weeks, if that."

Rosie swallowed, her head spinning from the champagne she'd drunk, as well as the dizzying speed with which Thomas was changing the conversation. She'd just agreed to marry him, and now he was talking about shipping out. It felt like too much to think about, all at once. "Yes, of course I know," she said quietly.

"Maybe even only days," Thomas continued, like a warning. "And, Rosie... we're as good as married, aren't we? You know I love you to pieces, and you love me back." He was back to looking earnest, and Rosie stared at him, trying to understand what he was saying. Then he said it. "I've booked a room at a hotel here in town, for the two of us, Mr. and Mrs. Crewe... Rosie, will you spend the night with me?"

Her mouth opened, then shut. She stared at him, once again feeling that disconcerting mix of being completely surprised and yet not at all.

"Of course I would never pressure you into anything," he added quickly. "You know I wouldn't, don't you? I just want to be with you. When a man is facing his own mortality, well, it makes him realize what's important. And you are, Rosie. You're so important to me. The most important."

"You're important to me, too," Rosie whispered. Her mind was spinning again, but now not from champagne.

"Then you'll come? It's not too far away, a lovely room, just for the two of us."

"Have you seen it?" Rosie asked, a bit stupidly, and he nodded.

"I arranged it this afternoon, before I met your train."

Rosie nodded, unable to think how to reply. She loved Thomas, yes, she knew she did, and she wanted to marry him. Absolutely. And plenty of girls were in the same position as she was in now—or really, worse, at least in terms of the small comforts. She thought of the couples they'd had to step over, back in summer, lying in the grass of that public square. At least Thomas had had the kindness and courtesy to arrange a room, a lovely room.

And she wasn't a prude, she reminded herself. She'd seen a lot over the last few years; she was no longer naïve, an innocent fresher traipsing through university, put to the blush. She knew what he was talking about. She knew, even, that it would be understandable, expected, desirable for both of them. And yet...

"Rosie?" Thomas asked. "Will you come?"

She gazed at Thomas—the man she loved, with his kind blue eyes, usually glinting with humor but now looking so anxious and earnest, his hands clasped in hers, the cleft in his chin that reminded her of a film star. He loved her. *He loved her*.

She smiled at him. "Yes," she said. "Of course I'll come."

The hotel was near Paddington Station, a small, slightly shabby building with a beady-eyed woman at the desk. On the front steps, before they'd gone in, Thomas had slipped Rosie a wedding ring, a cheap thing of brass.

"They'll check," he explained, a bit apologetically, and Rosie hadn't been able to think what to say as she'd slipped it on her finger; it hung loosely, at least two sizes too big.

As Thomas signed the register "Mr. and Mrs. Crewe," she thought suddenly of Nancy, and how she and Violet had looked for her back at the Walper Hotel in Kitchener. There had been a man at the desk back then, sniffily informing them that the hotel would never give a room to an unmarried couple, and Rosie had tried to hide her shock and embarrassment.

She felt no real embarrassment now, perhaps because she felt a bit numb; she suspected, despite Thomas's elaborate preparations, they had not fooled the woman at the desk one bit.

She seemed weary rather than condemning, but also unsurprised.

Upstairs, the room was small but pleasant enough, with a double bed with a bedspread of pink chenille, a bedside table on either side. There was a bureau and a washstand and a single window overlooking the train tracks. Rosie quickly drew the blackout curtains across the small pane.

"Ah, Rosie." She stiffened just a little bit in surprise as Thomas took her in his arms; there was a certain proprietariness to the gesture, a satisfaction to his tone. "I'm so glad you're here."

"So am I," she managed, because she was—*of course* she was. She put her arms around him and pressed her cheek against his chest, grateful for the familiarity of him, the strength of his arms around hers. "But I'm a bit nervous, too," she admitted in a suffocated whisper, feeling she had to say at least that much.

Thomas chuckled softly. "You don't need to be, I promise."

He sounded, she thought, like the voice of experience. Violet would tell her not to be so silly; of course men had more experience in this sort of thing than women. It had always been that way, and it most likely always would be. In some ways, she supposed, it was reassuring. One of them, at least, should know what to do.

"You... you will be careful, though, won't you?" she asked, thinking of Nancy again. "You know, with precautions and things." She tucked her head against his shoulder, her face aflame. Apparently, she was still able to get embarrassed, after all.

"Of course." He tilted her chin up to face him and kissed her then, tenderly, and thankfully she felt her reservations begin to melt away. She loved this man. She wanted to spend the rest of her life with him. And even if he were to fall in

France—heaven help them both—she would not regret this night. She would not let herself.

Rosie returned his kiss and then Thomas deepened it, his hands coming around to the buttons the front of her uniform.

"May I?" he asked, and wordlessly, her heart feeling as if it were beating all the way up her throat, she nodded. Thomas looked up at her, his face suffused with love. "You're so beautiful, Rosie, and I love you so much."

"I know," she whispered. "I love you, too."

And then neither of them spoke for a long time.

CHAPTER SEVENTEEN

JUNE 1944

Beaumanor Hall, Leicestershire

"All right there, Lyman? Best hop on your set. It's a busy time."

Captain Sillicoe's tone was as brisk as ever as Rosie reported to J Hut for her twelve-hour shift. It was early June, and she'd only had eight hours off duty before she'd had to report again, thanks to the level of traffic they'd been getting on the receiving sets.

It had been three weeks since her forty-eight hours of leave in London, every moment spent with Thomas, many of them in the closest way possible.

She still blushed to remember those two days—and nights—when Thomas had awakened her to pleasures she had never known existed, and could barely think about now without going warm all over. She'd woken up that first morning, shocked not to be alone in bed, Thomas's very bare, male chest just inches from her cheek in a way that had felt totally unfamiliar. He'd stretched and then put his arm around her, drawing her close, so she could breathe in the warm, spicy scent of him.

"You're not regretting anything, are you?" he'd asked as he'd stroked her bare shoulder.

"No," Rosie had said, and she believed she meant it. Certainly, she'd enjoyed herself that night, even if she'd felt nervous and shy and not quite knowing what to do. "It's a bit like dancing, isn't it," she'd told Thomas as she'd snuggled against him, the morning light filtering through the crack in the blackout curtains. "I never knew where my hands or feet were supposed to go, and I always felt a bit ridiculous and awkward, but eventually, with some practice, I got the hang of it."

He had let out a shout of laughter and drawn her closer. "I suppose you need some more practice in this kind of dancing, then."

And they had practiced, most of the morning, and that evening, as well, only going out for food and a quick walk around Hyde Park, much of it now plowed up for Victory gardens. By the time he'd dropped her off at the train to Lough-borough the next afternoon, Rosie had felt like an expert indeed, as well as pleasurably exhausted, not having slept very much at all, yet very, very happy, especially when Thomas had kissed her goodbye and told her the next time he saw her, he'd have that ring.

She must have still had something of a silly grin on her face, hours later when she'd returned to Beaumanor, because Isabel had come across her, heading up to her room, and let out a hoot of laughter. "Did you meet your GI, after all?" she'd exclaimed, and Rosie had just grinned some more.

But that had been three weeks ago—three weeks of constant work, as the intercepts had come thick and fast, the radio frequencies positively buzzing with traffic as the day of the invasion, whenever it happened, loomed ever closer. Yesterday, after her shift, as Rosie had walked back to the hall with Susan, they'd seen at least a hundred planes cross the sky in an elegant, purposeful formation, all heading south, toward the Channel.

They'd both stopped and silently watched the planes go by overhead; there had been no words to describe the moment, both the seriousness and the grim reality of it. It was happening. Finally, it was happening.

Now, Rosie sat down in front of her set and reached for the pad of W/T red forms with their grids of blocks of five, used for transcription. She slipped on her headphones, turning the dial to the frequency she'd been monitoring every night for the last few weeks; as each listener gained experience, she'd been given a specific wave band to monitor, often coming to recognize the style of the transmission—and the transmitter—that she was intercepting.

The transmitter's style was called a "fist"—the way they sent the message, the certain pauses or sudden, quick bursts, sometimes as good, as Captain Sillicoe had said, as a calling card. Rosie liked to think she'd come to know one of hers in particular—the quick way he went through the vowels, the slight pause before an unusual letter like Y or X, even the seemingly staccato rhythm had its own cadence, a pattern she fell into and recognized, almost as if it were her own.

Sometimes, in her more fanciful moments, she tried to imagine the man who was transmitting his messages into the night, having no idea—or maybe he did—that she, a lowly CWAC in the middle of Leicestershire, was listening in. She pictured him, young, earnest and dark-haired, bent over his machine, tapping into the night. It provided a strange sort of intimacy between her and her unknown transmitter, one she knew was actually non-existent but which she felt all the same.

Tonight, however, as she tuned into his frequency and, within minutes, started recording his code, she felt, almost immediately, that something was off. It was like missing the step in a staircase, or every other word in a conversation. It didn't *feel* right, but as she assiduously transcribed the code, she wasn't sure she could even say why, only that she felt it, deeply and certainly.

She had no time to think of it, however, because all of her concentration had to be on transcribing the code, which went on longer than usual. After over an hour, there was finally a break, and Rosie pushed the pad aside as she took off her headphones for a few seconds' breather.

"Lyman, get back on it," Sillicoe barked.

"Sir... I think something was off with the code just now."

Captain Sillicoe frowned, his eyebrows beetling. "Off? What do you mean, off? Did you transcribe it or not?"

"Yes, but I know his fist, sir. It didn't feel the same."

"Just file the transcription," Sillicoe replied irritably, "and keep going. BP will figure it out."

Rosie knew better than to argue with her CO, especially when he, like everyone else, was operating on very little sleep, and feeling the crunch of the impending invasion.

"Yes, sir," she replied quietly, and she drew the pad toward her again, neatly ripping off the top page, and then replaced the headphones over her ears.

The next morning, after her shift, she mentioned the strange sensation to John Williams, who had become a friend over the last few weeks, thankfully dropping any romantic notions, as far as Rosie could tell.

"Have you ever listened to a signal and felt like something was off?" she asked him as she sipped her tea.

John glanced at her, tapping the ash of his cigarette in one of the sardine tins that had been placed on the mess hall tables for just that purpose. "Off? In what way?"

"With a transmission. I've come to recognize a certain fist; sometimes it almost feels like we're talking to each other, even though of course we're not." She ducked her head, a bit embarrassed by the admission, but John nodded, his expression intent now.

"Yes, I know what you mean."

"It sounded different today. I couldn't even put my finger on it, just felt it in my bones."

"Maybe it was a different signaler."

"But it's always been him, this time of night, on that wave band, for the last few weeks."

"Still, there could be plenty of reasons why it was someone different. He was ill, or had been transferred, or killed by an Allied bomb, for that matter." He smiled without any humor. "Plenty of reasons, I should think."

"Yes..." Rosie knew he was speaking sense, yet something—some sort of instinct she hadn't realized she possessed—made her resist the notion. "If it had been someone different," she said slowly, "that is, if it had been meant to be someone different because of a schedule or an accident or what have you... I would have sensed that. You know how it is. You get a feel for some-one, because they're all so different, aren't they? The signalers."

John gave a brief nod, his expression still seeming skeptical. "Yes, they can be, to an experienced ear."

"But this... this felt almost like someone was *trying* to be him. I know it doesn't make much sense," Rosie continued hurriedly, before he could object, "because I don't even know who he is or what he was saying." As much as she couldn't help but try to make sense of the letters she wrote, one after the other, in their indecipherable blocks of five, she couldn't. Some were in German; some were in code; many were in both. It all got passed on to the various codebreaking teams at BP, Station X—German speakers, puzzle-solvers, university boffins, according to John, who were brilliant at crosswords or chess. And yet Rosie kept sensing patterns in the letters, as if some-thing was just beyond her grasp but most definitely *there*. Still, she knew that didn't mean she could make *actual* sense of the transmission, more was the pity. "But sometimes," she finished, "you really do just have a feeling. Don't you?"

John drew thoughtfully on his cigarette. "So, what are you saying? You think someone was impersonating him?"

Rosie reflected on the suggestion; now that she was out of J Hut, without the buzzy hum of the wireless receiver and the headphones over her ears, tuned in to the dits and dahs, she felt less certain about it all—including the strong feeling she'd had in herself. "I don't know," she admitted. "Maybe?"

"But why?"

Why would one German impersonate another? There was only one reason she could think of. "To give false information," Rosie replied hesitantly, "don't you think?"

John was silent for a moment, considering. "Why wouldn't your signaler just do it himself, then?"

"Maybe he did, but because he knew it was false, there was some hesitation or something. Hence, my feeling that it was off. Or maybe it was someone else, who didn't want to have other people know what was going on. I imagine the Germans can be as hush-hush as we are, even to their own people."

John still looked skeptical. "But would he even know it was false? Some lowly signaler being given a message to transmit by a higher-up?"

"He could do, couldn't he? He's not like us, just listening and taking down someone else's words. He's communicating, for a purpose. He must know Morse, and he must know his own situation—whether he's on a ship or a base or what have you. He could very well know whether what he is sending is true or not. At least, he must have a clue." She smiled wryly. "Unlike us."

Something hardened in John's face and he drew on his cigarette, his eyes narrowed against the haze of smoke. "That's quite a charge," he said at last.

"That a German might be feeding us false information?" Rosie replied in surprise. "Aren't we doing the same, somewhere, somehow, to them?" She'd assumed with all the top-secret stuff, something like that was going on somewhere.

"Well, yes, I'm sure, but..." John paused. "To accept what you're saying, it would mean dismissing the intelligence as inaccurate, misleading, even if it wasn't. That's quite a decision to have to make—and, if you got it wrong, to live with."

"But someone can't make it," Rosie pointed out, "if they don't know. Can they? I mean..." She paused as realization filtered through her. "If there are no doubts about the genuineness of it before it is passed on, whoever is decoding it can't assess it properly, because they don't have all the information." Which meant, she thought, that her seemingly lowly part in the process—actually transcribing the messages in the first place, writing down someone's else words—might actually be quite important.

John gave her a conciliatory, but, Rosie thought, slightly patronizing, smile. "I think you're getting in a bit over your head here, Rosie. The codebreakers and analysts at BP certainly know what they're doing. They can spot a fake intelligence report a mile off, I'm sure of it, simply by the way it's written. Besides, there will be loads of analysts whose only job is to determine what is true information and what is false." He cocked his head, his smile turning into something almost like a smirk. "I think this is definitely above your pay grade."

Rosie tried not to be stung by his slightly superior tone. "Maybe," she allowed reluctantly. "I did try to say something of it to Captain Sillicoe, but he wasn't very interested."

"There you are then." John gave a little nod. "Remember, the dispatch riders are heading over there every night of the week, sometimes several times a night." He stubbed out his cigarette as he rose from the table. "Your report is probably already on its way."

. . .

Rosie didn't think much more about it, because there simply wasn't time or space in her head. She fell into bed and slept for seven hours straight, only to wake up, wash, bolt down a cup of coffee and a revolting Spam sandwich, and then head back to the hut for another shift.

"Watch out," one of the girls whispered as Rosie sat down in front of her set. "Captain Sillicoe is in an absolute fury."

"He is?" Their CO was often blowing off steam, and Rosie had learned some weeks ago that his bark was worse than his bite, but the warning still gave her pause.

"He got a dressing-down from another officer, one from M." M was the main set room, where many of the male listeners worked. "In front of us all. He was livid, let me tell you."

"A dressing-down? Why?"

"Because apparently someone in M figured out that some of the transmissions might be phony. You know, false intelligence and all that. And apparently, we should have figured it out by the fist. The man from M, of course, is a hero." She rolled her eyes while Rosie went cold.

"Someone in M?" she repeated slowly. John Williams was in M.

"Yes, they had to send a rider *after* the rider, to let them know, and mark the relevant transmissions."

"How did he know what transmissions to mark? And how would someone in M know if our transmissions were phony?"

The girl shrugged. "How should I know? He did some digging, I guess. It was all a big to-do, but we just pretended it wasn't happening. No one wanted to catch the captain's eye, let me tell you!"

"No, I don't suppose they did." Rosie reached for her headphones; she knew she couldn't spend any more time chatting, or even thinking about what had happened. Had John decided her gut feeling was worth considering? If so, why hadn't he mentioned her? Instead, it sounded as if he'd taken the credit himself, and let the blame fall on her colleagues and CO. But surely he couldn't have meant to do that, she reasoned. In any case, there wasn't much she could do about it now. She could hardly tell Captain Sillicoe that she'd voiced the concerns; he had already dismissed them.

Still, the whole episode rankled more than a little as Rosie got through her night shift and then headed to the mess hall for breakfast.

She'd just walked into the hall when she saw John himself coming whistling down the stairs. When he caught sight of her, his smile dimmed and for a second his expression turned guarded. Rosie felt a sudden bolt of certainty, of fury.

"Good morning, John," she said, meaning to sound pleasant but failing. "I heard from one of the listeners in J Hut that someone had to go after a dispatch rider, to let them know some of the intelligence might be phony."

John's guarded expression relaxed, turning almost indifferent. "Yes, I decided there was something to what you were saying earlier," he replied with a shrug. "And I let my CO know."

Rosie felt her hands clench into fists at her sides. "And you didn't bother to let him know that I was the one who brought it to your attention?"

John arched an eyebrow. "Oh, did you want some praise? A promotion, perhaps?"

"Instead all of J Hut, including *our* CO, got a dressing-down for not paying more attention," Rosie retorted. "When that wasn't the case at all, as you very well know."

John shrugged. "That had nothing to do with me."

"Didn't it?" Rosie demanded. "If you'd said you'd heard it from—"

"This isn't about personal glory," he cut her off coolly. "It's about winning the war."

"I know that, but—"

"So I'm sorry if your feelings were hurt," he cut her off again, not sounding sorry at all, "but there's more at stake. Besides, you told me you'd tried to talk to your CO, and he didn't want to listen. So he *was* at fault, it seems."

Rosie shook her head, annoyed he was turning her own words back on her. "And yet your CO listened to you."

John smiled in a slightly smirking way. Why had she not noticed how superior he could seem at times? And yet, she realized, she had, even if she hadn't wanted to acknowledge it; she'd sensed the chip on his shoulder, from not being military, from not doing more for the war effort, and maybe even, for not being a romantic interest for her. "Well, you know how it is," he told her. "Women can sound a bit hysterical sometimes."

"*Hysterical—*"

"An officer will always listen to a man before he does a woman," John stated, simply as fact, while Rosie stared at him in fury, but also despair. She might as well be right back in her father's office in Kingston, she thought. No matter what women had done in this war, what *she* had done, nothing had actually changed. Maybe nothing ever would.

"At least now I know not to trust you," she finally choked out, but John just looked bored.

"Oh really, Rosie, now you are being hysterical—"

"Quiet, everyone!"

Rosie turned to the voice of an ATS girl from the mess hall, a finger to her lips. "What..."

"It's on the wireless," the girl exclaimed excitedly. "D-Day. It's finally happening!"

CHAPTER EIGHTEEN

Rosie stood next to John, their argument forgotten as John Snagge, the BBC Home presenter's, somber voice came over the wireless.

"D-Day has come," he announced gravely. "Early this morning, the Allies began the assault on the north-western face of Hitler's European fortress. The first official news came just after half-past nine, when Supreme Headquarters of the Allied Expeditionary Force issued Communiqué Number One ... This said: 'Under the command of General Eisenhower, Allied naval forces, supported by strong air forces, began landing Allied armies this morning on the northern coast of France.'"

A collective gasp seemed to go through the room, although no one moved. No one even breathed. Everyone was completely still and silent, their gazes trained on the wireless that had been brought in and propped on one of the long wooden tables.

Snagge continued, "It was announced a little while later that General Montgomery is in command of the army group carrying out the assault. This army group includes British, Canadian, and United States forces."

Rosie turned slightly away from the wireless, her mind reeling. It was happening; *it was actually happening*. Thomas must be in France; he would have been parachuted over with the 101st Airborne, maybe last night, even. He might already be in enemy territory; he might, she knew, already be wounded or dead.

And Jamie! The presenter had mentioned Canadian forces. Had Jamie been sent over, too?

Her heart felt as if it were beating out of her chest as she listened to John Snagge quote Eisenhower's words to his troops: "Your task will not be an easy one. Your enemy is well trained, well equipped and battle-hardened. He will fight savagely. But this is the year 1944... The tide has turned. The free men of the world are marching together to victory. I have full confidence in your courage, devotion to duty and skill in battle. We will accept nothing less than full victory. Good luck, and let us all beseech the blessing of Almighty God upon this great and noble undertaking."

Rosie glanced around the room and saw the range of expressions on people's faces—awe, gravity, wonder, but most of all, hope. Finally, they were doing something. Finally, the end of the war—even if just the beginning of the end—might be in sight.

And yet, in this moment, Rosie felt only a plunging sense of fear as she thought of Thomas... Jamie... and all the other boys—husbands, lovers, brothers, sons—whose lives were in deadly peril. Who might this very moment be being gunned down as they waded to shore, or parachuted into some lonely French field...

"Rosie, you're as pale as a ghost." She blinked at Susan, who had walked up to her and was now gazing at her in a stern sort of concern. "You've been on shift all night, haven't you? You ought to get some sleep."

"I can't sleep," Rosie protested, and Susan shook her head.

"You must. You'll be no good to anyone if you don't."

Somehow, Rosie found herself being marched up to bed; Susan tucked her in like she was a child and promised to bring her a cup of tea after she'd had a few hours' sleep. Rosie thought she wouldn't be able to sleep with everything tumbling through her head—Thomas, Jamie, D-Day, and John's treachery, her own pointless fury. It all seemed so silly now, in light of such greater things, but it still mattered. Didn't it?

The last thought she had before she drifted off to sleep was that she still wanted things to change...

She woke up to Susan shaking her awake and handing her a cup of tea. "You'd best get a move on. We're going to be on double shifts from now on, with everything that's happening. It's more important than ever that we're all listening in."

The next few weeks passed in a blur; when Rosie wasn't listening in J Hut, she was either sleeping or eating, and not much else. The transmissions were coming in at a frantic pace, and every bit of intelligence garnered was treated as essential; no more jokes about filing things in the bin were made. She started dreaming in Morse code; the dits and dahs dancing through her brain, making their own staccato music.

The signaler whose fist she had come to know, that seemingly old friend, had disappeared off the wave band. Rosie knew she would never know who he had been, and whether she'd been right in suspecting him. It was all part of the war, she supposed, and on that matter John had been right; it wasn't about personal glory. It couldn't be. And yet she still felt resentful at his manner, and their friendship had completely cooled. One day, she vowed, women wouldn't be ignored or dismissed. They wouldn't be called hysterical for acting on an instinct. She would make sure of it...

But for now, there was a war to win.

. . .

A month after D-Day, when Rosie was practically fainting with exhaustion and longing to hear from Thomas, as well as Jamie, a letter arrived, filling her with both relief and hope.

"The 101st Airborne is back in England," she told Susan, her voice shaking with emotion. "Thomas is all right—he has forty-eight hours' leave, and he wants to come up to Loughborough to see me!"

"If you can get the time off," Susan replied darkly. "It might be nice for him, but we're all working around the clock."

"But I have to see him," Rosie said simply. "I must."

In the end, she managed to wangle only a single evening; she got off the nine-to-four shift and took the bus into Loughborough, meeting Thomas at a pub near the station. She'd barely gotten off the bus before he was sweeping her into his arms and kissing her passionately right there in front of everyone, including an elderly woman, who sniffed and tutted at them before moving past.

"Thomas," Rosie said, only half in protest, when he finally let her go. "You're making a spectacle!"

"I don't care," he replied, kissing her again. "I've been in France, I don't care about any of that now."

Underneath the joy of their reunion, Rosie sensed something dark and despairing that chilled her. "Let's go sit down somewhere," she said, taking his hand. "Catch up properly."

But when they found a table in a corner of the pub, Rosie with a shandy and Thomas with a double whiskey, he didn't seem to want to talk about anything at all.

"You don't want to know what it's like, Rosie, honestly, you don't." He tossed down a long swallow of whiskey. "It's better if you don't. No one wants to hear it. No one wants to talk about it."

"But you're safe," Rosie said quietly. "And you're here."

He nodded as he set down his glass. "For now."

"Don't say that. We must be nearing the end of the war, Thomas. We must be."

He let out a hollow laugh. "You'd like to think so, wouldn't you? Sometimes I think we're still at the damned beginning. Those Huns, Rosie... they're like nothing I've seen. The Waffen-SS... they're *fanatics*. They have this... this light in their eyes, like they're lit from within. When you see them up close, you feel like they're barely human. They're like... like robots or something. Zealous robots." He shook his head and reached for his glass again. "Let's not talk about it."

"All right," Rosie said quietly. When he spoke like that, she did not particularly want to talk about it, either. It sounded unutterably grim, as well as terrifying to think of him that close to a German soldier, a member of the dreaded SS. She didn't want to talk about that at all; she didn't even want to think about it.

She hadn't even finished her drink—although Thomas had had another double—when he grabbed her hand, pulling her from the table. "Let's get out of here."

"Where do you—"

"We'll find a place."

Rosie didn't realize he meant a hotel until they were turned away from a grimy-looking place by the station; this time, they didn't have any wedding rings. They tried two more establishments before Rosie suggested they leave it, and just go for a walk instead.

"It's a lovely night," she told him. "We can go to the park and look at the stars."

"I've seen enough stars to last a lifetime," Thomas replied bitterly. "I landed in a potato field in the middle of a starry night. Stars show the enemy where you are, and trust me, that's not very fun."

Rosie's heart lurched in her chest. "Was it so very awful?" she asked in a whisper, but he just shook his head.

They walked in silence through Queen's Park; its band-stand, aviary, and boating lake were now surrounded by Victory gardens, the seedlings of various vegetables just beginning to push up through the dirt. Rosie struggled to think of something to say, something light and fun, but her mind felt completely blank. She was intimidated and a little frightened by Thomas's grim silence, and exhausted by the double shifts she'd been doing. She felt as if she could fall asleep right there on her feet, and then Thomas suddenly turned to her, his arms gripping her waist.

"Rosie..." he muttered, and then he was kissing her—not in passion, but in desperation, the way a drowning man might cling to a life preserver. Rosie returned the kiss, wrapping her arms around him, longing to imbue him with her own strength that was already flagging, to help him through whatever he was struggling with, the demon inside him, or maybe the ghost...

They stumbled off the path, and then Thomas was pulling her down to the ground.

"Thomas..." Rosie protested, although only faintly.

"Please, Rosie," he gasped out. "Please, for me. I need you. You don't know how I need you." He was pulling at her clothes, and there were leaves and twigs in her hair, and Rosie knew she didn't have the heart, or even the will, to resist. She loved this man, and he did need her. She knew it; she felt it.

She put her arms around him and kissed him, offering herself to him, yet she could not help but think back to how they'd stepped over the couples in that square in London, and how she'd been shocked and scandalized and a bit censorious all at once. So much, she thought as she held Thomas, had changed.

She saw Thomas once more, in August, before he left to return overseas. He seemed a bit more cheerful then, or at least a little less despairing, although Rosie still sensed that hard, brittle edge to him that she didn't particularly like.

He'd arranged a hotel room in Loughborough, along with the wedding rings, handing hers to her silently on the steps of the establishment before they walked in.

"When are you going to get me a real ring?" Rosie asked after they'd been shown to their room. She'd meant to sound teasing, but she feared she sounded a little shrewish instead.

"There aren't that many sparklers over in France, I'm afraid," he replied rather flatly as he shrugged out of his jacket and tossed it on the bed.

Chastened, Rosie stayed silent, and Thomas grimaced and then took her into his arms.

"I'm sorry, Rosie, darling," he said. "I know how I sound. I know how I feel. I just..." A breath shuddered out of him. "I have to go back, and I don't want to. If that makes me a coward, so be it." He pressed his face into her hair, his body as tense as a wire against hers.

"Oh, Thomas. Surely that's the opposite of cowardice—isn't true courage doing something even if you don't want to, even if you're afraid?" Gently, she touched his cheek. "I'm proud of you."

"I don't deserve you." He kissed her hair, her forehead, her nose, and then her lips. "I don't deserve you."

"I feel the same way about you," Rosie admitted shakily, and then for some time they didn't have to speak at all.

Later, as they lay in bed, he lit a cigarette and blew smoke up to the ceiling, seeming more resigned than sated.

"They say there's going to be a big push into Holland," Rosie ventured, and he shook his head wearily.

"You know I can't talk about it."

"Yes, I know." She snuggled against him. "Surely it won't be too much longer, though, till the end."

"From what I've seen of those SS devils, it's going to be long enough. They'll fight to the bitter end, to the last man." He stubbed out his cigarette and took her into his arms. "But I don't want to talk about any of that," he said, so they didn't.

They said goodbye at the gates to Beaumanor Hall; Rosie clung to Thomas for a few moments, not wanting to let him go, wondering when she would see and hold him next. Thomas clung right back, kissing her at least a dozen times all over her face, before finally, reluctantly, they parted.

"I'll write," Rosie promised him. "You can receive some letters, can't you?"

"Yes, as long as you write them to the 101st Airborne. I'll write too, I promise. I love you, Rosie. I'll always love you."

"And I'll always love you." Her voice choking a little, she waved and then walked slowly back through the manned gates. The two soldiers who were on duty looked decidedly po-faced. Rosie kept turning back to catch sight of Thomas, until there was a turn in the sweeping drive and then she could not see him at all.

The next few weeks were busy, which kept Rosie from pining too much, and at least she'd had letters from Violet and Jamie; Violet's beau, Andrew Smith, had made it through Normandy safely, and Jamie, dear Jamie, hadn't gone to France at all. He was stuck working as a mechanic in airfield in Felixstowe, fuming about it, while Rosie couldn't be happier. She knew her mother would be, as well.

Work continued apace, and in September she was granted

another forty-eight hours' leave to visit Violet and Beth in London. They'd hugged and laughed, and cried a little bit too, because there had been, of course, reports of the Normandy casualties, boys Rosie hadn't known very well, but boys all the same.

"Geoffrey Bell, the year above us at Queen's," Violet told her over cups of tea in the kitchen at South Street. "Mother wrote to tell me. Do you remember him? And Vera—do you remember funny old Vera? Her brother died on Juno Beach. I don't think he even made it onto shore."

There were others, too—far too many others.

"It feels almost as if several boys have died, when one does," Violet said sadly, "because you don't know what they might have become. A banker or a farmer or a poet? All the opportunities are lost. They'll never be able to find out, and we'll never know."

"At least your Andrew is safe," Rosie said, trying to hold onto a shred of optimism. "You're as keen on him as you were before?"

Violet smiled and ducked her head, seeming almost shy. "Even keener. It's the quiet ones who can steal your heart, Rosie, so watch out."

Rosie let out a little laugh. "I'm most certainly spoken for."

"You're sure about Thomas?"

"Sure about him?" Something in her prickled at Violet's slightly cautious tone. "As sure as I can be about anything." She thought of their last farewell. "Why wouldn't I be?"

"No reason," Violet said quickly. "No reason at all. It's just he's so very handsome, isn't he... I don't know if I could completely trust such a handsome man."

"Well, I can," Rosie said firmly. "And I do. Thomas and I are going to get married one day." She'd tried to sound certain, but she feared her tone was one of bravado, and yet she was sure. She *was*. And so was Thomas.

"Married!" Violet managed to look surprised, impressed, and skeptical all at once. "He's asked you, then?"

"Yes, I wouldn't have told you otherwise," Rosie replied with a touch of asperity. "He asked me once a few months ago, when he was on leave, and he said he'd ask me again, good and proper, with a ring and everything. So I shall have two proposals!" She tried to smile, even as she saw on Violet's face what her cousin was thinking as clearly as if she'd said it out loud. *But so far you've only had one.*

"Well, it sounds awfully exciting," she told Rosie, touching her hand, and Rosie couldn't bear to see the sympathy on her cousin's face. "*Awfully* exciting."

Rosie managed, during that leave, to see Jamie, who had come to London from his posting at Felixstowe; it had been wonderful to see her baby brother now looking so shockingly grown up.

"Why, you have to shave!" Rosie exclaimed in wonder, touching his cheek. "And I think you've grown at least an inch."

"I am nineteen, you know," he told her with a laugh.

"Yes, I know, it just feels like it's been so very long." The last time she'd seen her brother, he'd been in high school. Now he was a man.

"How's your time been over here in old Blighty?" he asked as he lit a cigarette, a habit he'd picked up since enlisting and one that certainly wouldn't have been tolerated back at home. "Any GIs steal your heart?"

"Well..." Rosie let out a little laugh and Jamie raised his eyebrows.

"Go on, then! Tell me about him."

Rosie hesitated, because while part of her was absolutely bursting to tell her brother all about Thomas, how wonderful he was and how much she loved him, her cousin's quiet skepticism was still ringing in her ears. The truth was, Thomas hadn't actually asked her to marry him, not in a way Rosie could tell her brother, anyway, and while there might not have been engagement rings over in France, there certainly were some in London. If he'd really wanted to buy a ring, he could have, surely. The realization was uncomfortable, indeed.

"There's not all that much to tell, really," Rosie said at last. "There is someone, but he's over in Europe, and you know what it's like in wartime. Who knows what will happen." She tried to give an insouciant shrug, but her lips trembled and her brother noticed.

"You really love this guy, don't you?"

"I..." Rosie found she couldn't go on.

Jamie reached over and squeezed her hand. "Well, for your sake, I hope he comes back in one piece."

Rosie managed to nod as she dabbed her eyes as discreetly as she could. "Yes," she agreed, "I certainly hope so, too."

A week later, Rosie listened to the news of the Allies' attack on Holland on the wireless in the mess hall, everyone silent as they heard about "the greatest airborne operation ever undertaken."

"In June, it was the greatest amphibious assault," someone muttered. "Now it's the greatest airborne operation. When will it stop?"

Rosie pressed one hand to her queasy middle as she heard about the thousands of planes and five hundred gliders that had flown over Holland, dropping parachutists into the night so the sky would have looked like a sea of falling stars. A sea of falling men, over ten thousand of them, including Thomas—and some, maybe even many, who would land to their deaths.

"Poor buggers," someone said in a low voice. "Being dropped in it like that, on your own. I heard most of the D-Day drops went to hell—some men over twenty miles from where they should be, with no cover, no defense, nothing at all. They were completely alone, them against the whole German army."

"That's defeatist talk," someone else said reprovingly, and Rosie's stomach heaved in protest at the thought of Thomas landing alone, utterly defenseless, under a starry, moonlit sky, just as he'd said before, open to attack... She pressed her hand more firmly to her middle, and then, with alarm, realized she was in danger of losing what little breakfast she'd had.

Quickly, she walked out of the room, hurrying to the toilet, closing her eyes as she retched up her breakfast. She sat back on her heels with a gasp, wiping her streaming eyes, and then tensing as she heard footsteps behind her.

"Here."

Susan handed her a handkerchief and Rosie murmured her thanks, glad it was only her roommate who had seen such an unfortunate display.

"I can't seem to hear the news without losing my lunch," she joked feebly. "Or, in this case, my breakfast."

Susan was silent for a moment. "Has it happened before?" she finally asked.

"No, not this bad." Rosie dabbed at her lips, grateful that her stomach was starting to settle. "But every time they turn the radio on in the morning, my stomach seems to start squirming. I suppose I need to buck up a bit, especially if Thomas is going to be over there for a good long while. I can't fall to pieces just because of the news."

"You think that's why you're being sick?" Susan asked, and Rosie heard the skepticism in her voice. She turned slightly to face her, the handkerchief still pressed to her mouth.

"What else would it be?" she asked, her voice muffled behind the cloth.

Susan was silent for a long moment, seeming uncharacteristically reluctant to answer.

"*Susan.*" Rosie lowered her hand from her mouth, the handkerchief clenched in one fist. "What exactly is it you're wanting to say?"

And yet somehow, before Susan even said it, Rosie knew. She'd known for a while, she realized, even though she hadn't let herself think about it, not even a tiny bit, so once again she had that disconcerting, shifting sensation of being completely unsurprised and shocked at the same time.

"Rosie," Susan said heavily, but without censure, "what if you're pregnant?"

CHAPTER NINETEEN

"How far along do you think you might be?"

They had gone up to their dormitory; Susan was sitting on the bed, her arms folded in her lap, while Rosie paced up and down the small room, ducking her head under the eaves every time she turned, her mind racing.

Pregnant. She couldn't be. She just couldn't. And yet, of course, she could. She certainly knew *that* much about the birds and the bees.

Rosie closed her eyes, her arms wrapped around her waist. "I... I don't really know."

"Well, you must know the last time you, *you know,*" Susan replied, sounding startlingly pragmatic. Of all the people to have this kind of conversation with, Rosie would never have chosen Susan, and yet it was Susan, prim, stuffy, censorious-seeming Susan, who was acting remarkably unfazed about Rosie's predicament. Far more unfazed than Rosie herself.

"Well, I suppose then it had to have been when I saw him in Loughborough," Rosie admitted in a mumble, unable to keep from blushing at the thought. "The last time we saw each other. But that was only a few weeks ago."

"And how long have you been feeling sick?"

"Not sick, just a bit queasy..." Rosie protested, as if it made any difference.

"Queasy, then," Susan amended, a bit impatiently. "How long?"

She shrugged helplessly. "A few weeks, I suppose. More than two, I think, although not as badly as I was today. I haven't really thought about it..." But perhaps she should have.

"Then you can't have fallen pregnant in August," Susan pointed out reasonably. "It must have been before." Rosie thought of her and Thomas in the park back in July, the way he'd held her, the twigs in her hair. "You must be a good two months gone, I should say."

Two months! Rosie whirled on her suddenly. "How do you know so much?" she cried.

Susan shrugged. "I've been working as a secretary since I was sixteen. Sadly, girls get into trouble all the time."

Rosie sank onto her bed, dropping her head into her hands. "You know, I think that must be about right," she confessed quietly. "It would have been July, then, when...." She stopped, gulping, before she felt her face crumple. "Oh, Susan." Her voice choked and she scrunched her eyes shut, her hands covering her face, longing to block out the world, if only for a few minutes. "What am I going to do?"

"Well, I wouldn't do anything dangerous if I were you," Susan replied after a moment, and Rosie thought of Nancy, back in Kitchener, saying much the same. *I know some girls might think about getting rid of it, but I couldn't do that... you hear stories about it going so terribly wrong...*

She'd felt so sorry for Nancy then, Rosie recalled, but she'd never, ever once considered that she might find herself in the exact same position. She would have scoffed at such a notion— yes, maybe even thought she was a little superior, assuming such a thing was impossible for someone like her, with education, with ambition.

Did she *ever* learn? Did she ever *change*?

"I'm not going to do anything dangerous," she told Susan heavily. "I couldn't."

In her last letter, Nancy had written that she'd had a beautiful baby boy; why, he must be coming on a year old now. She and Sam had married before he'd headed off to England, and her parents were pleased for her. Nancy had had her happy ending... but would Rosie get hers?

Rosie straightened, wiping her eyes. This wasn't the disaster it had first seemed like, she told herself. Thomas loved her, and they *were* going to get married. A baby had always been part of their plan—that couple of kids—if not *quite* so soon, but who knew, Thomas might even be happy about her news. If he survived for her to tell him...

"I'll be dismissed, though," she realized aloud. "In disgrace." The realization echoed through her. Unwed pregnant mothers were *not* welcome in the Canadian Women's Army Corps, that much she certainly knew, and neither would they be welcome serving at Beaumanor Hall. During her officer training, she'd attended enough lectures warning girls about venereal disease, as well as scaring them with stories of immediate dismissal if they ever found themselves in the family way. As soon as it became known she was pregnant, she'd be given her walking papers. And then what would she do?

"Well, that needn't happen for some time," Susan said practically. "You're thin as a rail now and since it's your first baby, you most likely won't show for ages. With some oversized jumpers, taking the waist of your skirt out a bit, why, I think you could get to five months without giving the game away, and maybe by that time your Thomas will be back and can marry you. You'd still have to leave, of course, but at least it won't be in disgrace."

Rosie stared at her in shocked wonder. "Susan, how on earth are you an expert on all this?"

"I told you, I've known girls who have gotten into trouble."

"Yes, but... did you help them?" Rosie realized how surprised she sounded at the notion, and Susan clearly did, too.

She pursed her lips in prune-like fashion. "I suppose you think I'd condemn them for it."

"Well..." *Yes*, Rosie thought, but didn't want to say.

"You don't know me as well as you think you do," Susan told her with some asperity. "As it happens, I helped a young girl at the office when she got in the family way. She was only fifteen, poor thing. She had the baby, in the end, but she had to give it up." She took a breath, let it out slowly. "And the truth is, once upon a time, that was me."

Rosie's mouth dropped open and she could not hide her complete and utter shock. "*What...*"

"Not pregnant, mind you," Susan said quickly. "Gracious, no!" For a second, she looked scandalized, and far more like herself. "But the baby? Yes. I told you I was raised by my aunt, but that wasn't exactly true. It was what I was led to believe for most of my life, until I was twenty, but the truth is my 'aunt' was really my mother. She'd fallen pregnant out of wedlock—I'm not even sure she had a beau, to tell you the truth. I never knew my father's name. Her parents insisted she give me up, and her sister and her husband hadn't been able to have a baby, and so they were apparently happy to take me. But then they died in the flu epidemic when I was only a few months old. My mother took me back, but for propriety's sake, she continued the fiction that I was her niece. She only told me when she came over poorly, and thought she was going to die. She felt she had to confess... but she lived another eight years, and so it wasn't quite the deathbed confession she thought it was." Susan smiled faintly.

"Oh, Susan." Rosie shook her head slowly. "I had no idea."

"Well, of course you didn't, because I didn't tell you," Susan replied briskly. "And how on earth would you guess? Never mind. That's not important now. What's important is what *you're* going to do."

Rosie's hands crept to her middle. There was a baby in there, a tiny, precious life. Part of her, part of Thomas, curled up and growing like a seed. As appalling as she'd first found the news, she now realized what a wondrous thing it truly was. "I have to find a way to tell Thomas," she said slowly. "And if you really think I can hide it for that long..."

"With my help, you can," Susan replied firmly. "It's a good job I know about these things, and, more importantly, that I'm a dab seamstress. With a little needlework, no one will see your bump till you're as big as a house, at least."

Rosie wasn't sure she had Susan's confidence in that matter, but hiding her pregnancy for as long as she could seemed the best, and really, the only plan, she could come up with, and so she soldiered through the days, keeping her secret to herself.

Thankfully, the morning sickness eased up after a few more weeks, and she started to regain some of her energy. She also gained a tiny little bump—barely a swell under her skirt, but noticeably there. If she buttoned up her jacket, it was fine, but it wouldn't be forever, or not even for a few more weeks, if that. And then what would she do?

Soon after she'd realized she was pregnant, she'd written to Thomas. It had been a difficult letter to write, as well as a painful one, because even though she longed for him to be as happy as she hoped to be herself, she realized she couldn't be entirely sure. The last time she'd seen him, he'd seemed so jaded, with that angry, despairing edge. She understood its cause, of course, with the trials of war, but it was a reminder that perhaps she didn't know her fiancé as well as she wished she did. In the end, she kept the letter as simple—and as hopeful —as she could:

Dear Thomas,

I think of and pray for you every day over there, as I know you must do for me. My greatest hope is that the war will end within the year, and we will start building that wonderful dream you had of a white house with a picket fence, a dog, and a couple of kids. It's a nice dream, I think, and one, as it happens, I am already beginning to build. You see, the truth is, Thomas, that I am expecting. It was a complete surprise to me, although perhaps it shouldn't have been! I hope it won't be such a shock for you, and that we can talk about it properly when we see each other next. I am glad, Thomas, even if I'm scared, too. It really is a wonderful dream.

Your Rosie.

She felt both sick with apprehension and relieved that she'd sent it, and that the matter was no longer in her hands. Now all she had to do was wait for his response—and pray that he was alive and well, and when he was next on leave, he really would marry her.

A month passed with no word from him, which Rosie told herself was completely understandable, considering the nature of the situation. The news was full of the Allies' recent victories; the 101st Airborne was on the move, having been parachuted into Holland in September. They'd liberated Antwerp and several other towns and villages, and even penetrated thirty kilometers into Germany. It was wonderful news, celebrated as a great victory, but the pace of advance meant that troops wouldn't always get their mail delivered. All she needed, Rosie told herself, was to be patient.

But it was hard to be patient when every day her waistband felt a little tighter, and even the wonderfully pragmatic Susan clucked and shook her head as she let out a few more seams.

"You're only four months gone and you're showing more than I thought you would," she told Rosie, in something of an accusing manner.

"I can't help it, you know," Rosie replied, trying to smile although she felt desperately afraid. She didn't think she'd mind leaving the CWAC if she was married to Thomas; she'd embroidered many pleasant daydreams of their necessarily hasty wedding in London, the country cottage he'd rent for her and their baby while he went off to win the war. She'd knit booties and write letters and grow their baby, and then he would come back and take her to the States, where they would be a family.

It didn't particularly matter, in these daydreams, that she'd never had such domestic fantasies before, and in any case, she didn't really know how to knit. It was enough to know she'd be able to care for their child, and that they'd be together, and they'd be safe.

What she didn't want, however, and this Rosie knew with an absolute certainty, was to be found out and then summarily and disgracefully dismissed. So she continued to squeeze into her skirts and wear a bulky jumper; fortunately, it was now November and the weather had turned chilly, so her attire was perfectly excusable. But she still didn't hear from Thomas.

At the beginning of December, she felt the baby kick for the first time—a tiny flutter, like a tickle on the inside. She was on shift, in the middle of transcribing, and she dropped two letters in the message as she let out a gasp, before the girl next to her gave her a narrow look and Rosie hurried to keep writing down the code. A kick, an actual kick! An actual baby.

But no letters from Thomas.

All through December, Rosie did her best to keep her spirits up. She told herself Thomas might not have gotten her letter, or his own letter might have been delayed. She reminded herself how much he loved her, the promises he'd made. She told herself to be patient, to wait, to trust. What other choice did she have?

She lay in bed night after night, her hands laced over her middle, and willed Thomas to write—and her baby to grow. As unexpected as this child was, she knew she already loved him or her, quite desperately. And she would continue to do so, she vowed, no matter what happened, even if she ended up dismissed in disgrace. This baby was innocent—and loved.

"What will you do," Susan asked one evening, in her practical way, "if they find out?"

Rosie considered the question as she peeled an orange; Susan had managed to get her hands on one in the village shop and very generously given it to her, insisting a growing baby needed all the vitamins it could get. "I suppose I shall have to go home," she said after a moment. She thought of Nancy saying how her father would kill her, if her mother didn't first. Rosie knew her parents would be disappointed that she was about to become an unwed mother, but they wouldn't be *angry*.

"If you can get a passage home," Susan told her. "In these times, I'm not sure you could. Any space will be reserved for the badly wounded, I should think, if there are ships going that way at all. Everything's going to Europe now, and understandably so."

Rosie realized she had not considered that. "Then... then I'll have to have the baby over here," she said, but with a quaver in her voice. She was currently paid four pounds, five shillings a week, and she'd managed to save quite a bit of it, but certainly not enough to set up house somewhere, and provide for a child. Not nearly.

"There are homes for unwed mothers," Susan suggested

after a moment, "but I don't know what kinds of places they are, or whether you're allowed to keep the baby after."

Rosie shook her head with a shudder. She remembered how Gracie had told her about the home she'd gone to, back in New York, when she'd been in a similar predicament, and how awful it had been. Her baby had died, but in any case, she wouldn't have been allowed to keep it. Rosie had no intention of falling into the same awful trap. "No, I'm not going to do that," she said firmly. "I'll figure something out."

And yet Rosie was realistic to acknowledge it was certainly not going to be as easy as that. Unwed mothers were the pariahs of society, as if they had something terribly catching. She'd be lucky if someone would be willing to rent her a room, never mind being able to find some work to do, or a way to keep body and soul together. If only Thomas would write her! It would make such a difference, she thought, and he might even be granted leave soon. He'd been over in Holland for three months now, after all, and he'd been sent back once before, after the Normandy invasion. Perhaps he would be again.

The very next week, on the sixteenth of December, the Battle of Ardennes commenced. Rosie listened on the radio about the gallant soldiers holding onto the crucial town of Bastogne, surviving siege and snow and starvation, desperately waiting for a break in the weather so Eisenhower could send reinforcements. She didn't know for certain if the 101st Airborne was stationed there, but she sensed it. It would make sense why Thomas hadn't been able to write, if he was trapped somewhere. *Trapped...*

It seemed as if everyone at Beaumanor was holding their breath, waiting to hear about the fate of the battle, but Rosie thought no one could be as invested as she was, not even Violet back in London who was hoping to hear from Andrew.

Rosie hadn't written Violet to tell her about the baby; while she hoped her cousin would be supportive, she knew she couldn't be entirely sure. Violet, for all her daring ways, had something of a surprising prudish streak, and Rosie didn't fancy being under her judgmental eye.

Over the next few weeks, the Germans fell back, regrouped, attacked. The Allies held the city in the midst of a cold, snowy winter. The day after Christmas, the weather thankfully turned, so supplies and equipment could be dropped in. Rosie was five months pregnant now, and knew, with a sort of weary resignation, that it wouldn't be long before she was found out. The cold weather helped, but, as Susan remarked, a bulky jumper could only hide so much, and her bump was decidedly visible to the discerning eye, even underneath her heavy clothing.

"And, I'm sorry to say it," Susan had told her, "but you are starting to waddle."

Rosie did her best to avoid crowds, eating alone and going from shift to mess hall to bed without saying so much as hello. She kept herself swathed in jumpers and wore her coat in the hut, which many of the girls did anyway, because it was so cold. But it wouldn't work forever, she knew. It might not even work for another week.

And then, in January, a letter came from Violet. At first, Rosie was glad to read her news; she always looked forward to hearing her cousin's cheerfully gossipy missive—except it wasn't like that at all.

Dearest Rosie,

I am writing with sad—very sad—news. There's no other way to say it, and I won't sugarcoat it for you, or pretend it isn't what I know you must have been fearing, just as I have for Andrew. You know me, I'll always tell you the truth, even

*when it hurts, and this will hurt, Rosie, I know it will, and I'm
so sorry. I can't imagine you will have heard, because it's the
kind of news they only tell families and wives, don't they, and
you're not that. Not yet. But Andrew wrote to say that Thomas
was taken at Ardennes, and has most likely been killed. You
know the Germans, they don't take prisoners, not now, when
they're about to lose the war, and Andrew saw him cut down,
left in a snowy field. I'm so sorry, and I know it looks horrible,
to have it written out like that, but there's no good pretending
otherwise, is there? I know how much you loved him. I'm so
dreadfully, dreadfully sorry for you.*

All my love,

Violet.

Rosie didn't remember the next few moments. In one
moment, she was holding the letter, her head buzzing like the
static on the receiver set, and the next she was on the floor, and
Susan was slapping her cheeks, insisting, in her scolding way,
that she must wake up now, really she must.

"Rosie... Rosie! I don't want to have to call someone, and
you don't want me to, either. Wake up!"

"I'm awake." The words came slowly, as if surfacing from
the deep, as she blinked dazedly up at Susan. She was sprawled
on the floor of their dormitory, the pages of Violet's letters scattered next to her, feeling very tired, everything in her aching.
"I've never actually fainted before."

"Well, you gave me a fright. I came up here and you were
stretched out on the floor, out cold. I thought—well, never mind
what I thought. You need to eat more, I think—"

"It's not that." The contents of the letter came rushing back,
and wincing, Rosie scooted up into a sitting position. "It's
Thomas, Susan. I received a letter from Violet, who heard from

Thomas's friend Andrew... Oh, I can't say it." A lump was forming in her throat and yet she didn't think she would actually cry. Some sorrow went too deep for tears.

Wordlessly, she gestured to the pages lying on the floor, and after a second's pause, Susan took them up and read through them quickly. Rosie wrapped one arm around her knees, resting the other on her bump. *Poor little fatherless baby...*

"Oh, Rosie." Susan's voice was quiet, without any of its stinging briskness. "I'm so sorry."

All Rosie could do was nod, her gaze on her knees. They were both silent for several long minutes, and Rosie began to feel the cold creep in through the floor, into her bones. Outside, it was getting dark; they needed to draw the blackout curtains, yet she felt as if she couldn't move.

Then she heard Susan gasp, and she looked up, but Susan wasn't looking at her; she was looking at the floor.

"Oh, Rosie," Susan said, and she sounded, for the first time, actually frightened.

"What is it?" Rosie asked, at the same time she felt a dampness between her thighs, on her skirt.

"Rosie," Susan said, "you're bleeding."

CHAPTER TWENTY

MARCH 1945

London, England

"The major will see you now."

Rosie walked slowly into Major Davis's office at CMHQ. The last time she'd seen the stern-looking woman had been when she'd been informed she had been recommended for a special posting. Then, the major had been briskly approving; now, the mood was quite different, her face set in weary, disappointed lines, yet Rosie found she couldn't even summon the energy to care.

When Susan had seen that she'd been bleeding back at Beaumanor in January, she'd insisted she had to see a doctor, even though it meant revealing she was pregnant. And Rosie had been too scared to think about anything else; with cramps banding her stomach and a terror stealing through her soul, she'd let Susan rush her to the village doctor, who had sent her to hospital in Loughborough, where, in the space of a single night, she had lost her baby and almost bled to death.

The weeks after were a blur of pain and fear; she remembered the nurse's disapproving look, her cold, grasping hands, the drip of blood into a metal bowl. She remembered how the nurse had whisked her daughter away—she'd learned it was a girl later, and only by demanding to know—so she saw nothing but a tuft of Thomas's blond hair and a pale, wrinkled cheek. She remembered the doctor telling her, as if it were her fault, that she'd almost died from the blood loss, and she remembered him saying, sniffily, that "judging by the creature's size and condition," the baby must have died several weeks ago, and so it had nothing to do with the shock of Violet's letter, or her fall.

"No doubt the fall brought on labor," he'd told her, "but the baby had died sometime before, in utero, perhaps an accident with the umbilical cord. These things do happen, and in your case, *Miss* Lyman, I think it is certainly a mercy."

Rosie had not been able to reply to such a cold statement; she'd simply turned her head, resting limply on her pillow, away from him and closed her eyes.

She'd stayed in the hospital for nearly a month, as weak as a kitten and feeling utterly hopeless. Susan had visited her, told her all the news from Beaumanor about the war, how the Canadian forces were liberating cities in Germany, along with the Soviets and the Americans, and apparently Hitler himself hadn't made a public appearance since January, and some even wondered if he was still alive.

"There has been terrible news coming out of Germany about these camps they had for the Jews," she had said, but then added hurriedly, "but you don't want to hear about that right now. The important thing is, we're winning, Rosie. The war will be over soon—some say maybe in weeks, certainly no more than a few months."

Such news had served as a thread to keep her tethered to reality, if only just, but Rosie found she preferred to float on a sea of nothingness—sleeping as often as she could, and simply staring into space when she could not—because at least then she could forget that her fiancé was dead, her baby was dead, and she was most likely going to be dismissed from military service in complete disgrace.

But she could not stay bobbing in that sea of nothingness forever. Her strength improved, even if her spirits did not, and four weeks after she'd arrived, she was briskly told that someone worthier needed her bed, and hospitals weren't hotels for fainting lilies, especially ones who had gotten themselves in trouble.

Back at Beaumanor, she was told with brisk, unsmiling efficiency, to report to CMHQ in London; her services would not be needed there any longer. Captain Sillicoe, in a moment of surprising kindness, had stopped her in the hall to say gruffly, "If I had my way, you'd still be on the set, because you're one of my best listeners and right now we need all the ears we can get. But it's not my decision, and your Quacks have their own way of doing things, so there you are."

Yes, here she was, Rosie thought dully as she stared at Major Davis. Here she was, indeed.

"Your position is being terminated, effective immediately," the officer said without preamble. "As I'm sure you know."

"Yes." Rosie didn't bother to say anything else, or offer any excuse, for she knew there was none she could give that would be accepted. Her fate had already been decided. Perhaps it had been decided months ago, when she'd slipped that brass ring on her finger and agreed to go into that hotel, the course of her life forever changed.

Why, she wondered with a sudden savage spurt of bitterness, were women always the ones holding the bag? The *baby*? Or not, in her case, but even then, it didn't matter. She'd still receive the blame. Thomas would never even be mentioned.

"You won't be the first girl to have gotten yourself in this situation," Major Davis said, with some kindness, "or the last. But as I'm sure you know from the officer training you had, the

Corps simply cannot allow any whisper of gossip concerning their servicewomen's loose morals. It's bad enough, what people have always said back home about the Corps, and it has negatively affected both recruitment and morale. We can't have them proved right, not in the slightest. I'm sure you understand."

Rosie simply nodded, swaying slightly where she stood, for the trip from Loughborough to London had exhausted her, and although she'd been strong enough to leave the hospital, she still did not feel strong. "Am I to be sent back to Canada?" she asked.

"Yes, ideally it would be as soon as possible," the major replied. "That is the protocol for situations such as yours." The hesitation in her voice made Rosie wearily wait for more. "However, the war is almost over," she said after a moment. "God willing, this is the final push, and all our resources, understandably, must be used to that end. It makes sense, therefore, for you to stay in this country until the end of the war, when transport can be more safely and easily arranged."

"All right," Rosie said. She found she didn't much care where she was, although she realized she was not particularly looking forward to going home and telling her parents what had happened. She knew they would be supportive, but they would also be shocked and disappointed. It was one thing, she supposed, to be willing to invite a troubled friend like Nancy into your home; it was another when it was your daughter who had gotten herself into such trouble.

"Naturally, you cannot stay in barracks," Major Davis continued. "It would set a most unfortunate example. But I trust you can make your own living arrangements for the short term. If you let us know your situation, we will alert you when transportation can be provided, which, as I said, will be as soon as possible."

So she was, more or less, being hung out to dry, Rosie realized. Again, she could not summon the energy or emotion to care. She thought of Gracie, the sorrow on her face when she'd talked about the baby that had died; back then, Rosie had felt a flicker of pity for her aunt, but not much more.

Now, when she had experienced the same grief, when she had felt and touched and *tasted* it, so it lay on her tongue and burrowed into her eyes; it crept into her very bones, twined through every sinew so it was an absolute and essential part of her, she realized how it made you a different person. And it was a person, she came to realize, that people did not seem to much care to know, because even in the midst of war, when everyone had tasted some kind of grief, dealing with someone else's soon became tiresome.

She saw that with Violet, whom she had to tell, of course; there could be no hiding it, considering her present circumstances, and in any case, Rosie knew the gossip would get back to her. After her meeting at CMHQ, she arranged to rent a room in a widow's house in Clapham. It was the sixth place she'd tried, after being turned away from all the others, her potential landlords suspicious and condemning of a woman alone who wasn't in uniform and had nowhere to go. Finally, the widow, a woman in her forties with a careworn face and a pragmatic manner, told her she could stay in her guest room, with breakfast and supper included, for two pounds a week.

"No visitors, and no smoking or drinking," the woman, Mrs. Mason, had stated flatly. "I run a respectable house, but I am fair."

Rosie had agreed, having no desire for any of those things, and then she'd gone to see Violet, telling her everything over a pot of tea in a Lyons Corner House, a dismally pedestrian setting for so deep a sorrow.

"Oh, Rosie." Violet looked both saddened and shocked as Rosie finished her litany of tragedies. It sounded like one of those melodramatic operas, she thought with a flicker of something almost, but not quite, like humor, and yet it had happened to her, every single bit of it. "I had no idea. Why didn't you tell me?"

Rosie shrugged. "I was waiting for Thomas to come back."

"Yes, but when you were in hospital..." Violet protested, "and even before! I would have helped you, you know. I would have visited you, at the very least."

Rosie pushed her teacup around on its saucer, unable even to take a sip. "I don't know how you could have."

"And they've let you go without anything? That's despicable—"

"I don't blame them, not really, and fortunately I have enough saved to manage for a few months. Everyone says the war is going to be over soon, anyway."

"It had better be," Violet replied darkly. "Ever since they've started launching these V-2 rockets, I've been desperate to get out of London. They're so much worse than the doodlebugs—at least you could hear those coming. But with these new rockets, there's no warning, they land in broad daylight, and they can take out a whole street." She shook her head, shuddering as she reached for her tea.

"Yes, I've seen." The street next to her landlady's in Clapham had been devastated by a V-2 rocket; there was hardly anything left. Six people had been killed, including a three-year-old-child.

"It's just all so awful, isn't it?" Violet remarked quietly. "All that excitement around D-Day, thinking it was nearly the end, and that was almost a year ago. We just want it to be over now. Everyone's so *tired*."

"Yes." Rosie managed a nod, although she felt so empty inside, her voice came out flat and emotionless. Better that, though, than raging or wailing, which was what she knew she would do if she let herself feel—anything.

"Oh, Rosie, I know this must be so very hard for you." Violet touched her hand briefly, reminding Rosie of the wing of a butterfly, barely felt and gone in an instant. "But... in a way, it's for the best, don't you think?" she continued uncertainly. "With Thomas gone, you wouldn't want to have to raise a baby on your own, and of course not being wed..." She bit her lip. "Of course it's terrible, I'm not saying it isn't at all, but... there is a silver lining, isn't there? At least, in time? You can move past this..." She gazed at Rosie with hope in her eyes, as if willing her to smile and nod and agree. Laugh, perhaps, too. *Oh yes, it was a close shave, wasn't it? All's well that ends well, though, thank heavens for that!*

Rosie stared at her cousin for a long moment, knowing she had no words to say, no reply to make. There were no silver linings, she thought, absolutely none at all, but Violet wouldn't understand that. She wouldn't want to, Rosie realized, because she didn't want to deal with this new Rosie, this lifeless woman who had become so haggard and grief-stricken, and well, not much *fun*.

"Rosie..." Violet began, her tone managing to be both abject and a little bit impatient, and Rosie reached for her purse.

"I'm sorry, but I should go." She took a few coins out of her purse and dropped them on the table with a clatter.

"Don't go!" Violet exclaimed. "Rosie, please. You know I didn't mean to upset you—"

"Take care of yourself, Violet," she said, and she walked out of the tearoom without looking back.

As the weeks passed, Rosie found herself thinking less about the daughter she never came to know—it was simply too painful— and more about Thomas. She punished herself by picturing his last moments the way Violet had described them—cut down in a snowy field somewhere in Holland, forgotten, frozen. Or had he simply been shot and killed in an instant, his life snuffed out in the matter of a second or two?

She remembered him as she'd first met him, laughing and leaning against the bar in Rainbow Corner, and then later, with her lying in his arms, feeling perfectly content. She thought of him as she'd last seen him, with that hard, desperate edge, yet still clinging to her, and her to him. Would he have lost that jadedness when the war was over? Would she have helped him to, or would he have been forever changed, as she now felt she was?

At the end of March, she decided, suddenly and certainly, that she wanted to write his family. She knew better than to tell them about the baby, of course, but Thomas had told her he'd written about her in his letters home, had assured her his parents were excited to meet her, and in this new, bombed-out world where she felt completely adrift, with no role, no child, no fiancé, she craved a connection of some sort, even one as tenuous as this.

She realized she didn't know their address, but Thomas had told her he lived in a small town in Connecticut—Greenwich, just like in England—and Rosie hoped that a letter addressed to Mr. and Mrs. Crewe of Greenwich, Connecticut would reach its intended recipients, and that they would be glad to hear from someone who had loved Thomas as they had.

She poured her heart out in that letter, more, she realized even as she wrote it, than she should have, since she was writing to strangers, but she knew they loved Thomas, just as she loved him, and just like with the signaler whose fist she had come to know, this knowledge forged an intimacy in her mind that, in her sensible moments, she knew wasn't really there at all.

And yet she still wrote—of how she and Thomas had met, of the dream he'd shared with her, of the ring he'd been going to buy. She wrote that she'd like to meet them one day, if they were willing, and how lovingly Thomas had spoken of them.

She said how she thought of their son every day, and she'd always love him, until her dying day. She signed and sealed the letter, posting it quickly, before she could change her mind about all the florid and flowery phrases she'd used, the sentiments she'd gushed on about, so unlike her, and yet strangely necessary at the time.

They might not even reply, she cautioned herself, but all the same, she knew the simple act of writing had, in some way, made her feel better, almost like a bloodletting, a necessary outpouring of her grief.

At the end of April, when the Soviets were already in Berlin, the Americans by the River Elbe, everyone waiting with held breath for the final end that would surely come any day, Rosie received her reply.

Her heart lifted with hope when she saw the unfamiliar writing, the postmark from the United States, and she slipped the letter out of the envelope with an expectant smile on her face.

Miss Lyman:

I do not know how you came to know about us, for I doubt very much it was through my son, but I am writing to make it clear that my wife and I have no possible interest in meeting with you, or hearing anything about you, ever again. Our son Thomas Crewe was engaged to a lovely young woman here in Greenwich, and had been for nearly a year when he went overseas. She is, as you can imagine, utterly grief-stricken by his death, as are we, and your letter was a most unwelcome and unpleasant shock, and one we have no intention of sharing with her. Whatever happened between you and our son, if indeed anything did—and I very much question the veracity of your sordid story!—it is a matter in which we have absolutely no interest. Please do not write or communicate with us ever again. If you do, please be assured we will be contacting our lawyer.

From,

Thomas Crewe Sr.

For a second, Rosie was back in the dormitory in Beaumanor, a buzzing in her brain, the world going in and out of focus. The letter started to slide from her hand. Then she took a deep breath, blinked the world back into view, and very neatly folded the letter and slipped it back into its envelope.

Engaged to a lovely young woman...

No, she could not think about that. She simply could not. She would not. She sealed it up in a box in her mind, just as she had the letter in its envelope, and did not think about it at all.

"There you are," Mrs. Mason said as she came up to Rosie in the front hall, wearing her second best dress and a slightly squashed hat. "It's time for the party."

"The party..." Rosie stared at her blankly, the letter still in her hand.

"For the war orphans," Mrs. Mason reminded her a bit impatiently.

Then Rosie remembered that her landlady had invited—really, insisted—that she attend a party for war orphans in the East End where she'd been volunteering for the last few months.

"I've let you mope for nearly a month," she'd told Rosie severely, "because I could tell you had your own grief, and heaven knows I understand what that's like. But it's no good staring out the window for the rest of your life, my girl. You need to do something. There's a little party for the war orphans in the East End I've been invited to help with, and I want you to come with me."

Rosie had agreed, because she could tell her landlady would brook no dissent, but she had not particularly relished the idea of attending. In the month since she'd returned to London, and this half-life of hers, she had, despite what Mrs. Mason had said, roused herself at least a little. She'd begun to go for walks, gazing out at the damaged streets and beginning to accept, slowly, the nature of her own loss, as well as the realization that no one in this war was immune to grief. Her situation was terrible, but it was not unique, but even so, she knew she did not want to go spend time with motherless children whose lives would be even more hopeless than hers; she didn't think she could bear it.

And now this new grief, that cast all the others into question. Had Thomas ever loved her at all?

No, she could not think of it. *She could not.*

"Yes, I'm coming," she told Mrs. Mason, her voice only a little faint, and she slipped the letter into the pocket of her skirt and went to get her hat and coat.

They took the Tube to the East End, where Rosie had never been, and as they emerged from the station, she was shocked by the amount of devastation, whole streets cratered or completely levelled, houses in a row of terraces without walls or completely gone, reminding her of missing teeth; the area had been far harder hit than any other she'd seen in London.

The party was in a gloomy little hall, with nothing more than some paper streamers and a plate of Spam sandwiches to make it festive, a horde of children galloping around excitedly so Rosie took an instinctive step back. She knew she did not want to be there, she didn't want to be anywhere, and the letter lay in her pocket, as heavy as a stone.

"Come on, then," Mrs. Mason said briskly. "We can put the party food out at least."

Rosie helped her lay out some sorry-looking cakes on a plate as the children raced around. In the midst of them all was the most magnificent woman she'd ever seen—topping six feet, with steel-gray hair and a lively, intelligent face. She seemed completely unfazed by the commotion all around her, a slight smile playing about her full lips as if she were very much enjoying the noise and activity.

It wasn't until the children had sat down, the room falling to sudden silence as they attacked the sandwiches with an enthusiasm that clearly came from hunger, that the woman came over to greet Rosie, who had retreated to the side of the room; Mrs. Mason had gone to refill the children's cups of milk.

"You look a little bit lost, my dear," the woman said with a smile. "Are you sure you're in the right place?"

Startled, Rosie wasn't sure what to say. She'd been simply existing for so long, and especially since she'd received that letter; she had no energy for emotion, no energy for anything at all. She couldn't let herself have it, because she had no idea what would happen. She might collapse or implode; she might scream and never stop. So she stayed silent.

The woman cocked her head, her dark brown gaze sweeping slowly and thoroughly over her. "My name is Marie Paneth," she said, and Rosie realized she spoke with a slight German accent, certainly an oddity in these times. "And you are?"

"Rosie Lyman," she replied after a moment. Marie Paneth seemed to be waiting for more, and Rosie found herself suddenly seized by a wild recklessness. "And you're right," she added, realizing she had nothing—absolutely nothing more—to lose. "I am lost, and not even a bit. I am completely and utterly and *hopelessly* lost and I don't know what to do." And then she simply stared at this unknown woman, this complete stranger, wondering what on earth she would say to such a statement, and one that had come from the depths of her being, that she couldn't even find it in herself to regret.

Marie Paneth smiled gently and took Rosie's hand, drawing her more into the room and its happy chaos. "Then, I think," she told her, "you are actually in the right place, after all."

CHAPTER TWENTY-ONE

JUNE 1945

London, England

The world was celebrating—or at least London was. In the three weeks since VE Day had been announced, there had been endless parties, carousing in the streets, parades and laughter and a wild and exultant joy as everyone had rejoiced in the end of the war. Rosie had witnessed it all as if from afar, grateful, of course, that the hostilities had finally ceased, yet unable to bestir herself any more than that.

Since the party for the war orphans in April, she had come to the play center Marie Paneth ran in Shoreditch almost every day to help with the children—making food, playing with them, or simply sitting and watching them draw. It had been a wonderful distraction from her own grief, and had provided her with a comforting sort of numbness she drew around herself like a cloak. When she was with the children, she found she didn't need to think. She could keep herself from remembering. After a while, she could even keep herself from feeling almost anything at all.

Marie Paneth was a great proponent of letting children express themselves however they chose—through play, through art or music, or simply by sitting still. It suited Rosie perfectly, to watch them and let them be, because that was all she wanted for herself.

She'd thought the grief of losing both Thomas and her daughter had been bad enough, but receiving the letter from the Crewes had cast those griefs into a fresh and awful light, and made her doubt everything—if she let herself think about it. Still, in the sleepless nights where she stared up at the ceilings, the questions came. Had anything at all been real? Had Thomas received her letter and ignored it because the last thing he'd wanted was for her to have his child? The dream of the house and the picket fence and even the damned dog—had it all been for someone else, this lovely young woman who had been waiting for him back at Greenwich?

She absolutely wasn't willing to let herself think about it, and in those waking hours in the middle of the night, her mind skated over these questions and then backed away gratefully. During the day, as a child clambered into her lap and another one thrust her drawing in her face, Rosie managed not to think about them at all.

Of course, she knew this numb limbo would not last forever. There was talk of some CWACs going to the Pacific and others being sent to Europe, to assist in the management of the demobilization of soldiers, along with the many camps for displaced persons, or DPs, that were being set up across Germany. Others were simply looking forward to going home.

Rosie had met with Violet once, an awkward and stilted conversation over cups of tea. Violet was hoping to stay in London until Andrew was demobbed; Beth had put her name forward to go to the Pacific. Rosie suspected transport would be arranged for her sooner or later, although sometimes she wondered if she'd been forgotten by the Corps; perhaps she could disappear into the East End of London and no one would even notice, much less care. It was not an entirely unappealing thought. She felt as if she wanted to disappear from herself.

Unfortunately, her small amount of savings was running out, and she was not willing to cable her parents for more. She had not told them about any of it—Thomas's death, her pregnancy, the loss of her baby, her dismissal. Jamie, of course, knew there had been someone, but that was all, and she wasn't about to tell him anything more, although she'd seen him once, right at the end of the war. He'd come to London and they'd gone out to dinner, and Rosie had almost managed to act like her old self.

When Jamie had asked her about "her GI," Rosie had smiled and shaken her head. "It didn't come to anything, after all," she'd said, and thankfully her brother had left it at that. He was looking forward to going home, and hoped to be demobbed in the next few months, and Rosie had made similar noises, although she didn't feel ready to go home at all.

She hadn't written her parents at all in months, which she knew would have distressed them, and yet even so, she could not bring herself to write lies, which is all she knew she'd be able to do. She'd never even told them about Thomas, hadn't dared, and now she wondered if somehow she'd always known, or maybe just feared, that none of it had been going to last.

But, at some point, as summer burst upon a bedraggled yet hopeful world, she knew she would have to do something. She would have to go home, or at least go somewhere. Find a way forward, even when she felt completely stalled inside.

"I wonder," Marie said to her one day as she was washing up in the little kitchen, after giving the children at the center lunch, "if you've thought about what you will do next."

"Next?" Rosie repeated, swirling suds in the washbasin. "I have not thought about any 'nexts' at all, really." She had not told Marie what had happened to her, but she had never felt she'd needed to. Something about the woman's worldliness—she had been born in Vienna, lived in Amsterdam and Indonesia, traveled to Paris and New York, been married, divorced, had children, as well as affairs, and, as a Jew, been forced to emigrate to England in 1939—made Rosie think she'd guessed the nature of it, at least.

"Well, there is always a next, whether you think about it or not," Marie replied with a faint smile. "This center will be closing down—relatives will come for these children, others will be taken to orphanages. The government has already decided it will no longer be needed."

A low sigh escaped Rosie. "I suppose I shall have to return to Canada," she said heavily. She had told Marie that much, at least, about her situation and family.

"You sound as if you don't want to."

Rosie thought of her parents waiting back at their house on Elizabeth Street, her father's law office, the lovely limestone buildings of Queen's. It all felt like a lifetime ago—two or three lifetimes, even. She could not imagine going back, taking up where she left off, not in any shape or form. "No," she said at last, "not really. But I don't know what else I would do."

"I have a suggestion."

Rosie glanced at Marie, her dark eyes alight, that small, knowing smile playing about her mouth. Over the last few months, she'd seen what a force Marie Paneth was to be reckoned with—towering over all women, and most men, once named "The Belle of Vienna," she was a formidable presence who incited awe in almost everyone she came across. Rosie was amazed such a woman had taken an interest in her.

"What is your suggestion?" she asked, a faint flicker of curiosity licking through her like a flame.

"I have been asked to assist at a school that is being set up near Windermere," she said. "Do you know the place?"

Rosie shook her head, although she recalled her mother's old friend Ruby McCallister had mentioned it.

"It is in the Lake District, very beautiful, but with very English weather." Marie smiled briefly. "Very rainy. They are repurposing some barracks that had been built for seaplane factory workers to make this school." She paused. "It is a school for children, Jewish children, most of them Polish, who survived the camps." She raised the dark slashes of her eyebrows. "You have heard of the camps?"

The photographs, stark and awful, of the liberation of Bergen-Belsen and Buchenwald, had been in the newspapers since April. Rosie swallowed and nodded. "Yes, although only a little."

"These children survived those camps, but their families did not. They are orphans, utterly alone in the world. They are being flown over here, to Windermere, to recover and to heal, at least until January, when they will most likely be placed elsewhere, in homes or hostels."

"That sounds... admirable," Rosie replied helplessly. "I'm glad there is a place for them to go."

"And there is a place for you to go," Marie returned gently. "The school needs volunteers for the next few months. These Windermere children need love and care. And I believe broken calls to broken, *meine schatzi*. Don't you think?" She cocked her head in that deliberate way she had, her gaze sweeping slowly over Rosie, who stood there, wrist-deep in soap suds, considering the surprising offer.

Broken calls to broken. Yes, she was broken. She knew she was, shattered into pieces, broken into tiny bits. These last few months had been helpful, in their own way, but it had been more of a much-needed numbing than anything else. She still felt as if she were a shattered version of herself, all cracks and splinters, and there was a terrible, wild grief inside her, a howl that slipped out through the cracks in her weaker moments, when she let it. How could she possibly help children, children such as these who were even more broken than she was?

"I don't know that I'd be much use at all," Rosie said at last.

"The school is being run almost entirely by volunteers. It needs people—willing bodies to make beds, or cups of tea, or, God willing, a child smile. These children have seen unimaginable things, Rosie—such horrors as neither you nor I could ever envision."

Broken calls to broken. Rosie stared down at the basin, a soap bubble popping gently, disappearing into the water. Marie waited, patient, gentle, but also firm. Rosie wondered if she would even take no for an answer. She knew she did not want to go back to Kingston just yet. She couldn't, not like this, and maybe not ever. She had to heal herself, and she wasn't even sure how to begin, but perhaps it would only come in the healing of others. At the very least, she thought, she could be of some use to somebody, even if it was just making a cup of tea. And it was a place to go that wasn't home.

"Well, Rosie?" Marie asked, in her rich, accented voice. "I leave for Windermere, to get ready for the children, next month. Will you come with me?"

Rosie stared out at the small, grimy window of the center's kitchen. Outside, there was nothing more than a square of concrete courtyard surrounded by crumbling brick, but in her mind's eye, she was seeing a kaleidoscope of memories—laughing with Violet as she showed her the brochure for the CWACs; her father's apologetic smile as he told her there would be no Lyman & Daughter; the freezing barracks in Kitchener, the swamping sense of loneliness and uncertainty she'd first felt there; the months in St. Anne's and Hamilton; the boat over to England... Laughing with Beth, reuniting with Violet, walking up to Thomas at Rainbow Corner and telling him she needed to learn how to flirt. Kisses and happiness, the first time she'd transcribed a code successfully, a sense of wonder, hope, determination, despair. Grief, wilder and deeper than any she could have imagined. A future that loomed utterly unknown and impossible.

And now this.

"Well?" Marie asked again. "I can give you time to think, of course."

"I don't need time to think," Rosie told her. "I'll go." She lifted her head to give Marie one swift, blazing look. "I want to go. Thank you for asking me, Marie."

"Good girl," Marie said in approval. "I thought you would. I will leave you to make such arrangements as you need. We leave the second week of July."

Rosie nodded, hardly able to believe she'd agreed to such a thing, and yet amazingly, glad that she had. That sudden burst of something almost like happiness was an emotion she hadn't felt in a long time, and even though she knew it was fleeting, she was grateful for it, fiercely so. It reminded her she could be strong, when she wanted to, if she could just remember how.

As she walked home that afternoon, through the bombed-out streets of Shoreditch, she found herself looking around as if for the first time. It was a beautiful day, summer in full blossom, the sky cornflower blue, the world full of birdsong, the buildings a mix of crumbling brick and complete rubble. In a bombed-out house that had been levelled to its very foundations, a little boy with coal dust on his cheek scrambled over a broken ledge, looking for his ball. With it triumphantly in his hand, his gaze met Rosie's and he gave her a cheeky grin. After a second's pause, Rosie smiled back. Joy was everywhere, she realized, tangled up with the grief, if you were just willing to look for it, recognize it for what it was.

She took a deep breath, lifted her face to the sky, and kept walking.

A LETTER FROM KATE

Dear reader,

I want to say a huge thank you for choosing to read *An Island Far from Home*. If you found it thought-provoking and powerful, and would like to keep up to date with all my latest releases, just sign up at the following link. Your email address will never be shared and you can unsubscribe at any time.

It was so much fun to revisit my Amherst Island series from the perspective of the next generation! Ellen's story first called to me many years ago, and I was so glad to have the opportunity to continue it with Rosie.

www.bookouture.com/kate-hewitt

I hope you loved *An Island Far from Home* and if you did, I would be very grateful if you could write a review. I'd love to hear what you think, and it makes such a difference helping new readers to discover one of my books for the first time.

I love hearing from my readers—you can get in touch on my Facebook group for readers, through Twitter, Goodreads or my website.

Thanks again for reading!

Kate

KEEP IN TOUCH WITH KATE

www.kate-hewitt.com

facebook.com/KateHewittAuthor

twitter.com/author_kate

ACKNOWLEDGEMENTS

So many people help to bring a book to readers, and as always I am very grateful for the whole amazing team at Bookouture who have helped with this process, from editing, copyediting, proofreading, designing, and marketing. In particular, I'd like to thank Isobel Akenhead, my first editor with Bookouture, and Jess Whitlum-Cooper, my second! Both of them have worked on this book and I am so grateful for their input. Most of all, I'd like to thank my readers, who buy and read my books. Without you, there would be no stories to share. I hope you enjoyed Rosie's journey as much as I did. Thank you!

Ingram Content Group UK Ltd.
Milton Keynes UK
UKHW011810060423
419751UK00004B/271